The Inventor's

Quest

Written By

Tony Franks-Buckley

Edited By

Gavin Chappell

Artwork By

Stephen Cooney

Hidden Wirral Myths & Legends

The Inventor's Quest is part of the Tales of Hector Hornsmith Series.

©Tony Franks-Buckley

Twitter@TonyFrBuckley

Dedication

For the Children of Wallasey

Special thanks

I must thank several people upon my journey whilst writing this book, firstly to my friend Gavin Chappell, who has played an important role in the research, thought and publication of this book. I would also like to thank Danielle Louise Thomas, whose voice has inspired me on a great scale. Laura, another important role played in the last couple of years during the completion of the book. Uncle John, as always you inspire me and try and teach me right from wrong. Gareth Hibbs and the rest of the Ashville lads. Friends of Hidden Wirral Members, Michael Bennett, Garry Fields, Michael Boyd. Last but not least my Mum, Dad, family and friends who have helped me along the journey in life. This book was written for you all.

Introduction

There was an inventor who was not just any inventor, but the cleverest of unknown inventors in the world. How can this be if he is unknown, you ask? Well, because none of his inventions have ever been invented. This did not matter to the inventor; he knew that he would be known for something spectacular one day, he just did not know what it would be.

The year is 1892 and England is under the rule of the great monarch Queen Victoria. The last hundred years have been a wonderful time to live in England; it has been an era of innovation and expansion that could not be matched by any other country in the world.

Many men have become rich, yet many have remained poor, but England has become greater and stronger than ever. The Victorian time was an age of prosperity and everyone sought their fortunes in one way or another.

In the north-west region of England there is a little town on the Cheshire coast called Wallasey or Walla-sea, if you want to know how to pronounce it. In this quaint little town live all sorts of people, rich merchants, farmers, trades people and even circus and theatre entertainers.

There is one man who is different from them all. His name is William Withens and he is known to his family and friends of the town simply as "The Inventor."

William was a very popular man with the locals; he was of a very friendly nature and the locals knew they could always rely on his expert knowledge. Whenever they had a problem, they would go and see William Withens "The Inventor," who could fix anything.

William had previously owned a small shop in the village of Wallasey, in which he would think up his new inventions and try to perfect them. The only problem is that he enjoyed helping the people from the town, he could not attend to his own inventions that had yet to be invented, never mind that they needed fixing.

The only solution he could think of was to move his workshop away from the busy village and find somewhere more peaceful, where he could work from home. It was here that his adventures truly began.

William Withens and his family had not long settled into their new home of Montebello Manor, following their short but exciting move from the other side of Wallasey. William was an inventor who invented many things. Nothing of great significance to the outside world, but to his family, they were great and useful things, especially to his wife Melinda who supported his work greatly.

Since leaving his village shop, it was not very often that William would be seen outside of the house. He was always hard at work on his next big idea, hidden away in his small but sufficient workshed.

William was reasonably tall, with a medium build and quite scruffy looking, but by no means a poor man. Even though he had not yet successfully created the big idea invention, merchants and shop owners would pay him for improvements that he made to their devices and machinery. William was also respected locally for the vegetables and fruit that his family sold in the local market two days per week, then at home for the remainder.

This was the reason why the move to a bigger house became necessary, in order to increase production, but also most unfortunately for William it was so he was able to accommodate the rest of the family, who had all decided to invite themselves to live in his house.

William moved from his small but cosy farm house to Montebello Manor, where there was more than enough room for all of the family to live, as well as for him to conduct his work and research.

And when I say all of the family, it was not just William's beautiful wife Melinda and their two sons Mark and Michael, but also William's parents Grandma and Grandpa Withens and not forgetting his two brothers Alfred and Benjamin. The two brothers resided in Montebello after losing their cottage in a cards game.

But William really didn't complain. Everybody worked hard on the farm and without their help, he would not have as much time to spend inventing, which was his main concern. Even though Grandma and Grandpa Withens' age was increasing, their love for fresh fruit and vegetables ensured that they were in good shape and they helped out, working on the farm. Grandma would wake up early every morning and collect the eggs from the hundred or so chickens that roamed the barn, Grandpa would do the more strenuous work of milking the dozen golden coloured Jersey cows in the field behind the house. The quality of the milk was the best around and Grandpa took pride in making sure that every last drop had been squozen out of the cows in order to sell as much as possible to the local residents.

William's brothers Alfred and Benjamin used their muscles and previous labouring experience to carry out the longer daily activities of repair works and tending to the vegetables and fruit trees. They had previously worked for local farmers in the village of Wallasey. When they lost their cottage, William decided it would be best for all if they came and worked for him, paying for their rent and also getting a decent wage, which was quite often all spent in the public house. But William did not care what they did with their money, so long as they worked hard on the land and maintained the Montebello Manor so there was no need for William to do much work, allowing him to concentrate on creating and testing his important inventions.

The house, as mentioned before, was called Montebello Manor. It was a large sandstone building four floors high and one of the biggest properties in the area. The house originally belonged to a rich merchant and slave trader from Liverpool who moved over to New Brighton to escape the stresses of city life. He, along with other rich merchants, was invited by the founder of New Brighton, James Atherton, to come over and build their properties in a new and exciting area that was going to become a seaside resort for the middle classes. Montebello is not normally a place that you would associate with a simple living family such as the Withens. But William Withens wasn't an ordinary man.

William would spend nearly all of his working day in his secret invention room, but it was not really a room, it was a cave. When the Withens family moved into the manor house a little over two years previously, by chance William found a secret cavern in which he could hide all of his new inventions without interruption from the village folk and the rest of the outside world.

William's two sons, Mark and Michael, ran excitedly around Montebello Manor, exploring all the new rooms of their home. The boys made their way from the top of the house in which they ran to first to claim their new bedrooms, down the two sets of stairs and through the door to the cellar.

Both of the boys were very active and jumped up and down ecstatically on the uncovered wooden floorboards. I say uncovered, that just means that they had no carpet.

"Look at me, Michael; I can jump like a cricket," Mark shouted as he jumped around the room like a bow-legged cricket.

"And I'm a tiger," Michael said as he pranced round, imitating the movements of an energetic tiger.

There was a loud crack, followed by a huge bang. Mark had disappeared through the rising clouds of dust and was trapped in the floorboards.

"Ouch! My legs, my legs!" he screamed loudly. "Michael, grab me quick, I'm falling," he shouted to his younger brother.

Michael panicked as he clutched the arms of his older brother, who had become lodged up to his shoulders through the floorboards.

"Help! Somebody help!" Michael shouted out as loud as he could.

Footsteps above could be heard running above as the ceiling creaked with each step.

The door swung open and William Withens rushed to the rescue of the two terrified boys. It was this very moment that the inventor's life would take an unexpected turn and his dreams would become more of a reality.

"What happened, and what have you done to the floor?" he shouted as he pulled Mark to safety out of the splintering floorboards.

"I'm sorry, father, I didn't mean to," Mark sobbed.

"No matter now, boy. More important thing is you're alright," he said as he dusted down his eldest son. William loved his two sons; he called them "His greatest inventions," and was very proud of them indeed.

William peered down to see what damage the boys had made this time. They were always causing some sort of damage, not on purpose. "Just unlucky coincidences," as William would call it when anybody would make a complaint against them. The light was scarce as he peered down, but he was able to make out a tunnel through the thick silver cobwebs that engulfed the area below.

"That's strange. I am certain there was never a mine in New Brighton," he said to himself out loud. "Run upstairs and fetch a lantern for me, will you boys?" he asked.

Being an inventor it was his duty to investigate everything of a strange nature, and the possibility of a tunnel running beneath his house was very strange indeed.

Michael returned back to his father with the square metal-and-glass-cased lantern, Mark did not return as he had whimpered off to his mother to cleanse the cuts and remove the splinters in his legs. The lantern burned bright following the ignition from a phosphorus matchstick, William attached a small rope from his trusted satchel and lowered the lantern into the dark passage. Cobwebs snapped as he dropped the lantern through onto the floor of the tunnel. It was not as deep as he first thought. William peered down and saw the tunnel ran in two directions. He removed a couple of the broken floorboards that were splintered from Mark's unfortunate 'coincidence' and was now able to lower himself down into the passageway, ordering Michael to stay put.

"You stay here; you've had enough fun for one day."

Michael grumbled as he eagerly watched his father lowering himself gently into the dark hole. William was now inside the tunnel and cobwebs clung to his jacket, which he quickly brushed off as he picked up the lantern. He walked along the dark passage for around five to ten minutes. Nothing but darkness ahead and more cobwebs. Then at last, he saw something in the distance.

"And what might you be doing down here?" he said, as a few glimpses of wood appeared in rhythm with each swing of the lantern. He moved in for a closer look. He had reached a wooden door.

"Why and when has this door been put here? This is most peculiar. I am definitely certain there was never any type of mining facility in Wallasey and never was it a place known for natural gems nor coal," he said out loud.

The brief glimmer of excitement did not last for long, because the door was sealed and locked shut and had cast iron latches. Continuing was impossible without a key, a key that he did not have. William had no option but to head back in the other direction. If only he had brought some tools.

Feeling more optimistic, he made his way past the opening in which young Mark fell through earlier and went further into the tunnel. This time he was following a route of a left curving direction. After travelling for around fifteen minutes, despite the cobwebs remaining unchanged, the tunnel had become colder and damp and soon was no longer a tunnel. Carefully taking a step forward William trod across splinters of rock and blocks of sandstone; he was in a square passage. It was a considerably large room and appeared to have been created by hand. William could tell by the scrape marks on the stone walls that it had been scratched away using tools. By further investigation, he followed the breeze of air and found a circular opening on the opposite side of the square passage.

William took his lantern and held it up as he looked around the area, which was damp due to the water trickling down the sides. There were several markings on one of the mossy walls that were currently unreadable.

"Why didn't I bring my tool bag?" he said again, frustrated.

William saw a glimmer of light at the other end of the circular passageway, so he stepped through avoiding a few rocks that were roughly edging out of the ground, also hearing the odd crunch here and there.

"Bugs! I bloody hate bugs!" He daren't shine the lantern to the floor to see what they were; he carried on through for several paces. Beams of light greeted him as he reached an opening.

"My good lord," he said as his eyes adjusted to the light. Was he really seeing what was in front of him? William removed his spectacles and rubbed his eyes with his hands to make sure it was not a mirage and he was actually seeing what he thought he saw.

A look of complete surprise appeared on William Withens' face. An underground cavern was before his eyes, a flood of red and yellow colour from the stone surroundings met his eyes that they were completely focused. He could also hear running water somewhere; he looked across to see a glistening waterfall emptying down into a pool. Speckles of green from plant-infested areas divided the colours in the rocks. It was magnificent, never before had he seen such a place. His thoughts flowed vigorously.

"I'm underground and yet there is complete light down here. How is this possible in an underground sealed area? Have I travelled upwards without knowing?"

William stepped further into the cave and his unanswered questions became clear. Circular objects had been placed around the cave. Having studied Egyptology briefly at university he recognised it as the Egyptian mirror system.

Thousands of years ago in the time of the Pharaohs, Egyptian slaves would work within stone structures such as pyramids and tombs, which became resting places for their gods. In order to paint hieroglyphs on the walls, they needed complete light; much more than a few lit torches or lanterns could offer. They daren't make a mistake for fear of death by their gods.

The mirrors were perfectly placed around the cave with each mirror linking to the next, reflecting and bouncing the light from one to another. It was a simple but very effective process. William followed the path of the mirrors with his eyes as he stepped further into the cave. There were many mirrors, but one in particular pointed to an opening in the top of the cave. The opening had been perfectly crafted in the form of a shaft, with a beam of light coming straight down to meet the angled mirror below; it really was a marvellous technique.

There were old bottles, bones and bits of general rubbish scattered around the floor, but apart from that the cave looked like it had not been used in a long time, maybe even a few centuries; he could not tell, it was an empty shell. William soon realised the potential greatness that the cavern could offer.

"Nobody can interrupt me down here," he said to himself with a smile on his face. He dashed round with excitement, jumping up on rocks as his enthusiasm grew.

"My work will be more secure than ever. Just think of the possibilities. There is running water, I can set up a drinking supply system, and I can even use it as a power source. There is plenty of light. I could even grow food. I could live down here. No, wait! Melinda and the children. Cross that last idea out, good but not relevant."

William was more excited than ever, even more excited than when he first became an inventor. This would be his own secret chamber which only he would know. He could be certain to keep his inventions secret and away from the outside world.

"This is the greatest thing I've ever seen," he said, looking around the room, planning where he was going to place all of his tools and apparatus. "I can only imagine what I can invent down here. Finally, I'll have my chance to amaze the world."

His mind worked overtime as streams of ideas ran through his mind, things he had desperately wanted to invent for such a long time, but had never had the room or time to do so, but this was all about to change.

This was the beginning of a new and exciting time for the inventor William Withens. Anything and everything became possible.

Chapter One

The year was 1894 and two long but exciting years had passed. The Withens family had settled in their new home of Montebello Manor. The manor house was much cleaner and brighter after its restoration from the derelict state in which it had been left, new wooden floorboards in the basement included.

Before the Withens family had moved into the house, the surrounding fields had been left empty and overgrown; a waste of good useable land. William Withens was not only an inventor, but he was also a keen farmer. "Food is the most important ingredient of life," he would say to himself, and many of his inventions were used to make food grow bigger, juicier and better. William, upon first viewing the house and surrounding land, knew that here he would be able to increase his crop yields dramatically. This had already become true; the fields were filled with various crops which they sell on Melinda's market stall. People would come from the other side of the village to purchase the Withens' crops as they were the best around. Montebello was situated off St George's Mount in New Brighton, a rural area filled with many fields. A busy access road ran between the fields, and passers-by would stop and stare across the Withens fields at the unusual devices that were in constant daily use. Sometimes they would sit for hours in marvel at the exciting machines, such as the wind powered carrot lifter, or the steam powered potato puller. There were many wonderful mechanical and wooden devices working throughout the farmland.

The Withens family had become respected within the local community for the quality of their vegetables, fruit and even the fresh eggs for their ripeness. Mrs Melinda Withens and Grandma Mabel Withens would be out each day on the stall selling to the locals, but never on a Sunday. Sunday was the day of rest, and more importantly, church in the morning followed by a family dinner in the afternoon. This was an important tradition for the Withens family.

"Come on, boys. We're going to be late," Melinda shouted at Mark and Michael who were still getting dressed.

"Just like their father, always leaving things till the last minute," Grandpa Withens responded, shaking his head behind his morning newspaper. He was right as well, it was 8:37 on a Sunday morning and William was not even in the house and mass was starting at 9:00.

"Ring that darn bell, will you please, Grandma," Melinda said frantically.

"Every Sunday morning it's always the same. We do this every week! Maybe just one day we could all be ready without me having to ask," Grandma moaned, preparing the beef roast for the oven.

"You panic too much, my dear Mabel. Look at me! I'm sixty-seven years old and do you see me worrying about anything?" Grandpa said.

Grandma moved across towards the back door of the kitchen and gave a yank on the rope labelled "Workshed."

William was returning to the workshed as he was greeted by a chorus of ringing bells. The bells set off an alarm in his head, as he remembered what he was supposed to be doing over an hour ago.

"Oh dear, is that the time already? I must get my church clothes on," William said in a panic. He had been working down in the cave on his new project since six in the morning, skipping breakfast for the second time this week, something that he very rarely did, as he loved breakfast, but some inventions were really important, and this was one of his most important yet. Many inventions that William had created had been put to good use around the house and fields, but William had returned from the cave on possibly his best and favourite invention ever, the underground transport system better known as S.T.A.N. William had created his own version of the magnificent steam train, which had first been used by the wonderful George Stephenson. William had created a smaller version and was now able to reach his new private workshop in the cavern via this transport, and was able to create and hide all of his new inventions away from the prying eyes of the outside world.

The small steam train was simply called S.T.A.N because its full name of Steam Transport Alternate Navigation was too much to pronounce, so S.T.A.N became his choice of name. Each day, William would prepare S.T.A.N by filling the burning furnace with the coal by which it was powered. It would take one sack of coal to keep the fire burning at optimal temperature for most of the day, but when William was moving much of his tools and gadgets down into the hidden cave he used one and a half to two sacks of coal per day. Mr Marshall the coal seller did not complain, though. S.T.A.N relied on heat in order to move;

the more heat created, more steam and more steam created more speed. It was a simple but effective process.

S.T.A.N had been created when William was transporting his machines and tools down to the cave. The original transport of a horse and rail cart was neither fast nor efficient when transporting from the workshed all the way down to the cave. It was the slow journey that gave the inventor an epiphany moment and came up with the idea. However, unlike a steam train which generally had just one engine at the front of the carriages, William thought, *Why not put one on each end?* This became the alternate way to transport using steam power, an engine on each end, and there was no longer a need to disconnect from the carts. This ensured that William was able to set up his new secret workspace much faster than expected, despite the many hours, weeks and months needed to lay all of the tracks.

William rushed back to the house and got changed quickly and the whole family headed to the church via horse and cart. It was a fifteen minute journey to St Hilary's church situated on the other side of the village and as usual they were expecting to be late because it was now eleven minutes to nine.

William's brothers Alfred and Benjamin were sitting on the front of the cart with Alfred controlling the horses and Benjamin smoking away on his pipe. William, Melinda, Grandpa, Grandma, Mark and Michael all sat within the carriage.

"Michael, will you please stop playing with your tie? It's staying on and don't think otherwise." Michael stopped what he was doing and folded his arms in a huff.

"Sorry Mother," he responded in a sulky voice. The rest of the journey to the church was silent.

The Withens family arrived late and piled in through the church doors, with a collection of turning heads greeting them for interrupting the priest as he recited from the Bible. They shuffled into the empty benches situated at the back of the packed room.

"As I said, honour your father and your mother, as the LORD your God has commanded you, so that you may live long and that it may go well with you in the land the LORD your God is giving you. Deuteronomy 5:16," Everybody in the church responded with an "Amen," performing a cross sign upon their chests.

"And now to local matters," the priest said with a smile upon his face

"Irene and Imelda Flynn would like to invite everybody to their gathering, this coming Saturday, in honour of St Patrick. A selection of stew and soda bread will be available to consume. Music and games for the children will also be provided, and everybody is welcome."

Irene and Imelda Flynn were two sisters who moved to Wallasey as children during the great famine in 1845 and had stayed ever since. The church service carried on through all the local news and events, with more prayers and a few hymns. The service finished at eleven o'clock.

As usual the families gathered outside and talk amongst themselves. A moment of silence broke the flow of speech as a gentleman and his family passed through the crowd, heading towards a silver carriage outside the church gates. William shook his head with disbelief. "How that man is not struck down by the Lord upon entering the house of God, I don't know. He was surely spawned by the devil himself."

Whenever this man came near William, he would feel nothing but anger. Melinda could always sense when William was angry and it was usually whenever this revolting man was near.

"Just look the other way, William," Melinda said as she pulled William to face away from the grinning man in the carriage. William did as he was told and rejoined the circle of friends who were happily chatting away about the last week's events.

The Withens family said their goodbyes and headed home for afternoon family games, followed by the traditional roast dinner.

Chapter Two

The weekend had passed. Everybody was working around the manor and the boys were back in school. William was carrying out repairs to the underground railway track that led from the cave to the workshed. For a while, William had been thinking about the locked door situated at the other end of the tunnel. He knew that he would need something strong to prise the door open, for it was thick oak wood with cast iron bolts; it was a well locked door.

"I must get my tools; I'm going to have to hit it with some force," he said to himself.

He finished the repair works on the broken track, which meant that S.T.A.N was operable again, so he returned to the workshed aboveground to collect his tools. The Steam Train Alternate Navigation was at the end of the track, covered up inside the workshed. Nobody was allowed into the workshed, not even the family, for safety reasons; well, that is what the family thought. William collected all of his required tools and was busy roaming around the room collecting them.

"Lump hammer, yes, I'll need you." He picked it up, placing it in one of the carts attached to S.T.A.N.

"A few iron rods, this should help with leverage." They also went in the cart.

William would have to lift the door from the hinges on which they were resting. He filled the cart with everything else that he required and he grew more anxious about finding out what might be behind the closed door that had been placed in the middle of an underground tunnel. William stoked the furnace with coal which roared while steam seeped out from all around the engine, following the refill with water. He leapt onto the seat and put the machine into a forward motion. S.T.A.N pulled off down the opening and into the tunnel. Three of the six carts were filled and the rest was left empty for anything that might be found behind the closed door.

Previously it had taken William five to ten minutes to reach the door on foot, so it was not long until he reached the end of the track a couple of yards away. William adjusted the nearby mirror to shine towards the door. After he lay two heavy pieces of wood to be used as levers, the iron bars were ready to be positioned under the door. Thick rope was needed and was suitably attached to the end of the iron bars, with the other ends tied to S.T.A.N.

"Right, come on, old faithful, you haven't let me down yet," William shouted in a positive voice as he climbed back aboard the machine. S.T.A.N roared into action, the pressure forcing down on the iron rods, which slowly lifted the door from off the hinges and with an almighty bang, it released and fell to the floor. Dust and dirt engulfed the tunnel. William coughed and wafted his handkerchief through the clouds, trying to make his way back towards the door. With the mirror adjusted, the light shone dimly through the newly opened tunnel.

"Well, I'd best grab what I need; the journey ends here for you," he said grabbing his satchel and lantern out of S.T.A.N. It had taken nearly two hours' work but William had got the door open and was proceeding down the tunnel. The lantern led the way through the complete darkness of the passage. William walked for twenty minutes down the straight path, wondering when it would stop. Finally, the passage opened into a larger passage. He held up the lantern and was greeted by three different passages.

William stopped to catch his breath and cough up some more of the dust that had engulfed him earlier.

"Right, no time to stop and rest, there's a job to be done here," William said getting back on his feet. He shone the light around the room. It had been carved perfectly and above the three passage ways were chalk markings. The tunnels had been labelled from left to right RI, HH and PR. He stopped and wondered which tunnel he should take.

"If in doubt, straight down the middle," he said, heading down the passage labelled HH. Unlike the others, the tunnel rose ever so slightly higher with each pace that he took. It became obvious that he was heading upwards, but he was not sure where he would end up.

It took another ten to fifteen minutes until William reached the end of the tunnel, where the opening was above his head, but it was sealed close by two wooden doors. William pushed up on the doors and they both swung open. Flashes of sunlight strained his eyes that had been acclimatised to the dark. He climbed out through the door and found himself in the midst of trees.

"Where is this?" he wondered to himself.

He came out of the trees into the long grass of the large surrounding gardens, filled with flower beds and wooden benches. In the background there was a large house, more like a mansion. It was four or five regular houses wide and three floors high, somewhat bigger than Montebello Manor. William walked up the stone path to investigate further. The building looked empty and unused. Even the windows had been boarded up. There was a plaque on the wall:

Welcome to Hornsmith Manor.

"Hornsmith. I've heard that name before, but where?" He tried to think for a while.

"Hector Hornsmith! That was his name; I remember my father talking about him. So that must be what the HH meant in the tunnel, it was a marker for Hornsmith Manor."

He walked around the outside of the building, admiring the detail that had gone into the structure of the magnificent manor house. Sandstone blocks perfectly shaped gave a curve effect to each corner. Patterned windows, many different shapes perfectly placed to gather the sunlight. There were even two circular stained glass windows depicting boats upon the sea. It was a most unusual building and a lot of effort had been put into creating it.

After a couple of hours of exploring the outer grounds of the building, dinner time approached and William knew his family would be wondering where he was. He had found some of the answers to what he looked for; it was time he went home, and that he did.

Following a delightful boiled ham with all the trimmings, William retired to his study for the evening.

"Hector Hornsmith... His name's in here, somewhere," he mumbled as he rummaged through all of his saved newspaper cuttings. "Ah, here we go. The opening of Fort Perch Rock," he said as he found a relevant newspaper article. "Hector Hornsmith was the official guest of honour at the opening of the Fort," it said in *The Wallasey News*, on Saturday 17th Oct 1833:

"I thank you all for coming on this momentous day, no more will we be attacked by pirates. No more will we be scared by threats from the French. It is on this day that I, Hector Hornsmith, declare the new defender of the River Mersey open."

There was a picture of Hector Hornsmith on the front of the newspaper, with the Mayor of Wallasey. Many people had flocked to the area to view the new battle station of the Royal Navy, which had been erected to protect the trade route of the River Mersey against pirates and smugglers, but more importantly, from invasion from the French.

"Just who was this Hector Hornsmith? How much did people really know about who he really was? What link has he got with the tunnels and where did the other two tunnels lead too?"

William was asking himself too many questions to which he did not have the answers. What was certain though, was that he would be spending as much time as possible to find out the answers. William retired to bed, his head buzzing with so much information that he was unable to think clearly any longer.

Chapter Three

Following a good night's sleep, William woke in a positive mood. It was clearer in his mind what he needed to do next. Today he would investigate further in the tunnels. Now the door was open, he was eager to learn where the other tunnels led.

"Another day in the shed is it, dear?" Melinda asked as she served William with a plate of cooked bacon and eggs.

"Yes, my dear, I've made a breakthrough on my new invention, I think this is going to be my biggest yet."

"Ah..." Melinda had heard this all before, so she just responded with her usual motivational speech. "That's wonderful news; I always said you could do it."

Melinda was proud of her husband, but she wished he would spend more time on matters that needed attending to rather than hoping for the next big idea. But she would never say so; she wouldn't like to hurt his feelings, for she didn't know about the previous inventions that had been stolen from William, which could have made them much wealthier than they were.

It was twenty seven minutes past seven in the morning and William had finished his cooked breakfast.

"That was delightful. Just what I needed to help me through my day. Simply marvellous, delicious and beautiful. The beautiful part being you, dear."

"Anything for my clever inventor to start his day." Melinda smiled.

"I'm heading into the village. Is there anything you would like me to pick up for you?" William asked.

"Oh, come to think of it, yes. I really could use some fresh bread rolls from Flowerday's. The Flynn sisters dropped us round another pan of soup; I thought we could have it for tea."

William always looked forward to eating food prepared by Irene and Imelda, because they always used vegetables grown on his farm and it always tasted different. Maybe it was the Irish style of cooking.

"Yes, that won't be a problem. Will eight be enough?" he asked.

"Well, Alfred and Benjamin are down at the public house later so they will be eating out. Just get the six."

"They are going the public house yet again?" he said shaking his head.

"Apparently it's cards night again, third time this week."

"No wonder they never have any money! They are terrible card players."

"Well, it keeps them out of trouble, I suppose, so we shouldn't complain."

William nodded, putting on his old musty sheepskin coat, and recalled why the two brothers were living in his house, having lost their cottage in a card game.

"Don't forget your scarf and hat. Best to keep warm as possible today."

"I even have my extra vest on today and a second pair of socks."

It was raining outside so he daren't catch a cold again. The last one had kept him bedridden for several days.

"I shall love you and leave you then, my dear. See you this evening," he said leaving through the front door. William headed into the village today via his horse and cart. His order was available from Mallon's Mirrors. The horse had been covered with an overcoat and was unhappy with his removal from the barn into the pouring rain. The cart struggled through mud that became ever thicker as the rain mixed with the stone and clay of the lane.

"Morning, William!" A voice wailed from an oncoming cart. It was Angus McGregor, the cattle farmer who lived across the fields from Montebello Manor.

"Good morning, Angus. I bet the cows are having fun in this weather." The carts stopped beside one another.

"Had to put one of the old girls to sleep last night, but not to worry. I've some nice slabs of beef for you here," Angus said, patting a big parcel with his hand.

"Thanks very much. Melinda is up in the house, I'm sure she will be happy to see you. Take yourself some carrots and potatoes, have yourself a nice stew."

"That'll be fine, William, just fine," Angus shouted as he pulled away towards the manor house.

William entered the village, greeting the locals as he did on every occasion. Even though it was a little past eight o'clock in the morning, the village was very busy. William headed round to the rear of Mallon's, so that the cart was ready to load his order.

"Ah, William, I am glad to see you. I trust Melinda gave you my message," Morris Mallon said with a glowing smile as William walked through the shop door.

"Hello, Morris. I do apologise for being a day or two late. I've had a few things to attend to."

Morris Mallon was not bothered at all as William was his best customer, but he never knew what he did with so many small mirrors. For even him, the maker of the mirrors never had more than one in each room of his house.

"Come through to the back; your items are there," Morris said as he guided William through to the back storage room. There were mirrors of all shapes and sizes, dotted around the room.

"Charlie, start packing these boxes onto Mr Withens' cart would you, please?" Charlie was Morris Mallon's only son.

"Tell me, William, what exactly do you do with all these mirrors?" Morris asked.

"A magician never tells his secrets. Neither shall I, but one day, my dear friend, all will be revealed," William said.

Morris could hardly wait; it had been bugging him: he wanted to know just why over the past few years William Withens had ordered hundreds of six by nine inch mirrors.

"How much do I owe you for this lot then, Morris?" William asked.

"Let's see. One hundred and fifty six-by-nine mirrors. That will be six pounds and twelve shillings please."

William took out his wallet to hand the fresh crisp notes to Morris.

"Here. Take seven pounds, I insist." William always got the mirrors for next to nothing so a tip on top of the price was sufficient.

"Thank you, William. Would you be requiring any more in the future?"

William could not guess how many he would need, for he did not know what length the undiscovered tunnels would be.

"Best put me an order on for three hundred more."

Morris wrote the figure down in his large order book.

"That is fine; I shall send a message when your order is ready. Have a good day, Mr Withens."

William waved goodbye and returned to his horse and cart. Through all the excitement, William had nearly forgotten about the bread rolls for tea.

"Damn, I must go back and get the rolls." He had already passed the shop and was nearing the edge of the village.

"Mr Withens, Mr Withens," a voice shouted. A man was running behind the cart as it turned. He peered over his shoulder to see who it was.

"Mr Withens! Ah, I'm glad to have caught you." It was Gregory Griffith, the schoolmaster from Wallasey Grammar. "It's about your two boys; they have been playing in the chemistry laboratory again."

William shook his head in disbelief. What had the boys done now?

"Mr Griffith, it's a pleasure to see you once again," he said as he got down from his cart.

"Yes, it's a pleasure to see you too. It was this morning during Mr Manning's Chemistry test." The schoolmaster was out of breath from chasing the cart.

"Just what has this got to do with my boys? They did not have chemistry today." William knew that Mark had art and Michael had woodwork.

"That is precisely my point, Mr Withens. Your boys have been in the chemistry laboratory and switched around some contents of the chemical bottles.

"Mr Manning was performing a simple limestone test in front of the pupils, only when he thought he was adding a jar of vinegar to the barrel of water and limestone. He was in fact adding a jar of hydrochloric acid. The room is destroyed and will take days to clean up the mess." Mr Griffith was really worked up.

William laughed under his breath because he knew just what a mess it would have made when mixing hydrochloric acid which is much stronger than vinegar; the reaction would have been much greater.

"I've had to send the whole class home from school; their uniforms were soaked through from foaming bubbles."

Again William laughed in his head. He daren't laugh out loud.

"Alright, Mr Griffith, please send me the bill for the damages. I do apologise for the boys' behaviour, I'm sure they did it in good spirit."

"Good spirit indeed," the headmaster replied. Mr Griffith was satisfied, for Mr Withens made many contributions to the school's science and industrial departments; this is probably why the two boys had never been expelled.

"Alright, Mr Withens, but please will you tell Mark and Michael to stop these silly games? Poor Mr Manning is in a right state of confusion."

William agreed and headed back on his way to the bakery.

Mrs Flowerday's bakery had been passed down through the family for four generations; it has been popular for many years.

"Good morning," William said as he stepped into the crowded shop.

"Hello, Mr Withens, what a pleasure it is to see you again. Have not seen much of you recently. Is everybody well at home?" Mrs Flowerday asked.

"Everybody is fine thank you, working hard as always," he replied as he took off his hat.

"Have you seen who has bought your old workshop? Apparently it's going to be a clothing store. Poor old Mrs Perkins is not happy about it at all. Thirty-four years she has had her shop in this village."

"I can only imagine there is one person who could do such a thing," William said shaking his head.

"Yes it is he. Terrible man he is. Doesn't care about others as long as he is making his money."

"Well, one day somebody will have the last laugh over him."

"We can live in hope that the good Lord sees fit to do so." Mrs Flowerday clasped her hands and looked up above to the heavens.

"Melinda would like six of your finest bread rolls, please," William said.

"Certainly. Would you prefer brown or white?"

William checked to see how much change he had left in his pocket.

"I'll take six of the white, please, and could you throw in six of those delicious looking cream cakes also?"

Mrs Flowerday wrapped up all of William's order. He paid and left the bakery.

William rushed straight home. He had a busy day ahead. He had a new batch of mirrors for the tunnels and he needed to get to work on them straight away. Leaving the mirrors lying around would make people curious about the work that William was conducting. He must protect the secret of the tunnels as best as he could.

Chapter Four

William went back down to the tunnels following an adventurous morning in town. The mirrors were transported using S.T.A.N and were fitted in the unlit tunnel leading to Hornsmith Manor. Each mirror was placed ten yards apart on either side of the tunnel in a zigzag pattern. William could hear a noise coming from further up the tunnel. It sounded like somebody talking.

"That's odd. These tunnels are sealed. Who could possibly be down here?" He picked up his lantern and went to investigate.

"Who goes there and what you doing in my tunnels?" a voice shouted.

"Hello down there! I'm William, William Withens," he shouted.

"Just what did you do to this door? You're not supposed to be down here. A right mess you've made."

William was up close to the person. It was a frail old man with a walking stick.

"You're the Withens boy from the other side of town, are you not?" the old man said.

"Yes, I'm he. Who are you?"

"Never mind who I am, look at my door," the old man said shaking his head.

"I'm sorry about the door but I wanted to know what was behind it. I didn't know that people still used it."

"Do you make a habit of breaking down locked doors?" the old man said inspecting the mirrors. "This is a clever contraption you have made. There's not been light in these tunnels for many years," he said pointing to the old burn marks on the wall.

William was hoping he could finally get some answers to what the tunnels were for. He sat down on a work stool that he had taken with him.

"Here, please take a seat; I've much to ask you."

The old man was happy to sit down and take the weight off his sore feet. William told the old man his story from the beginning from when he first found the tunnels; they were speaking for some time as well. Once William had finished telling the old man his story, he was ready to ask why there were tunnels running beneath Wallasey.

"Can I ask what your name is?" he asked.

"My name is Barney Browne. Be a good lad and help me back to my home and I'll tell you everything you would like to know. The cold down here is making my bones ache."

William helped the old man stand.

"So you live at the end of one of the other tunnels?" he asked as they walked down the tunnel.

"Yes, I live at the starting point of the tunnels, Mother Redcap's."

William looked up at the engravings above the door.

"RI. That is the Redcap's Inn."

The old man chuckled looking up at the markings.

"Yes, Hector mapped all of the tunnels with markers. Without them you would be sure to get lost."

"All of the tunnels? Just how many are there?" William asked.

The old man was back to his feet and walking at a slow but steady pace.

"There are hundreds of tunnels beneath Wallasey, stretching to all corners. How do you think they moved around unnoticed?"

"They? Who are they?" William was confused

"When we get back to Redcap's Inn, I'll tell you everything." The old man was too tired to walk and talk at the same time, so William agreed and they made their way to Mother Redcap's Inn.

They both walked for about fifteen minutes before they reached a door. William helped Barney through what looked like an ale cellar filled with barrels, then assisted him up the wooden staircase which led into the main room of the Inn. William sat down at a table by the window. The old man prepared them some drinks.

"This place has a wonderful view across the river," William said.

Barney returned with the drinks and sat beside William at the table. "Yes, she boasts a beautiful scenic view."

"My children's rooms have a beautiful view across the river also. We are up on the top of the hill, behind McGregor's cattle farm. Do you know it?"

"Yes, for many years I've eaten the delightful beef that his family has produced."

They both took a sip from the rum, which created a burning sensation as it ran down William's throat; he did not often drink such a strong liquor.

"It looks pretty new in here. Did you build it yourself?" William asked.

"Ah, yes. I rebuilt her to try and resemble the way she used to look, but I was afraid that the Royal Navy would blow her up again."

"Royal Navy? Why would they blow up a building?" William asked in interest.

Barney took another swig of rum before he carried on speaking; the walk down the tunnels had made him rather thirsty.

"As I said, I began to rebuild this place in 1830, but as you can see by the new woodwork, I had to get her partly rebuilt again six years ago in 1888 because most of the building was destroyed by fire."

William was relaxed and intrigued by what he was hearing; he was finally getting some answers to what he had been pondering about for the last two years.

"The original owners were Captain John (Bones) Gray and Polly (Mother Redcap) Jones."

"Captain, you say. Was this a ship owner's house?"

Barney laughed. "You could say he was a ship owner but not the type you are thinking of."

William decided not to interrupt and let Barney tell his story.

"Captain Bones, after finding the place disused, ordered Hector Hornsmith his friend and crew member to rebuild the broken inn for his lover Polly and he gave it to her as a place for him to return from his voyages."

Barney drank some more rum. He was starting to warm up. "But mainly Captain Bones used here as a place for Polly to reside, so he always knew where she would be he was on the seas."

"Is that Polly, that picture above the fireplace?" William asked.

"Yes, that picture is one of the remaining artefacts that I was able to salvage from the bombardment of cannon fire. This place would not be the same without her picture hanging in her usual spot."

"She was a beautiful looking lady," William said staring at the picture.

"That she was. Also a remarkable lady; could lift a barrel over her head, arms like an ox.

William sat back at the thought; she must have been a right battle-axe of a lady.

"So how did you come to live here then, Barney?" William asked.

"I was rescued by Captain Bones at sea. I was aboard another ship with my family when it was destroyed by the Royal Navy and I was left to die."

William interrupted Barney, before he went any further.

"Hang on; you were attacked by the Royal Navy? Why would they do such a thing?"

"My parents were pirates; I was aboard a pirate ship." William spoke to a real live pirate, sort of.

"Anyway, when they rescued me in 1819, they brought me back to live here and I've been here ever since for the last seventy-five years." Barney Browne was eighty-seven years old, he had been only twelve years old when his parents were killed.

"So what were the tunnels previously used for?" William asked.

"Originally, before Captain Bones and his crew arrived on the banks of the River Mersey, the tunnels were much smaller. I never did find out what they were for. But Hector Hornsmith and the crew lengthened the tunnels so that they could live underground and get to places around Wallasey without being noticed."

"Was it only Captain Bones and his crew that used them?"

"The tunnels had never been found by an outsider; that is until you managed to find your way into them. For years the Royal Navy and the man who killed my parents, Lord Captain James

Vernon, sailed up and down the River Mersey in search of Captain Bones and his crew, but they were always searching on the wrong side of the river." Barney pointed across the river to Liverpool.

"It was on that fateful day in 1827 that one of the crew members aboard Lord Captain James Vernon's ship, *The Barfleur*, saw a member of Captain Bones' crew rowing back across the river from Liverpool and followed him into Redcap's Inn."

"Did many people travel across the river to this inn?"

"Only the people in the know would step foot in here; too dangerous for others who would steer well clear, just like the locals did."

William took another swig from the near empty glass of rum.

"It was here that the spy from the Royal Navy befriended a few of the crew members, buying them rounds of drinks, and extracted several stories from them, which alerted the spy to Mother Redcap's Inn being the home of Captain Bones and his crew.

"This was the end of Mother Redcap's as we knew it. The spy returned to Lord Captain James Vernon and not long after, a bombardment of cannon fire followed."

"What happened to Captain Bones and Mother Redcap?" William asked finishing off his rum.

"They left several days after the siege; luckily they were underground at the time of the attack, checking over the recent haul of loot they had gained." William's eyes lit up at the sound of loot.

"They stayed hidden until the coast was clear, then took half of the loot that was placed in the treasure room and left the rest for me to keep so that I could rebuild Redcap's Inn, in case they ever returned."

"So what happened to the rest of the treasure?" William said in anticipation as his eyes glowed from the thought of gold, silver, diamonds and rubies.

Barney laughed.

"My dear boy, look around you. I sold the treasure piece by piece to rebuild this place. It's all long gone."

The smile on William's face soon disappeared.

"But I'll say this, there is a possibility that some of the crew members wandered off into the tunnels and hid their loot. I've never found any, but then again I've hardly searched all of the tunnels because there are so many of them."

William smiled again; he might after all be able to find some treasure.

"What about Hector Hornsmith? Why had the Royal Navy never pursued him?"

The old man pointed to a picture on the wall. "See, Hector was clever. Even though he was a pirate, he was also a member of society. Hector Hornsmith led a double life and at the time of the attack from the Royal Navy, he was on the other side of Wallasey with his wife."

"He sounds a real character," William said.

"As you can see by the picture, he became a very well respected member of society. It looks like you have already been to Hornsmith Manor. I saw you from the window when I was up there yesterday, and this is how I knew someone had been in the tunnels."

"Ah yes, that was me," William admitted.

Barney Browne picked up the empty glasses off the table, returning to the bar and poured out some rum.

"So why is Hornsmith Manor empty and why have you got the keys to the house?" William asked, as Barney returned to the table.

"Hector gave me a place to stay during the time when Redcap's Inn was uninhabitable. Together we protected the caves by ensuring all entrances were sealed, so nobody would find them if they went looking."

"Was it just you and Hector then?" William called over to the bar.

"Hector enlisted many of the crew members who decided to stick around and he paid them to build the house which became Hornsmith Manor. The men had nowhere else to go and they followed Hector's example and became men of God, repenting their sins."

"Men of God, you say?"

"Yes, they all became members of the church." William wondered what types of pirates they actually were. "Many of them are buried in the grounds of St Hilary's as pillars of the community; they were good builders and were involved in many of the buildings that Hector built around Wallasey."

William saw why Hector Hornsmith was such a well-respected man, considering nobody knew that he was also a pirate.

"What happened to his family then after he died, and why is his manor house boarded up?" he asked.

"Hector and his wife have long passed away, and his children moved away and started new lives as goods merchants down in London. They very rarely come back anymore and they asked me as a trusted friend of the family to look after the premises, which I've done as a payment to Hector for the help he gave me."

"Why did you not move in there? It looks a lovely place to live."

"I often look in from time to time, but as you can see I'm an old man now. The tunnels are much too long to travel and I could never leave my beloved inn."

Looking at the views across the river, William saw why Barney was so attached to the building.

"What are you going to do about Hornsmith Manor then? Surely such a building should not be left to ruin."

"That is true. Such a shame to see it left unused. Hector worked so hard to build that place for him and his family, I wish I could do more to keep it looking as vibrant as it once was."

"I agree," said William as he looked into his glass.

"Maybe if I give you the keys you could do this for me. It is quite possible that many of Hector's secrets are hidden within Hornsmith Manor, and you may find more answers to questions you are looking for."

"Really? You would let me look after the building?"

"And why not? You seem like a decent young man. I'm sure you would do a grand job. After all, you already know about the tunnels."

William gladly accepted. It was an offer that he could not refuse. Barney took out the key hidden around his neck on a chain.

"Here you go. Just the one key for every door."

William took the key and placed it in his pocket.

"Barney, thank you for the drinks and for everything that you have told me, but I must return home. My wife will be wondering where I am." It was nearing tea time and William had been gone all afternoon.

"Remember, the secret of the tunnels must remain hidden. No one must ever know about Hector either; his good name must not be tarnished."

"Thank you, Barney. I promise I'll come and see you again soon." He left the room, headed back down the tunnel and returned home as fast as he could.

Chapter Five

The time had just turned six o'clock; William's eyes were slightly open.

"Come on father, wake up." Two voices could be heard entering the room, which began to fill with sunlight as Melinda drew back the curtains.

"It's Tuesday; we only have three days left to get her ready," Mark shouted in an excited voice as he jumped around the room.

"Ready? Get what ready?" William was still blurry eyed and not at all awake. The cold in the room was not helping either.

"The race, Father! It's this Saturday, remember?"

With all that had been going on recently, William had completely forgotten that is was the annual Wheel Cart Derby this very weekend.

"Can we see her, father? Can we?" Michael said.

William rose out of bed and had his daily morning stretch and loud long yawn.

"Breakfast and morning chores first, boys, then we will get her out."

The boys looked at each other at the thought of having to do chores.

"Go and help Grandma collect the eggs, mother makes breakfast."

Usually the boys would be moaning at this point, but not today.

"Right. Come on, Michael, I'll race you," Mark shouted.

"Last one there is a rotten egg," Michael said. The boys ran out the room, more enthusiastic than normal when asked to do their chores, sliding down the banisters to reach the bottom hall as fast as they could. Continuing his morning ritual, William got dressed.

The two boys ran through the courtyard and headed into the barn. Grandma had already been in there for fifteen minutes, collecting the freely laid eggs from around the barn. There were more than a hundred chickens in the large barn and for Grandma each morning was an egg hunt which sometimes took her several hours.

"Grandma, Grandma, we're here to help you. Right, Michael you go that way and I'll go this way," Mark ordered as he passed Michael one of the egg baskets.

Grandma Withens stopped and stared in surprise at seeing the boys happy to help her for a change. Some of the chickens had decided to stay nestled on their newly laid eggs, but this did not deter the boys as they pushed the birds out of the way, causing lots of clucking and crowing, with feathers flying about.

"Now, now, boys. Be gentle. We don't want to break any of them," Grandma said.

But the boys were too busy to listen and carried on filling their baskets.

"Fetch some more baskets, Grandma, I'm nearly full," Mark shouted. Grandma did not refuse; she enjoyed having her work done for her, so she fetched six more baskets from off the barn shelf.

Meanwhile, William was sitting downstairs with Grandpa, who had finished his morning work, milking the cows.

"Ah, nothing like a fresh glass of milk in the morning, is there, boy?" Grandpa said as he finished off his glass.

"Pa, what did you know about Hector Hornsmith?" William asked.

"Hector Hornsmith, hey? Now that is a name I've not heard around here for many years." Grandpa was sixty-eight years old and had born in 1826, a year before Mother Redcap's was destroyed by the Royal Navy.

"So you knew him, then?" William asked.

Grandpa put down his slice of toast and turned his chair to face William.

"Hector Hornsmith was a pioneer of a man around here. I worked on his manor house from time to time. Very nice place he had indeed."

"You worked for Hector Hornsmith and you never told me about it."

Grandpa simply shrugged his shoulders "Well, you never asked, so why would I have reason to tell you?" This was typical of Grandpa Withens, he never shared his stories and never spoke much about his past.

"I'm looking after his manor house as a favour to a friend..." William said.

"Oh, that's nice," Grandpa said as he made a start on his next piece of toast.

"Well, as always, Pa, it has been riveting. I've got to go and make a start on the boys' cart. I'll see you later."

Grandpa nodded in response and William made his way out to the workshed.

William looked around at the mechanical parts that were lying around the workshed. The cart had been left untouched following last year's victory. Last year was a close race and William knew that the rival team, "The Savilles," would have paid for a better cart than last time. "What can I use? I should have started weeks ago," William said looking at the bashed up cart that had only just passed the winning line. The boys were shouting outside for their father, but they were not allowed inside the workshed, so thankfully they could not see the sorry state that the cart was in.

"Father, father, please let us in," they shouted as they knocked repeatedly on the door.

"I'll be out in several minutes, boys. Go and see your mother." William had to think quickly on what he was going to do.

"No, you won't do, and you won't do either," he said to himself as he rummaged through lots of old mechanical parts. Then, the solution was right in front of him.

"The steam shooter." He had one of S.T.A.N's failsafe devices in his hand.

"Yes, this could just do it. On a device as small as the cart with only two passengers aboard, it will increase speed in a time of need." He was right as well; the device was used as a kick-start for when S.T.A.N was not releasing enough power to make it up the steep parts of the underground tracks when overloaded. Whereas S.T.A.N would have eight devices attached to it, the cart would only need two.

"The boys will be pleased this year," he thought to himself. But first he had to get the cart back to working condition. The bumps and dents had left the cart looking rather unloved and unusable.

Melinda was in the kitchen, preparing the packed lunches for Mark and Michael.

"One apple each, boiled ham and onion inside two slices of bread, and last but not least, a jar of fresh milk each." Melinda ensured each day that the boys had a filling lunch at school, a luxury that many schoolchildren never had. "Alright, boys, come and fetch your lunches; it's nearly time to leave for school." The boys drifted into the room in disappointment; they had been hoping to see their new cart before school time.

"Thank you, mother," they both said, one after the other.

"Why the long faces?" she asked.

"Father was supposed to have our cart ready for us to see today, but we still have not seen it," Mark said, upset.

Melinda tried to reassure the boys. "Well, you know your father; he likes everything to be perfect. He will have it ready for you soon, I'm sure."

"Alright, mother, I suppose." They both walked out of the door and headed off for a day in school.

William spent the whole day fixing the cart, replacing the broken pieces of wood and reshaping the wheels that were no longer in a circular shape. He needed to make sure that the cart would be better that last year. Unlike his rival Henry Saville, William built his own cart for his boys; rather than paying for somebody else to build it for them. The race for the last three years had been close; the Saville boys won the first two and last year, Mark and Michael won the race by the closest of finishes. But to be beaten by the Saville family was much more than a race defeat to William, it was about the awful use of money. Henry Saville had more money than he ever needed and always thought that he could buy his way to success in everything that he and his family did. More importantly, even without evidence, William knew that Henry Saville was somehow behind the theft of the inventions from his workshops.

"A really horrible man he is, indeed," William thought to himself.

Whenever something had gone missing from the workshop in the village, Henry Saville had previously been in the shop bothering William, trying to find out what he was working on. William would never tell anyone his planned inventions, never mind the rude and ignorant

Henry Saville. William spent the afternoon trying not to think about times when Henry had annoyed him, but with each hammer blow to the wooden cart, he found some kind of happiness and a release of built up anger inside himself.

That evening, after finishing dinner, William took the boys into the living room.

"Well, boys, how was school?" he asked as the boys climbed up onto their chairs.

"Wasn't too bad actually, father. Did you know that a crocodile has sixty-six teeth?" Mark asked.

"Really? That is fascinating stuff."

"Yes and also did you know that its real name is *Crocadolus arecute*?" Michael said. Michael was happy that he had remembered something when telling his father.

"No, Michael. I've told you, it's pronounced "*Crocodylus acutus.*" It's how it's pronounced in Latin." Mark was always correcting Michael, something that annoyed him greatly.

"Marvelous, boys. The reason why I've asked you to come in here is because I want to tell you something." The boys sat up straight and looked towards their father.

"Now, I know you think that I've not been paying much attention to you recently, but your cart will be ready and better than ever. I've a

The Inventor's Quest

new strategy this year that will help you greatly."

The boys were really excited now.

"Really? Is it going to fly?" Michael anticipated.

"No, not quite flying, but by one press of a button it will move faster than you can pedal." The boys were really excited at the thought of the new wheel cart they would have this year.

"Now go and get changed for bed, you have school in the morning." The boys kissed their father good night and headed upstairs to bed.

The next few days and nights, William focused all of his attention on the wheel cart. He removed the dents and scratches that remained from last year's race and gave it a new lick of paint. It was now red, white and blue. It looked like a grand British invention. In the nineteenth century, Britain was the greatest nation on earth, so it was only fitting that the great wheel cart on earth shared the same colours as the British flag and its glorious empire.

The next few days flew by and the boys got more excited as the race day grew ever closer, speaking to their friends in school telling them how their father had built them a bigger and better cart than last year.

"Apparently, Father has given us something we have never had before this year," Mark said.

"What would that be, Withens, a new pair of pants without holes in them?" a voice said.

"Shut it, Saville, nobody likes a big bully like you," Mark said. John Saville scrunched his face up, pulling a tongue at Mark.

"So what is it then, Mark?" another voice said as the class turned round to look towards Mark.

"I'm not sure, but Father has been working on it all day and night for the past three days. What about your cart, Rupert, what have you done this year?" he asked.

"Both I and Robert have worked hard on a new cart; our last one was crushed when a man fell out the back of the public house and into our yard. Most terrible incident it was, indeed."

Mark looked over to the table beside him and Penelope Marshall was busy drawing.

"How about you, Penelope? Are you going to race this year?"

"Our father has made us a nice pretty car this year. He let me pick the colours as well, didn't he, Christopher?" she said as she looked over to her brother.

"It's an absolute farce; I refuse to drive such a thing." Christopher was not happy. Penelope had been allowed to decorate the cart as she liked. Ribbons and bows was not what Christopher was hoping for, but unfortunately for him that was what she had picked.

The teacher arrived in the classroom and the day of schoolwork began. The children sat forward, keeping quiet; well, that is apart from John Saville's younger brother James who was busy picking his nose. The day dragged out; minutes felt like hours; they all watched the clock in the corner of the room as they were all excited about tomorrow's race.

Chapter Six

It was Saturday morning and the day of the Wheel Cart Derby had arrived. William was the last to wake up and he soon headed downstairs for breakfast. Mark and Michael had been too excited to sleep and were waiting around the breakfast table for their father to arrive.

"Father, you're awake! Can we see her now? It's Saturday morning," Michael asked.

William poured himself a cup of tea while eating a slice of freshly made toast.

"All in good time, boys, I've just sat down for breakfast. I tell you what, you go and help grandma again with the eggs and I'll have finished breakfast and have her ready for you to see by the time you finish." Mark and Michael shot out of the door faster than a steam train at full speed.

"Might be a good idea to comb your hair today, hey, William?" Melinda said as she served up a full plate of bacon, eggs and wild mushrooms.

"I'll be wearing my best waistcoat and top hat today, my dear," William responded giving his bacon a pinch of salt and a dash of pepper.

"This is an important day for the Withens family."

"Don't be too hard on them if they don't win." Melinda was worried that William was putting too much pressure on Mark and Michael and would be upset if they did not win.

"They are my boys. Win or lose, they make me proud each day. They are much more human beings than those two Saville brats will ever be." He was right as well; John and James Saville were nothing more than a pair of spoilt rich children. Always getting what they wanted and dressed in new clothes each week.

"How a person could be measured by wearing new clothing each week," William said.

"It's not the boys' fault if their father dresses them as businessmen," Melinda replied.

He did as well; they did not wear normal children's clothes, they dressed more like a middle aged businessman who was going off to work and not school. The Savilles were not a very well-liked family in the community; they lived on the other side of town from Montebello Manor. First there was Henry Saville and his wife Petunia; they had three boys and two girls. The eldest boy was called Benford, and he was away working down in London in one of the banks. Then there was John and James, a pair of bullies. The girls were much younger and very much like spoilt princesses.

Henry Saville has been known to be a real nasty and hard driven man. His workers quite often went on strike in protest at the low wages and long hours that they are given. Henry Saville would flaunt his extreme wealth in the faces of others. He owned his own personal carriage, but not just any normal carriage; it was near solid silver. He also owned a mansion that was much bigger than Montebello, which was of considerable size itself. The outer gardens contained a boating lake, a maze, and numerous rose gardens. But not many people were allowed to enjoy the pleasures within the garden; this was saved only for the rich merchants who would visit Henry for business reasons. The land was also surrounded by large hedges and cast iron gates; nobody could get in, especially with the four guards that surrounded the perimeter.

But what he had done to William had created a resentment that only William knew. Even his wife Melinda did not know the whole story as to why they had to move house so quickly. Back when the Withens family had lived in Wallasey Village a couple of years ago, William was working on a new device that was going to revolutionise the factory process across

Britain. The new conveyor would be able to move things much faster down the production line using a rubber belt powered by steam. But William was unable to finish it because the device was stolen when he was at his regular church meeting on a Sunday morning.

When he returned to the workshed on the Monday morning to complete his work, the window on the door had been broken and the device was gone. This was not the first time that it had happened, but William was determined to make sure it was the last by moving house and keeping his workshed on his own premises. He could never prove that Henry Saville was behind the robberies, but he knew quite well that he was responsible.

The boys had finished helping Grandma collect the eggs and they were waiting patiently, sitting on the wooden fence that surrounded the horses. William was inside his workshed, preparing the cart and giving it some last minute checks.

"Wheels attached and turning smoothly, check."

"Wooden side panels repaired and painted, check."

"Steam boosters attached to left and right rear ends, check."

"Pedals and chain connected and rotating, check."

"Steering wheel attached and working, check."

The cart was ready. Mark and Michael looked up in anticipation as the workshed doors opened; the cart came through the doors, glistening in the Saturday morning sunshine. Mark and Michael made their way over to the cart and gave it a good look over.

"She looks beautiful, father," Mark said as he ran his hand along the newly painted wooden panel next to the driver's side.

"What is this, father? I've not seen this before," Michael asked as he pulled on a metal cylinder on the back of the cart.

"Don't yank that, Michael. It's extremely delicate." Michael took his hand away immediately and stepped back from the cart.

William gathered the boys around the front of the cart and explained how to use the new device attached to the cart.

"Alright, boys; see this red button on the steering wheel?" The boys leaned over into the cart.

"This button is connected to the small furnace attached to the back of the cart that sends steam from the water cylinder through the small pipes that go around the underneath of the cart and to the two cylinders on each side of back of the cart. Have you got all that?"

Mark and Michael were slightly confused but they understood what they did because it was similar to a steam train, on which they had made several journeys.

"Alright, but what do they do, Father?" Mark asked.

"Well, when you press the red button, it will give you a boost of speed that will increase how fast you are going by up to an extra sixty percent, so you need to make sure that you are on a straight road when applying the increase of speed, otherwise you're likely to crash." Mark was slightly worried because he was driving.

"Alright, so I press the button when I'm on a straight road, got it."

William and the boys pushed the cart onto the waiting horse and carriage that Alfred Withens had brought around. They were ready to leave for the start of the race.

The Withens family all gathered onto the horses and carts and set off for the starting line situated on Seabank Road further down the hill from Montebello Manor. The first was driven by Alfred Withens, carrying the wheel cart, Mark, Michael and William. The other cart was driven by Benjamin Withens, with Grandpa, Grandma and Melinda Withens.

It was only a short journey along the pathway of the Manor and down the hill of St George's Mount, so the Withens family was the first to arrive. William, Mark and Michael got out of the back of the cart and placed the wheel cart on the road. Benjamin and the rest of the Withens family drove past and headed towards the finish line, which was on the New Brighton pier.

Meanwhile, the Withens family readied their cart at the starting line. The Saville family arrived in their silver carriage, with their servants rushing round, getting the cart ready for the race. Henry Saville was dressed in one of his best suits from London. He walked towards William holding his golden handled walking stick.

"Ah, Mr Withens. I see you're using the same cart as last year."

William turned from the cart wiping his hands on an oily rag to face the smirking Henry Saville.

"So what have you bought this time, Henry? Still smarting over last year's defeat, are we?"

Henry laughed loudly. "Last year was last year, Withens. This year I've hired a much better qualified scientist who will ensure that my boys bring that trophy back home to where it belongs." Henry was always replacing people like he replaced old clothes, especially ones that had not done their job to his standards.

"We will see, Henry," William said. He turned back to finish getting the cart ready.

"Show starts in ten minutes, Withens. See you at the finishing line." Henry walked back over to his silver carriage and headed off to the New Brighton pier.

It was five minutes to eleven and all of the contestants were ready awaiting the eleven o'clock horn shot to start the race. The sun glistening across the River Mersey in the distance. William finished relaying his instructions to Mark and Michael and left with Alfred down to the start of the race. The scientist spoke to John and James Saville, giving them the run-through of how the cart worked; the servants rushed round strapping them in and placing their protective hats and goggles on. Edgar and Neville Brown were next in the row and their cart was very basic. Mr Brown, their father, had been lost at sea on a fishing expedition when his boat capsized during a freak storm. Next in line were Christopher and Penelope Marshall, the son and daughter of Mr Marshall, the local coal merchant. At the end was Rupert and Robert, the Bell twins. They were the sons of Brian and Bella Bell, who ran the local Magazines Inn.

The five sets of contestants were ready and waiting for the Mayor of Wallasey to start the race. He was in full voice.

"The course will begin here at the joining of Seabank Road and Rowson Street. It will then go down the hill and taking a right turn will proceed to the bottom of Victoria Road. Once they reach the bottom of the road, it will then be a straight finish to the end of the pier."

The local mayor, Lord Cuthbert Coulthard, counted down the seconds on his pocket watch. It was nearly eleven o'clock. Each year the Mayor sponsored the race, which offered a prize of twenty pounds to the winners. The last few seconds were counting down and the Mayor shouted out in a loud voice.

"Three, Two, One, Go," and then fired his pistol.

The crowds cheered as the carts began to move with the drivers peddling away to reach the beginning of the hill. The Saville boys had taken an early lead, ahead of Mark and Michael

Withens who were just behind. The Rowson Street hill was on a forty-five degree angle and was very steep. All of the carts were gathering speed, travelling down the hill. The roadsides were packed with locals cheering as the carts went by. The carts of the Withens and Saville's were neck and neck, with John Saville shouting abuse over at Mark Withens.

"We will have you this time, Withens!" He steered over towards the Withens cart, causing Mark to steer further away from the centre of the road.

"Cheating again as always, Saville. You and your family are nothing but cheats."

He was right, as well; last year the Withens cart nearly got pushed off the road and into the river, and it looked like John Saville was going to try and do it again.

The turning into Victoria Road was approaching and both carts slammed on the brakes, causing screeching noises. The Saville cart went round the right hand corner smoothly, thanks to the excellent and expensive brakes that had been attached. Then the Withens cart followed, shuddering as it battled with the ninety degree angle. It was bad news for Edgar and Neville Brown; their cart failed to slow down in time and smashed through the crowds of people and into the row of oak trees. The other carts were still struggling behind and it looked like a two-way race again. Mark Withens peddled as fast as he could and gained ground on the Saville Cart. With a little over half the race left, the Withens cart began to make its move. They edged past the Saville car with James shouting:

"Let them have it, John. Go on, let them have it!"

John looked down inside the cart and pulled the lever next to him. Two openings appeared at the front and the back of the driver's side of the Saville cart and a spike appeared out of each opening. John Saville laughed to himself as he started to ram into the Withens cart, making punctures into the wooden side.

"You're mad! What are you doing?" Mark shouted across to John Saville.

"I'm showing you who is the boss! That's what I'm doing," he shouted back as he plunged the spikes into the cart again, scraping away the wood, causing it to splinter severely. The Withens cart was severely damaged. A few more scratches and it would fall apart.

"Do something," Michael shouted at Mark. They were nearing the halfway point of Victoria

Road and at this rate they would be lucky to make the end of the road.

John Saville prepared one last attack on the Withens cart; one more hit and they would be done for.

"This is it, Withens, say goodbye," he shouted, laughing as he swerved over to the Withens cart.

"Mark, if you don't do it, I'll..." Michael shouted.

"Do what?" Mark replied looking confused.

"The button," Michael said. He pointed to the red button on the steering wheel. The Saville cart was inches away from connecting with the Withens cart and Mark had no choice but to push it.

"Hold on, Michael, it's going to get rather fast." Michael grabbed hold of what he could and Mark pressed down hard on the red button. A loud hiss of steam sounded out and the cart jolted forward in an incredible speed.

"Woweee," Michael cried out as he held on as tight as he could to the shuddering cart.

"See you at the finishing line," Mark shouted at the stunned looking John and James Saville. The steam blast had sent the cart into an extremely fast motion and the sides rattled as they approached the bottom of Victoria Road.

The crowds were everywhere, cheering and clapping as they saw the Withens cart approaching.

"We're going too fast," Michael shouted.

"Hang on," Mark said, as his face shuddered in the wind.

Mark Withens had trouble controlling the steering and they were veering all over the road. Bits of broken wood began to fall off, hitting people as the cart went by. Mark tried to put on the brakes but they were not working, they would not slow down. They had reached the start of the pier and people were panicking as the cart smashed from side to side into the sides of the walkway.

It was obvious that Mark and Michael were going to win the race, but that was not important anymore; slowing down was. The cart was going way too fast to be able to stop at the end of the pier, despite hitting and bouncing off the sides of the walkway; they simply were not slowing down enough. The crowds at the end of the pier cheered until they saw the cart heading in their direction. Many jumped over the side and into the river to prevent being hit. The cart passed through the tape on the finishing line and the music rang out from the band that was playing at the back of the pier. The music soon ended as the cart hurtled towards them sending more people flying out of the way. The band members had dropped their instruments and were running to wherever they could find safety. The cart hurtled through the scattered instruments and straight into the railings behind, catapulting the boys out of the cart and into the air. For several seconds the boys were suspended in the air with their arms and legs moving frantically as they dropped back to drop back down to earth. A loud crash was heard as the boys could fall no more.

Thankfully, upon falling Mark and Michael went straight through the canopy of the pavilion, somewhat breaking their fall. The boys appeared from out of the pavilion in a dazed state. William ran with joy towards them.

"My boys, you did it, you did it! We won." Mark and Michael were embraced by the outstretched arms of their father.

"But the state of the cart! She is done for now," Mark said as he looked round the pier. The cart was scattered into many pieces, most of which were now floating in the River Mersey. The rest of the contestants had arrived at the back of the pier and being reunited with their parents. However, there was much shouting coming from the crowd. It was Henry Saville giving his boys a right talking-to.

"You've let me down for the last time! All of the money I've spent on building you a new cart and you still couldn't even win. Next year I'll buy myself a new driver as well as a better cart." Poor John and James were very upset as their father dragged them off down the pier.

The Mayor Cuthbert Coulthard stood upon the stage and addressed his audience. "It is with great pleasure that I can award this year's prize to the winners, Mark and Michael Withens. Who, despite nearly destroying our iconic pier, were able to win in a humbling and gracious manner. I award you twenty pounds and the fabulous New Brighton Wheel Cart Silver Cup."

The crowd cheered and once again. The Withens family were the winners of the New Brighton Wheel Cart Cup for the second year running.

Chapter Seven

After spending Saturday and Sunday in celebration, it was now Monday morning and things had returned to normal. The boys were back in school, Melinda was out selling vegetables and fruit on the farm stall and William was back in his workshed. William was loading up S.T.A.N with lengths of timber and rods of iron. He knew that he must get back to Hornsmith Manor, fix the damage to the tunnel entrance to ensure that no one would find a way into the hidden network of tunnels, just as he had promised Barney Browne he would do. He made his way through the tunnels to Hornsmith Manor and spent the morning fixing the doorway that he had previously broken open. Following the completion of the repair work, William decided to visit inside of the manor house. Now that he was a key holder, he was able to come and go as he pleased. Barney Browne had told William Hector Hornsmith was an excellent architect and had designed and built the manor house himself.

Seeing the tunnel networks made William's imagination run wild, thinking about what could be hidden within the manor house itself. William closed the fixed doorway and made his way to the front door of Hornsmith Manor. He opened the large oak door with the key, which gave a loud click as it unlocked. He turned the brass handle and went through the opening, which creaked each inch it opened further. The hallway was dark as he walked in; there was a marble floor covered with symmetrical patterns and a beautifully crafted wooden spiral staircase heading upwards from the centre of the hallway and sweeping round both sides up to the floor above. As William walked further into the room he looked at the walls, which were covered in portraits of what looked like Hector and his family members. Many of the items within the hallway were covered in cotton sheets and had clearly not been uncovered for some time.

However, at the end of the hallway there was an old grandfather clock covered in dust and no longer ticking. On each side of the clock were two doors. William proceeded to enter the door to the right, which was slightly open. He walked through the open door and into what was the kitchen, and what a beautiful-looking kitchen it was. The room had been set out in a very spacious and neat manner. Despite all the dust and dirt that had collected over the years, it was clear to see that it had once been a happy family environment in which many meals had been prepared. Leading out to the left of the room was a glass room that overlooked the back garden. William had noticed this glass structure when walking up from the tunnel opening. The room was covered in glass panes, something in which you would normally find plants and flowers. But there was nothing botanical about this room; it had a large dining table and a piano. It was clear to see that as well as being the setting for family meals, guests would also have been invited round and entertained with music they would feast. William went over to the piano and pressed down on a few keys that let out little out-of-tune beats, sending dust rising into the air. Clearly this piano had not been played in a very long time.

William walked back into the kitchen and across to the opening on the other side of the room. It was a smallish room filled with empty jars, still labelled from their previous contents. Many were labels of fruit jams; this was expected considering the number of wild berries that were growing in the garden. Just as Melinda Withens would make her homemade jam, it was clear that the Hornsmiths had done the same. William returned to the main hallway to explore the rest of the house.

There were six doors situated on the bottom floor of the house; the kitchen door, another leading into the front room, which was filled with more items covered in cotton sheets and a rather large fireplace, which would have generated sufficient heat for the spacious room. Another door on the left hand side of the main hallway led to a room which looked more like a family living room, several bookshelves lining the walls filled with many different genres. There was also a fireplace with a cast iron kettle suspended over it. There was a door that led to a cloakroom. William had one similar in his house; there were that many people living in his house that the coats and shoes needed to be housed in their own room. The last two doors were both empty rooms, most likely storage rooms at one point.

William headed up the spiral staircase to check out the second of three floors of the house. There were more pictures on the walls as he walked up each step of the staircase. Many were of local landmarks of the area, such as the Perch Rock Fort, St Hilary's Church, the view across the ship-filled River Mersey. William had arrived on the second floor landing and there were four more rooms. The first was a bedroom, more than likely for guests as it contained just a large bed and fireplace. The second room was the children's bedroom, filled with toy chests and two cabin beds set out like the inside of a ship, with many nautical items displayed on the walls such as anchors, ropes, ship flags and a barometer. The last two were an empty room and the master bedroom. There was nothing more of interest on this floor so William headed up to the last floor of the house. The third floor of the house was much bigger than the second. Many more rooms were available; most likely servant's quarters, which was normal for a house of this size. However there was one room which was locked at the very end of the hallway. William only had a key to the front door; Barney Browne had only given him that key which he said opened every door.

Since he was an inventor, locked doors generally were not a problem for William. He had the ability to open any locked door with his tools, apart from the large door in the tunnel, of course. Those types of locks can never be opened with a few mere tools; brute force was the only answer. But there would be no need to pull open these doors, they were simple latchkey locks; a thin piece of metal wire would be sufficient. William opened his trusty tool satchel, which contained just about anything an inventor would need in tricky situations.

"Right, let's see. What have I got in here?"

William rummaged through his satchel and pulled out a foot of copper wire and also a pair of pinching pliers. Upon carefully inserting the wire in the keyhole, he positioned the two ends in the top and bottom parts of the lock. Using the pinching pliers, he simultaneously turned both ends to the left, creating a clicking noise as the door unlocked. William opened the door and walked through into Hector Hornsmith's study.

William's eyes lit up as he entered the room. It was like a small library. The walls were lined with bookshelves, there was a writing desk neatly compiled with several books, newspapers, an oil lantern and pad of writing paper. William sat down on the chair in front of the desk and looked through the pile of papers that had been neatly arranged. Many of the paper cut-outs were of Hector himself, articles mentioning how he had built or played a part in the opening of many local mansion houses and buildings.

"This man was really admired around here," William said to himself.

He scanned through the papers. One of the papers came away from the pile in William's hand and dropped to the floor. As William bent down to pick it up, he noticed a switch placed under the desk.

"Hello there! And what would you be doing under here?" he said examining the brass switch placed on the right underside of the desk. "Well, I came here looking for answers, so let's see what you do." William pressed the button and a loud click came from behind him.

The bookshelf had become detached from the wall. William arose from the chair and proceeded to examine the area. The bookshelf was a cover for a doorway which led into a dark room. William returned to the desk and retrieved the oil lantern; he opened his satchel and took out his box of matchsticks to light the lantern. He then walked through the door, illuminating the room more with each step he took.

"What the dickens is this?" William muttered to himself. The room was empty apart from a large wooden compartment in the centre of the room. He walked over to the device. It had four wooden walls and contained only a lever. He pulled the lever and the device lowered into the floor.

William entered another room. He pulled the lever back to the middle position to stop the moving motion, and exited the wooden compartment. The room was darker than a moonless sky and was much bigger than the room above.

William walked over to the wall on the right hand side of the wooden compartment. A lantern was attached to it. He put down the lit lantern and returned to his satchel from which he pulled out a candle. Using the already lit oil lantern, he used the candle to transfer the flame from one lantern to another. The room gained more light and everything became more visible. There were two wooden chests, a pirate flag and a wooden ship's wheel dotted around the area of the lantern. William walked over to the other side of the room where again there was a lantern hanging from the wall; he lit the lantern to gain more light.

The room was now fully illuminated and it was double the size of the room that he had come down from.

"How can a room of this size be hidden within a house?" he wondered to himself. William thought about the way in which the house had been structured. There were only four rooms on the second floor that were no way big enough to fill the entire area, yet it would not look suspicious to those that would be occasionally visiting the house. There was a desk with wooden shelves above situated on the left hand side of the room. William walked over as he spotted several books that looked quite aged. He picked up the book titled "The last diary of Hector Hornsmith," scanning through pages that were filled with information and drawings. He turned to the last diary entry, dated 31st December 1839.

To whoever may be the person reading this, you have found my secret rooms and my diaries, this will mean that I'm long moved on from this world to the next. By now if you have come this far, you will know who I am and my adventures at sea with my good friend Captain John Gray.

You may be thinking about the vast amounts of treasure that was accrued over the years. I'm sad to inform you that much of it has been split accordingly between the Captain, myself and the crew members. Much of which was wisely invested in the area of Wallasey by myself and many of the crew members that chose to stay.

However, not all has been lost. My private fortune is still to be found and if you are worthy of its wealth, you will be able to undertake and complete the challenges that I've put in place in order to prevent the treasures from falling into the wrong hands.

Only a man of true heart and mind will be worthy of this fortune and he will be challenged by the need for thinking, strength, wisdom and heart. If you contain all of those abilities, here is the beginning of the quest for the Treasure of Hector Hornsmith. If you follow each clue it will lead you to your next step; get the clue wrong and your quest will be over. Your first clue is as follows:

The beginning starts with ringing and the chimes of the singing, but you will not find what you seek before eight and you will not gain entrance without the three. On the tower you will find thee, where a vessel will transport ye.

Signed

Hector Hornsmith

William had found the all-important clue that he had been searching for. The quest had been set by Hector Hornsmith. It may have taken over fifty years to be found, but William Withens was the discovered and would undertake the challenge. But he knew that if anybody else found out about the diary of Hector Hornsmith and the quest, they would become a dangerous enemy. William knew that he had to act quickly and secretly and be careful to ensure that nobody was watching his movements; he was going to have to start the quest as soon as possible.

Chapter Eight

While William had been searching inside Hornsmith Manor, a train had arrived at Liverpool Lime Street station. Steam was pouring from it as it halted at the end of the track. Crowds of people were waiting to board the train back to London, and some were eagerly anticipating their loved ones dismounting from their carriages. In particular there was a group of people waiting for one carriage door to open. The carriage door swung open and in the doorway stood an elegant looking lady wearing a bright red dress with a large straw summer's hat to match her long curled blonde hair.

Ellie-May Grangeworthy had arrived on the twenty past two train from London to Liverpool; elegantly she stepped out of the carriage onto the platform one foot at a time. Dressed in the latest fashion from the Continent, she turned heads with her good looks and wealth, standing out from the crowds dressed in their dark clothes. Following in her footsteps were several small but stocky men, carrying several large chests containing her valuables. She walked on through the station, moving for nobody, expecting everybody to get out of her way. Outside the station she made her way to the main doors. A carriage awaited her arrival and a man stood firmly with open arms to greet her. It was Henry Saville.

"Ellie-May, my dear! Was it a pleasant trip?" Henry asked. Henry Saville had entrusted Ellie-May Grangeworthy to become the new boss at his cotton factory.

"Dreadful, it was absolutely dreadful. Do you know, I had to share my journey with some ghastly man who spent the whole journey reading his newspaper and smoking his pipe, interrupting me while I was reading my Bronte novel? He introduced himself as Sherlock Holmes and kept mumbling about somebody called John Watson. I could not have cared less about either of them, I just wanted to read my book."

Henry Saville shook his head with displeasure.

"Will you be making a complaint to the head of department in transport?" he asked as he helped Ellie-May into the carriage.

"They will be hearing from me very soon. When my father hears of this he will be most annoyed."

"Ah, that he would, my dear. That he would."

"Well, don't just stand there, boy, help me into the carriage," Ellie-May barked.

The young lad was catching his breath after he had just finished loading the stacked cases and chests containing Ellie-Mays valuables onto the second carriage.

"Yes, my lady, I'm sorry, please forgive me," he said helping Miss Grangeworthy into Henry Saville's silver carriage. The carriage pulled off and they made their way towards the Pier Head of Liverpool.

The carriage containing Henry Saville and Ellie-May Grangeworthy travelled through Liverpool to the dockland area. They crossed the River Mersey by ferry boat with the second carriage following behind.

They made tracks from the New Brighton Pier towards Miss Grangeworthy's new home, somewhere that she had not seen before.

"Lovely little seaside resort you have here, hey, Henry?" Ellie-May said as she peered out of the window at the view over the river.

"Well, it's a prosperous area, but I don't have much time for the locals. Thankfully I've secure surroundings around my house to keep the peasants out."

Ellie-May nodded in agreement. "Ah, yes, the lowly peasants. Can't live with them, can't make money without them." They both shared a chorus of laughter.

The carriage pulled up at its destination and Ellie-May peered out of the window at her new residence. They had halted at a set of iron gates and behind them was a large beautiful house.

William Withens was busy reading some of Hector's diary when he returned to the study room from below; he was startled by a noise outside and jumped up to peer out of the third floor window. William saw two carriages. One of them was clearly Henry Saville's. Nobody else in the area had a silver carriage.

"What is he doing here?" he muttered to himself.

He quickly gathered the collection of Hector Hornsmith diaries that he had brought up from the hidden room and hid them within his satchel.

"That despicable man, Henry Saville, is trying to steal my work again. But how would he know? Surely he does not. Who would tell him? Barney wouldn't tell him and I've only just found out about the treasure myself. I must keep calm and not let it slip about any of it."

William was getting himself into a blind panic; he needed to calm himself down. When he peered out of the window again, the silver carriage had pulled away from Hornsmith Manor and then there was movement within the house. Barney Browne had made him the new housekeeper and it was his duty to protect the place. He left the study room and headed down the two flights of stairs to the hallway. Once he reached the bottom of the stairs, he was met by the glaring eyes of Ellie-May.

"And who might you be, then?" she asked.

William thought the same.

"May I ask who you are? My name is William Withens and I've been entrusted to look after this house by its owners."

Ellie-May had a real scowl on her face; she hated being spoken back to.

"Well, William Withens, I'm the new owner of this house and your services are no longer required, so I suggest you pack whatever belongings you have and make your exit as soon as possible before I have you arrested for trespassing."

William did not know how to react but there was now an army of men and women coming in and out of the house with an abundance of Ellie-May's belongings. It was clear that it was no longer going to be an option to come and search through the hidden rooms that he had found and he knew the only thing he could do was to collect as many of Hector's personal papers as he could carry. He stumbled down the stairs with several books and rolled up papers filling his arms.

"I hope that is your property," Ellie-May shouted.

"They are mine. I often do my work here because it's more peaceful than home." It was the only thing that William could think of saying.

"Well, William Withens, you shall have to find somewhere else to do your work from now on." Ellie-May took a glance at the items that William was holding, but did not pay too much attention to the details.

William left through the door of Hornsmith Manor for what could possibly be the last time; his only hope was that the entrance to the tunnels would remain hidden now that the house had new unexpected occupants. William had no option but to walk home from Hornsmith

Manor. It was not worth risking making his exit through the tunnel. But he knew more importantly he needed to return to Mother Redcap's and warn Barney Browne about the new tenant at Hornsmith Manor. It was going to take a good twenty minutes to reach Mother Redcap's on the river front and it was due to go dark in a few hours, so William needed to hurry. Walking around the river front in the dark was something that William did not fancy doing. So many locals in the public house have come in from the dark telling their tales of encounters with evil spirits, and then there was the Black Rock mermaid, but that's a whole other story.

William reached the premises of Mother Redcap's. Barney Browne sat in the window looking out over the river. William entered through the front door, dropping the items from out of his tired arms.

"Hello Barney, how are you today?" William asked as he entered through the door.

"Ah, young William. I hear your boys had a momentous victory in the race the other day," he said as he turned to face William. They chatted for a while about what happened in the race, because Barney had been unable to make it to the event.

"The reason why I'm here, Barney, is because I've just come from Hornsmith Manor; did you know anything about the land being sold to Henry Saville?"

Barney shook his head in disbelief. "Never in my eighty-seven years of life have I met a more vile man than Henry Saville. I've no idea why the Hornsmith children agreed to sell their father's land to him of all people. I received a letter just yesterday from them, thanking me for my help over the years and saying they had no plans of returning home. When Henry Saville made them a reasonable offer they could not refuse." This upset Barney because he knew that his friend Hector would never have allowed it.

"I've found several of Hector's diaries," William said, taking out a couple of the books from his satchel.

"He was always writing in his book. Carried it everywhere with him he did," Barney replied as he emptied the last of a bottle of rum into two glasses.

"I need to be honest with you, Barney; I found the books in a hidden room within the house."

Barney smiled and took a large gulp of the dark coloured liquor. "I know you did. Who did you think helped build an area of such secrecy? Hector would not have been able to complete such a design all on his own. It was lucky that we managed to complete and hide it before any of the other builders arrived to finish the work." He was right as well. It took Hector and Barney several months to complete the foundations and framework of the manor house, cleverly creating the hidden rooms within the design and sealing them off before the rest of the construction crew joined into complete the work.

"Well, why did you not tell me of such a place? It would have made things so much easier. It was only by sheer luck that I found the room behind the bookcase." William was quite upset.

"My boy, you have read the final entry in the diary, I presume. Does it not say only the man of true heart and mind would be worthy of undertaking the quest?"

William nodded in agreement.

"Well, there you have it. I could not guide you; you had to find it yourself if you were truly able and worthy to take on the quest."

After a short silence in which William thought about what he had read in Hector's diary, he realised he had more questions that needed answering.

"So you knew about the treasure and you knew about the quest. Why did you never take the quest yourself?"

Barney hobbled slowly over to prepare the fire as the room was dropping in temperature as the night time crept in. "I've never had the need to take on the quest; I've always had everything I needed in life right here. Remember, a man with wealth of fortune always has a heavy price to pay. Look at Henry Saville. Money has consumed his mind; it's all he thinks about."

"That is for sure," William replied.

"Before you undertake this quest, you have to decide if you can bear the responsibilities of having more money than you would ever need."

William had a big decision to make. Would finding the treasure really be worth risking the happy life he already had? Never in this world would he want to turn out like that evil man Henry Saville.

"I'm willing to take on the challenge, Barney. I'm an inventor, it's my duty to discover things. I'm strong minded enough to find it and I'm strong enough to not let greed consume me."

Barney believed William; he knew that in his heart he was a good man.

"How about you join me on the quest, Barney?" William asked.

"My days of going on adventures are long gone, my boy. I just need my rum, warmth and my view out onto the river with my book. That is all the excitement I need."

William smiled; it was pleasing to see somebody enjoying the simple things in life.

"Alright, but can I ask one more favour? Could I possibly borrow your horse so I can get home? I couldn't possibly carry all these things home."

Barney agreed and they both sat and finished a glass of rum each.

William rode home through the dimming light of the setting sun; all he could think about was the quest.

Chapter Nine

The next morning arrived and William was feeling rather tired, having spent most of the night in between sleep thinking about the quest. Melinda was already downstairs cooking breakfast, the boys were out helping Grandma collect eggs and Grandpa was out in the other barn milking the cows. William dragged himself out of bed at the smell of fried bacon from downstairs. His sleeping pattern might have been out of sorts, but his stomach sure wasn't. He looked out of the window and rubbed his eyes to double-check what he was seeing was correct.

"Snow in October! That cannot be correct," he said to himself.

The snow was still falling and looked as if it had been falling all through the night. There was a white sheet covering everything. He got himself dressed and quickly forgot about the snow, having more important matters on his mind.

Once washed and dressed, he headed down the stairs to a full bodied breakfast table. Melinda had served a breakfast feast of bacon rashers, eggs, mushrooms, fried onions and toast. William sat down with everyone else who were already tucking into the delicious looking food.

"Good job those hens lay their eggs in the barn. We would never have found them outside, would we, boys?" Grandma said as she bit into a piece of crisped bacon.

"They still don't leave them in the same place though, do they? We have to have a different search every morning." William smiled at Michael's comments.

"Well, Michael. The reason why they do this is because hens like privacy when laying their eggs. They will wander off and find somewhere on their own as a suitable spot to rest," William explained to Michael.

"Strange day we are having here, hey William," Grandpa said.

"Strange?" William said with a confused look.

"The snow! It's snowing in October. Have you not noticed?"

"Ah, yes. Sorry, I wasn't thinking properly. Yes, very strange day indeed, Pa."

"Is everything alright dear?" Melinda asked.

"Just did not get much sleep last night. I'll wake up soon."

"Here, have some more bacon. That will wake you up," Melinda said placing two extra rashers of bacon on William's plate. They all finished breakfast and went about their daily duties, the boys heading off through the falling snow to school.

Several hours had passed. William looked out of the kitchen window. "Well, thank heavens for that," he said to himself. The snow had finally stopped falling. "I won't be using the cart today, that's for sure." The kitchen door opened and in stepped Melinda Withens, dusting off the snow from her sheepskin coat.

"It's been a wild morning, William. When was the last time we ever got snow in October?" she asked.

"I'm not sure, my dear. It certainly hasn't happened in my lifetime."

The door opened again. This time it was Grandpa Withens.

"Holy Moses! I've not seen snow this time of year since I was a child."

Melinda was brushing the leftover snow off of Grandpa's coat.

"We were just saying the same thing, Pa," William said. The Withens family sat around the kitchen table for the afternoon, discussing issues with the farm, drinking hot milk to keep warm.

The next day, more snowfall throughout the night had left a crisp white sheet throughout the fields around Montebello Manor. Grandma and Grandpa Withens had been out early, tending to the livestock. The animals had been taken out of the fields and placed in the barns, out of the cold. Mark and Michael Withens had been given their day off by the headmaster due to the doors being unable to open. This pleased the boys very much and they were taking full advantage of a day with no school. Across the fields from the manor house, Mark and Michael were sliding up and down McGregor's hill on a wooden sled, built by their father. William and Melinda were in the barn, brushing down the horses.

William and Melinda shared a ten minute period of silence as they ran the brushes across the bodies of the horses. This was due to William thinking of the right words to use to tell his wife about his absence that would happen shortly.

"Melinda, dear," he said in a soft voice.

"Hmm?" she replied as she looked up towards her husband.

"There is something I need to tell you." He was quite nervous and Melinda could tell. "How would you mind if I went off on a little adventure for a while?"

Melinda stopped what she was doing and William now had her full attention.

"Go on, then. Tell me. What is it now?" she replied.

William went around the side of the horse and took Melinda by the hand to sit on the wooden bench at the side of the barn. William told the story from the beginning. They were man and wife and he could not bear for there to be secrets between them. For about half an hour Melinda listened to what William had to say and she was not really sure if what she was hearing was true.

"So you're saying that we are living above hidden tunnels and somebody has left you a treasure map and you want to leave everything and go and find it. That doesn't sound crazy at all?" she said in a sarcastic voice.

"This will be easier if I just show you. Come with me to my workshed," he said as he took her hand. They both walked across the courtyard to William's workshed, somewhere that Melinda had never entered since they had lived there. William opened the workshed's doors. Melinda was excited to be finally going into William's secret workshed. Little did she know what else she would see.

Melinda looked around at the familiar tools that she remembered from William's shop in the village, but something she had not seen before was a big opening leading downwards, with a large machine within it.

"William, what does this do?" she asked, running her fingers along the side of S.T.A.N, looking it over in great detail.

"Get in! I'll show you." William filled the furnace with fresh coal and helped Melinda into the front seat. He checked over the water content and tested the furnace to ensure that it was generating enough heat before they set off down into the tunnels. All checks complete, they went through the opening and down towards the cave. Melinda was in awe as they travelled along the tunnels, but she was more surprised by the mirrors lighting the way through the tunnels.

"This is magnificent, William; did you build this all on your own?" she asked, fanning the engulfing steam and smoke away from her face.

"Well, I did have some help, but I did most of it."

"I've never seen anything like it in my life. Did you dig the tunnels as well?"

"The tunnels were already here. I just needed to lay the tracks and attach the mirrors. You haven't seen the best part yet."

"There is more to see?" Melinda said excitedly.

They carried on till they reached the cave entrance; William brought S.T.A.N to a halt.

"Remember, you must tell nobody about any of this. It's our secret."

Melinda nodded in agreement and braced herself for what she was about to see. William added more coal into the furnace and manoeuvred the lever into the forward position; S.T.AN moved forward once again.

"It's absolutely beautiful," Melinda said as her eyes lit up.

They entered the light filled cavern, now packed with all of William's contraptions and inventions.

"You even have fresh water in here," Melinda said pointing to the pool, which contained a wheel that William used as a source of power.

"Look up. Can you see that tiny hole where the golden circle is? That is where the light comes from that illuminates the whole room and tunnels."

Melinda was overcome with excitement and still in complete shock as she gazed around the large cavern. They travelled around the cave on the track, taking a semi-circular route, passing several half built metal structures. With each distance they took, something new caught her eye. A wooden pen full of pigs was the next thing to surprise her. There were even chickens and a goat running round freely.

"Should I even ask you what they are doing down here?" she smiled at William.

"Alternate power source, hopefully one day," he replied as he pointed to the wooden crate of manure.

"Where exactly are we?"

"Well, by my calculations, I would say that we are somewhere by the sandstone rocks on the river front. You know, down from where we walked along the sand on that beautiful sunset, past the lighthouse several years ago."

Melinda knew exactly where he meant. They had spent the summer evening watching the sunset and the ships sailing out from Liverpool towards the sea.

S.T.A.N reached the end of the track. Steam hissed out as the wheels ground to a halt. William helped Melinda out of the driver's carriage and walked over to his wooden desk in the middle of the cave.

"So this is where you go every day for hours on end," Melinda said as she admired the desk area, carefully built in between two large rocks in the centre of the cave.

"These are the diaries that I found in Hornsmith Manor." William pointed to the books on the desktop. Melinda picked up the opened diary of Hector Hornsmith and read the last entry that explained the quest. After a few minutes, she knew that William was telling the truth and the possibility of hidden treasure was not just a bedtime story that a father would tell their children.

"How many did he write?" Melinda asked as she started counting the stack of books on the desk.

"Well, I've managed to find five of them, but from what Barney has explained to me, I think there will be several others. I didn't have time to look further, but I may try and sneak back into Hornsmith Manor when the coast is clear."

Melinda was engulfed in one of the earliest written diaries.

"Here William. Listen to this. Hector speaks of finding a place called Ye Black Rock."

William stopped what he was doing, turned to look at Melinda and sat down to listen to what she had to say.

"Go on, then. Read it to me," William said. Melinda started to read from the diary.

"The entry is titled "Finding Ye Black Rock," dated 23rd March 1796."

My name is Hector Hornsmith and I was born in Portishead near Bristol in 1759, I was a year younger than John. Portishead were a nice quiet little fishing village nothing like when I moved up near Liverpool, we had a lovely little stone cottage with a thatched roof, we lived about 10 minutes from the River which was where me and father would fish in the day and take tea home for supper it really was wonderful when we had a good day catching, however the winters were cold. I mentioned father his name was Peter married to my mother Elizabeth and I had one brother and one sister named, Elliot and Harriet. Mother used to spin yarn with Harriet me and father would go fishing, Elliot was older than me so father used to make him tend the chickens and vegetables so we all helped in our own way, when it was cold father used to let me stay at home with mother and Harriet and help spin wool this is why John made me make a weaving room for Polly, because of how I learnt from mother.

I had finished creating the weaving room in the garden it was more like an outhouse which had taken me around four months to build, what was handy is that lots of excess stone was left lying around from when the tunnels were excavated and used on the inn and the surround wall, so I managed to use plenty of the stones once they were cut down into shape, but with my leg being bad it took me twice as long as I expected. When I first stepped back and looked at it when it was finished, I was very happy with what I had built. The stone was smooth all the way round because I made sure it was chiselled down to near perfection, it was about ten feet high I know this because I'm about six feet tall and it was near twice as big as me, the good thing was I had a few helpers issued to me by Captain Bones, so I was able to get the stones into place much quicker. The roof was wooden and took several trees to create it due to the one room being of a good square shape, with just one door as an entrance also made of wood. Before we left I presented the weaving room to Mother Redcap after some of the sailors had filled it with plenty of wool and a spinning machine, she was very happy as she could now prepare her own wool to knit her own clothes, this also made Captain Bones happy as he knew she would have a new hobby to attend he went on his next voyage across the seas.

The captain rounded up all of the men and told me to make sure I had everything I needed as he did not know how long we would be as we were going to a place that we had never been before, I did not bother inquiring where; I trust his instincts and did what he said. We headed down below into the passages where the boats were afloat; it was quite nice weather with it being June so the waters were not choppy at all. There was about twenty of us getting into the four boats as some of the crew had already gone ahead to Liverpool to prepare the vessel for sail. Redcap was waving as we were leaving holding back the tears and Captain Bones shouted "Farewell my love, until we are together once again," and away we went to start our journey out of the cave. The tide was on its way in so there was a need to hurry before the water became too high and would prevent us from making it out, the passageway was only able to *allow one boat at a time to pass through and the Captain's boat would take the lead and the rest of the boats would follow. The best thing about the cave passage being only around eight feet high and around six feet wide, was that unless you were from around the area you would not know that they existed this is how me and the captain first found them rather by luck than expectance.*

Back when we first came into the River Mersey heading towards Liverpool, the storm was bashing our ship up and down on the waves, with the water crashing over the whole deck, lightning strikes the water, with claps of thunder as loud as I had ever heard before. The more we moved up the mouth of the river, we were constantly being pushed away from the port of Liverpool across to the opposite banks of the Mersey, which was putting us in danger due to the constant rows of rocks right along our path, the only thing we could do was drop anchor and ride out the storm. The storm kept getting worse so the captain made a decision of everyone getting off the boat and heading to land, the men gathered what they could and lowered the smaller boats into the water, we only had six boats and each boat could carry six people and there was over sixty people on board, so some men and women decided to take their chances and stay onboard, the captain went to find a safe route.

I as usual was ordered onto the captain's boat, the waters where wild it was about fifty strokes to reach land and I was not certain that we were going to make it, but the captain relayed his orders amongst the harrowing winds and clashes of thunder "row men, row, use all your might." The four other men rowed as hard as they could, I was in front of the ship looking for a good place to land, but the currents of the river kept pushing us further off course and closer towards the rocks. It looked like this would be our final journey as there would be no victory against the strength of the seas, then we were now only several strokes from the rock walls, I managed to notice a small opening, I quickly shouted the Captain, "John, I mean Captain Bones, look an opening." You might notice I sometimes forget to call John as Captain Bones. It was hard for me to adjust, and I still struggle now even though this happened a long time ago. The captain ordered his men to head for the opening, it was all or nothing now, if we did not make the opening, I most definitely would not be writing this now, however by the grace of God, we reached the opening in the rocks.

We got inside, it was blissful we managed to capture our breaths as we were secured from the wind and rain, it was dark though we could not see a thing apart from when a few flashes of lightning gave us a brief glimpse of our surroundings. We had passed into a cave; one of the crewmen had lit a lantern and began to move it round the boat in each direction. The boat was directly in the middle of a great cavern and sandstone walls were surrounding us in each direction, but straight ahead there was a platform pointed out by the crewman "Captain Bones, Captain Bones look ahead." the captain looked into the distance and ordered the crew to row over to the ledge. We all got out of the boat onto the platform and immediately there were tree roots scaling down the walls, which we all snapped off and through into a heap onto the floor to make a fire, thankfully there was quite a few so we were able to make a steady fire that quickly lit up the area.

We managed to get some warmth as we were all soaked through, I took a look around as I sat by the fire it really was a fine cave. It became obvious that somebody had been here before us but not in a long time, the walls to the north east of the cave had an opening which I got up and took the lantern to go and have a look.

There were steps leading down, I shouted John to get his attention. "Hey John, come look at this, there are steps leading somewhere." the captain came over followed by his men who were picking themselves up from off the floor around the fire. We started to descend down the steps with me leading the way; they were definitely manmade, the steps went down about fifteen times taking us into another room.

This room was very different as soon as I walked in I could feel the atmosphere change, I held up the lantern and I was in a round room with a stone table in the middle I held up the lantern towards the left of me and there was an unlit torch on the wall which I immediately lit, I carried on walking and came to another torch which I also lit, then again another one, I passed an opening as I kept walking round till I got back to where the captain was standing. The room was now fully alight and my eerie feeling from when I first walked in now made more sense, the room was a complete circle with a stone slab that looked like a bed directly in the middle. Everybody started looking around the room. It was not a blank room. As I looked up there was a symbol right in front of me, it was a triangle with a line running through it, I had no idea what it meant, I slowly moved round the room and there was another one it was exactly the same as the last one but it was upside down, I was starting to get interested now so I carried on round and there was another one, this time it has been a triangle just on its own facing upwards, then again another one identical to the last one just upside down again. I was fascinated, what odd drawings on the wall, I had never seen anything like them before and what an odd place to find them.

The time had passed through a few hours, the captain ordered everybody to head back to the cave opening to check on the storm and see if we could get back to the boat and get to port in Liverpool. I requested to stay behind so I could look at the room in more detail and see where the passage that we had yet to check, the captain granted me my wish and left with the others and headed off back to the boats. I continued to look around with complete bemusement as to what it was for, the symbols on the wall, the table in the centre of the room, it was one of the most bizarre places I had ever seen, I decided to go to the opening and see where it may lead.

Melinda looked up from the diary and took a few breaths. She was overcome with excitement.

"There is more to this than meets the eye," William said.

"How is that then?" Melinda asked.

"I know there is a network of tunnels and I've hardly been in any. There must be another cave entrance beneath Mother Redcap's."

"But we have walked along the beach on many occasions and not seen anything," Melinda said thinking back to the route along the beach which definitely did not have a cave entrance of any sort.

"Barney said that it had been damaged by cannon fire from the Royal Navy. Maybe it was that badly damaged the rock just fell in."

Melinda nodded in agreement as that sounded quite possible. They both sat around the desk reading from the diaries for several hours. Melinda had become really intrigued by everything that she had seen and learnt and was desperate to discover more. William had to make sure that she would swear on the children's lives, that she would mention this to no other. There was too much at stake. The last thing he needed was her getting giddy and excited and telling her friends at the local book meeting. She promised that she would not mention it to anybody.

That evening William and Melinda were sat around the table with the family eating a fabulous roast chicken that Grandma had spent the afternoon preparing. Roasted potatoes, carrots, parsnips, sticks of corn and peas from the pod were placed around the table. The smell was divine.

"Here, Grandpa, you do us the honour and carve the chicken," Grandma said.

She handed over a very sharp carving knife across the table. Grandpa Withens decided to give a little speech as he carved continuously into the cooked bird.

"It gives me great pleasure to be able to cut up this fine animal, for us to consume on this day. She once provided us with eggs and now she is the main course. Thank you, Chicken."

The rest of the family laughed as they all dispersed the bowls of food onto their plates.

"I see that you were over on Mr McGregor's hill today, boys. How are the sleds working?" William asked.

"Working beautifully, dad, but we need to find a bigger hill so we can go longer and faster," Mark said as he prodded his fork into the mound of peas.

"Well, it looks as if school is cancelled again tomorrow so if you help Grandma and

Grandpa with their morning duties, I'll let you go back out again tomorrow. I'm sure Mr McGregor will not mind." The boys were excited at the thought of no school again.

"I wish it snowed every day," said Michael.

The Withens family finished their meal and retired for the evening to the living room where they sat around the roaring coal fire, playing games and enjoying each other's company.

Chapter Ten

The next morning arrived and even though the snow had stopped falling, it still had a cold wintery feeling. William had enjoyed his regular cooked breakfast and was putting on his thick layers of clothing. Melinda fastened up the buttons on his sheepskin coat.

"Be careful as you go out there. The ice is settling in."

William put on his woollen hat and gloves and prepared to head to Sprigg's hardware store. He left the house and headed up the pathway out of the manor grounds. The wind breezed and the air was cold, but even though the snow was still very thick and was topped by a sheet of ice, William had no trouble walking. For he was an inventor and a few years back he had created a pair of walking shoes in case a day like this ever occurred. Until today they had been gathering dust in the cloak room.

With each footstep that William took there was a crunching sound. The wooden bases attached to the shoes were cross cut and each step cut into the snow like a potato being mashed. Without the careful cuts in the wood, which looked like a honeycomb, the walking boots would have been unable to manoeuvre through snow or ice.

"Hello there, Willie." A voice came from in the near distance. William was that wrapped up in clothing with his head down, he could not see who it was, but he could hear a horse and cart approaching.

"Oh, William, William," another voice shouted. He stopped walking and looked up. There was a tiny little cart and pony heading towards him. He knew straight away who that was. It was Irene and Imelda Flynn, the two sisters from across the village. The small cart stopped as they pulled up alongside William.

"Hello, ladies. It's a cold morning we have today, isn't it?" He removed his woollen hat so he could see the two ladies.

"Top of the morning to ya, Willie. Indeed, it's a most peculiar day. Never have we seen this type of weather in October," Irene Flynn said removing the black shawl that was wrapped around her head and shoulders.

"Your vegetables are ready for you in the house; Melinda went out yesterday morning to pick them especially for you." This excited William more than the ladies themselves because the Flynn sister cooked the best beef and vegetable broth he had ever tasted and they always sent some round for the Withens family each time they made it.

"That is grand, Willie. We will be sure to drop you some broth off in the morning." William and Melinda always provided the two sisters with the biggest vegetables they could for this very reason.

"Bye now, Willie, we will see you shortly. Giddy up now. Oscar," Irene Flynn said as she shook the reins of the pony. They carried on their journey up the path to Montebello Manor and William continued on his way.

William walked a couple of miles from home to reach the village; despite the cold weather it was surprisingly busy. Mr Marshall stood outside of his coal store, loading sacks onto his horse and cart.

"Good morning, William. What a day it is today," he shouted over as William approached him.

"Hello, Christopher. Must be a busy time for you at the moment," William replied glancing at the cart loaded full of sacks.

"Yes, had me startled. I've never seen anything like it, this time of year. I've nearly run out of coal. This is my last load until the next shipment arrives in a few days. But don't you worry; I've set aside your usual six."

William thanked Mr Marshall and carried on through the village.

As he walked on further, there was a beautiful smell of freshly baked bread. He was nearing Mrs Flowerday's Bakery. He waved hello as he passed by. Mr Porter was sweeping his floor in the shop next door.

"Morning, Mr Withens," he shouted to William, who waved back.

"Morning, Eliot. I'll be in for a trim next week. Melinda has been shouting at me to clean myself up." William needed a haircut desperately. His tatty brown hair was a lot longer than usual. It was on very rare occasions that William would make it through the village unnoticed; he had been very popular when his workshop was situated there, and he still was. People would bring all kinds of items into be fixed; William would end up spending most days working on other people's things rather than his own. Samuel Crowley was the owner of the next shop, who waved at William as he walked past, then continued to chop into his fresh hog that had arrived that morning. Finally William had reached his destination; he was at Sprigg's hardware store.

He removed his specially designed snow shoes and a bell rang as he entered. The shop was big inside and it had many different items on sale; it was a proper hardware store. Mr Sprigg perched up on his ladder restocking the candle shelf.

"You should be taking things a lot easier now, Mr Sprigg. Have you still not hired that assistant we were talking about?"

Mr Sprigg turned around from the shelf.

"Ah, William, I didn't hear you come in. How are we today?"

William passed up some more candles to give Mr Sprigg a hand.

"I'm very well, thank you. What were you saying about an assistant?"

William spoke up a bit so Sebastian Sprigg could hear him.

"I said... What happened to that assistant we were talking about?"

Mr Sprigg climbed down the ladder now that the shelf had been restocked.

"An assistant would be no good to me. Who else knows where everything goes like I do? Hey, young William?" Mr Sprigg had run the hardware store for over forty years and was in his late sixties.

"I'm going to have a look around and collect a few things that I need. Alright, Mr Sprigg?" William had no idea what he required for the quest, but he knew that some things would be essential for the journey.

"Another new project is it, William? I'm particularly pleased with the new woodcutter that you made for me; it's perfect and saves me so much time."

William had built Mr Sprigg a device that chopped logs into even portions. Mr Sprigg would never hire someone to chop the wood for him. He was a firm believer that it was always best to do something yourself, because then you don't have to shout at anybody when they do it wrong. Most of the items William planned to take on his journey, he already had in his cavern work space, but it was always best to ensure all possible situations could be dealt with.

There were five separate aisles in the hardware store; it was the size of four shops in one. William picked up a bundle of rope, which was always a handy tool and would help him reach places with safety. He also took some iron pegs, an iron hammer and some lighting flint. He returned to Mr Sprigg who was back up stocking the shelves.

"Can I take a handful of those candles, Mr Sprigg? Some of those matchsticks also, please?" Matchsticks are essential for lighting fires when it's too wet for a flint to create a flame. Mr Sprigg handed them down and William popped them into his satchel.

"Are you planning a trip into the forest, William?" Mr Sprigg asked with a smile.

"Let's just say I'm going on a little adventure. I can't say where, but I expect it may take some time."

"It sounds very intriguing," Mr Sprigg said.

"Sebastian, can you remember a man by the name of Hector Hornsmith?" William asked. Mr Sprigg stopped what he was doing and went into deep thought.

"Hector Hornsmith... Now that is a name I've not heard in a long time," Mr Sprigg replied.

"So you knew of him then?"

"Well, yes. I was only a young boy when I met him, but he was a brilliant man. Hector Hornsmith transformed New Brighton from a quiet little port into a haven for the rich. He built houses then invited rich shipping merchants to come and live in the area. He was a very wealthy man; I suppose building was how he made his money. Anyhow, he did a lot of good work in the area, and many of the buildings you see around here, he had something to do with. Why do you ask?"

William had to be careful how he replied; he did not want to let too much slip.

"I looked in on his manor house for a while until the new occupants moved in."

Mr Sprigg had taken a seat on his wooden stool. "Ah yes, Miss Ellie-May Grangeworthy. I had one of her servants in yesterday. From what he was telling me she sounds like a real mean lady." William nodded in agreement.

"I had the unfortunate pleasure of meeting her myself." William really did not like her or her rich and grubby kind like Henry Saville; they were a horrible bunch of people who cared for nothing but themselves.

"So you were at Hornsmith Manor. What a beautiful place it was. I often went as a child with my parents to social gatherings that used to be held in the garden area. We would have many a good day there. I always remember some of Hector's friends would have pieces of gold lodged in where they should have had some teeth. They glistened when they smiled. It was most peculiar." The mention of gold made William smile. The men must have been some of the crew members who remained with Hector. William and Mr Sprigg chatted for a little while longer about Hornsmith Manor and past times.

"Have fun on your adventure, William; be sure to let me know all about it when you return."

William put his satchel back over his shoulder.

"I'll be sure to see you upon my return, if it goes as well as planned; we should be having a very interesting chat." William said his goodbyes, put his special snow shoes back on and headed off home through the snow.

The Inventor's Quest

Chapter Eleven

Upon William's return from the village, the boys were across the way, taking advantage of the unusual October weather by making good use of their sleds. He headed through the snow-covered potato field across to McGregor's hill to greet them.

"Father, Father! Come and watch me," young Michael shouted. "Look how fast I can go now," he added as he sped down the hill through the snow.

William had made a sled for each of the boys; he got his idea when making his special shoes for walking in the snow. It was a wooden crate on two curved pieces of smooth wood; on snow-covered hills they really did gather speed.

"Boys, come here a minute please," William said.

He sat down on the tree which had fallen across the stream. The boys sped down the hill, racing each other towards their father.

"What's up, father? If it's about the old Flynn ladies' toilet, we didn't mean for it to explode. It was an accident, honest," Michael said. William had a look of puzzlement on his face.

"No, Michael, it's not that, but I'll be intrigued to learn more about it later."

"I told you not to say anything." Mark hit Michael in the arm for being a big mouth and nearly getting them into trouble.

"Well, what is it, father? What's the matter?" Mark asked as he pulled Michael up to join him sitting on the fallen down tree.

"I'm going on a trip tomorrow; your mother will be very busy looking after Grandma and Grandpa. So I want you both to behave and not cause any trouble." The boys looked at each other and both said simultaneously:

"We don't cause any trouble, Father."

William smiled. "What was it you were just saying to me about the Flynn's toilet?" Before William could finish the boys had jumped down and ran back up the hill with their sleds.

"We love you, Father! Bring us back a present," Mark and Michael shouted giggling together.

"My boys, I don't know," William said as he stood up, relieving his backside of the cold that was slowly setting in. He headed back over the potato field, past the pen full of pigs that were rummaging around looking for hidden food under the snow with their snouts. As he entered the courtyard of Montebello Manor, he heard a galloping sound coming from the pathway leading to the house. There was a horse and cart coming towards him as he turned the corner to the front of the house; it was Christopher Marshall, the coal merchant.

"Hello, William! I've got your coal here as promised," Mr Marshall said as he stepped down from his cart.

"Hello Christopher, hello Darby." This was replied by a woof and a wag of the tail from Mr Marshall's black and white collie.

"Six bags as promised. I'll bring more next week when my shipment comes down from Manchester on the canal." Christopher pulled down the hatch on the back of the cart, which released a ramp.

"Darby, fetch," he shouted at the dog. Darby leapt into action, running up the ramp and grabbing the bottom of a coal sack between his teeth. The dog growled and snarled as he pulled at the sack, using all of his strength to pull it down the ramp and eventually to the feet of Christopher Marshall. Darby repeated this a further five times Christopher Marshall carried the sacks to the coal shed. When they had both finished, Christopher Marshall rewarded Darby with a piece of cooked ham. This was something that he did each time a job was completed, probably why Darby was so eager to pull the sacks that weighed considerably more than him.

"Just what do you do with so much coal, William?" Christopher asked.

"Well, you know, a big house requires a lot of heat," he replied.

"You seem to go through twice as much as everybody else per week."

William had to make up a good excuse; he could not mention that he owned his very own underground steam train.

"Well, it's probably Grandma and Grandpa; you know how the cold affects older people."

"That it does, William; that it does. Well, I shall not complain. You can have as much as you like."

"I am glad you mentioned that," William said. "I would like to start purchasing ten sacks per week, if possible?"

"Expecting more of this cold weather, are we?"

"You could say that."

"I'll bring it round next Thursday. How about that?"

"That will be perfect, thank you. Melinda will be here."

"Going away, are we?" Christopher asked.

"Just got a few things to attend to, that's all."

"Right you are, William; I'll be on my way, then."

William paid Mr Marshall. They said their goodbyes and he went into the house.

"Oh good, was that the coal man?" A voice spoke out in the distance. It was Grandma Withens, cleaning in the cloak room.

"Yes, Grandma. We are fully stocked again. No need to worry about the cold."

Grandma Mabel Withens always liked to make sure there was plenty of coal, because without coal there would be no heat and without heat she would surely freeze like an icicle.

"Where have those boys got to?" she asked.

"They're over on McGregor's hill."

Grandma sighed.

"No doubt they will be treading more mud through the house when they return. I've been cleaning up after them all day."

William made a sharp exit into the study room, seeing that his mother was in one of her funny moods. He sat down in one of the chairs by the fire. The other one was already occupied by Grandpa Withens, reading today's newspaper.

"Have you heard the latest, William?" Grandpa said.

William looked over at his father.

"Not yet, but I'm sure you're going to tell me." He picked up the fire stoker to prod at the burning chunks of wood. Grandpa David Withens peered over his newspaper.

"They say that one day travel to the moon will be possible. These Oxford scholars do come out with some nonsense."

William sighed and shook his head.

"It's a newspaper, Father; don't believe everything you read in them."

Grandpa would often dismiss the debates in the newspapers as rubbish.

"Anyway, I've got you here. I'm leaving on a trip in the morning."

Once again David Withens peered over the top of his newspaper.

"Oh, that's nice," was his only reply and he got back to reading his paper. William expected at least a few questions, but nothing else was said.

They both sat quietly minding their own business for the next few hours. This gave William a chance to study one of Hector Hornsmith's diaries. More importantly, he needed to solve the riddle and find the first marker. If he could not solve it, he would not be able to start his quest. He knew that somewhere within one of the diaries, he would find a link to the place mentioned in the riddle. William read the passage again in Hector's diary to try and make sense of what it meant.

"The beginning starts with ringing and the chimes of the singing, but you will not find what you seek before eight and you will not gain entrance without the three. On the tower you will find thee, where a vessel will transport ye."

Grandpa Withens finished reading his paper and listened to William talking to himself.

"What's that you have there, boy? Is it a riddle?" Grandpa liked riddles; one got published in the paper each day.

"It's nothing, Father; I'm just working on a new project."

Grandpa sat back into his chair, and shut his eyes to relax in front of the fire. William scanned through the diary until he came to an entry dated 3rd March 1836. This grabbed his attention as it specifically referred to the building of a clock tower and a device that was placed within the clock face.

"Today I was given the honour of opening the new clock tower at the Seacombe Ferry Terminal. Having spent many months building the structure with my work crew, we had completed the tower a few weeks back. It was in this very building that I placed the first marker, a marker that will be guided only by the light. What I speak has been concealed from the stranger and only the rightful person shall see. My wife and children were all in attendance and we experienced a ride across the Mersey to the port of Liverpool. It has been a most marvellous day indeed."

William re-read the diary entry to confirm that he had read it correctly.

"So this is it, this is the first marker," he said to himself. "If this one is listed, so must the rest be. I must ensure that I take this with me on my travels; it could be more important than I expected." William closed the diary and leaped out of his chair, punching his fist in the air and giving out a little cheer. Grandpa opened his eyes to look at William. He shook his head and went back to sleep.

The marker had been found, it had to be Seacombe Ferry Clock Tower. *"On the tower you will find thee, where a vessel with transport ye,"* William said to himself. He looked back into the diary.

"But what does it mean when it says *The beginning starts with ringing and the chimes of the singing, but you will not find what you seek before eight and you will not gain entrance without the three?"* William strode up and down the study room, thinking to himself, trying to work out the rest of the riddle.

"The clock tower has chimes that ring every fifteen minutes and a clock has twelve numbers on its face. Eight and three; is it a quarter past eight or a quarter to three? It has got to be a quarter past eight because the smaller hand is

141

not fully facing the three when only at a quarter to. But is it night or day?"

He carried on pacing up and down the room thinking to himself. Grandpa was snoring loudly; this did not affect William as he was in deep thought. He stopped and read the diary entry again from when Hector opened the clock tower.

"It was in this very building that I placed the first marker, a marker that will be guided only by the light. What I speak of has been concealed from the stranger and only the rightful person shall see."

"There is no light during the night, only moonlight, but the moon does not face the clock tower, so it has got to be quarter past eight in the morning." William had figured out the riddle.

"I need to be in the Seacombe Ferry clock tower at the chimes of the quarter past eight bell."

And so the quest begins.

Chapter Twelve

Ellie-May Grangeworthy had spent the last several days settling into her new role as manageress in Henry Saville's cotton factory. Since her arrival, the already-bad feeling within the factory amongst the workers had increased. They did not like Henry Saville one bit, but Ellie-May Grangeworthy was ten times worse than he ever had been and she had been at the factory less than a week. The workers were forced to work harder for longer hours and hardly any extra pay. They had no choice to argue because they would be sacked in an instant if they did not do as they were told. This drove fear into their hearts.

Henry Saville inherited the Liverpool Cotton Factory from his father as he had done from his father. Ellie-May was not only the first female to hold any sort of management position within the company, but she was also the first non-Saville. Henry had been looking to take time out from his company to pursue other ventures, but his eldest son was not interested and his other two sons were too young. Henry also had no brothers or sisters, so he had had to travel to London to find somebody suitable.

Having experienced several unsuccessful interviews, Henry was travelling back from the centre of London to the outskirts where the second of his six houses across the country was situated. He had been travelling along nicely in his carriage with its pine wooded interior until his driver came to a sudden stop amidst a chorus of chanting and shouting. Men and women had gathered together preventing anybody from passing through.

"Driver, driver! Why have we stopped?" he shouted as he poked his head out of the window to see what was happening.

"It seems to be some sort of protest, squire," the driver shouted back.

The road was blocked by people; hundreds, maybe thousands of them.

"Bloody rotten peasants," Henry muttered to himself. But it was by fortune that the carriage was stopped, since it was here that he came into contact with Ellie-May. A carriage pulled up alongside Henry, who was leaning out of the carriage window looking towards the commotion. The carriage had silk curtains, which were pulled back and a plump, bald-headed man appeared.

"I say, good man, what is all the fuss about?" the man asked.

"Those pesky peasants are at it again, by the looks of things."

The bald headed man sniggered. "What are they expecting now, less hours and more pay again?"

"More than likely," Henry said. The two men shared a laugh together.

The protesters looked like they were there to stay and nothing was going to stop them, even the several policemen who had appeared on the scene, blowing their whistles but not managing to control the situation.

"Just run them down further. They will soon move out of the way then," a voice said from inside the carriage.

The plump faced man leaned out to signal the driver to move on, but the driver refused. The right hand door of the carriage swung open and Ellie-May appeared. Exiting down the three carriage steps, she went towards the driver. She pulled herself up onto the driver's seat, pushing the driver to the other side of the seat. Ellie-May grabbed the reins in her hands and shouted "Yah, Yah!" The horses bolted into action and went towards the gathered crowds. People turned to see the speeding horses and carriage heading towards them and they scattered all over the place jumping out of the way to safety wherever they could. Henry Saville looked on in awe of Ellie-May, who cleared a path in no time.

"Driver, follow that carriage," he instructed as he pointed to the carriage in front.

The driver responded by whipping the reins, urging the horses to move on. The two carriages had made their way through the crowds, who were gathering together once again as if the incident had never even happened. The carriages came to a halt and Ellie-May returned to the inside of her carriage, sitting next to her father. Henry Saville ordered his driver to open the door and made his way over to the other carriage.

"My, my, young lady. That was quite a performance," Henry said as he looked through the window. "I really admire the way you handled those peasants. It's by chance that I may have found the very person that I've been looking for. How would you like to come and run my factory?"

Ellie-May was leaning over her father towards the window. "My dear man, you could not afford me."

Henry Saville leaned further into the carriage. "I'll pay you handsomely, my dear; I'll give you whatever you require to keep my workers in order." Henry was desperate to secure Ellie-May's services.

After a while of thinking Ellie-May came to her conclusion. "I'll accept, but only if my conditions are met. I want my own house, but I want it to be a grand looking house. I also want full control of the factory; I answer to no-one and everybody will answer to me."

Henry had a gleaming smile on his face; he had found the perfect person for running his cotton factory.

"Those are reasonable terms, my dear, and they will be met, I've just the place in mind for you to live. I'll head home to purchase it immediately. Please join me in my quarters so we can sign the relevant paperwork."

"I say, what is your name?" Ellie-May said.

"I'm Henry, Henry Saville," he replied.

"Well, Henry, let's get moving. I'm famished. I trust you have some delicacies that I and my father can enjoy?"

"How does wine and cheese sound?" he said, rubbing his fat stomach.

"Some grapes and ham would go down nicely too," Ellie-May said.

"I'll have the servants prepare it."

Henry returned to his carriage. They travelled back to his country manor home to complete the deal and enjoyed an evening of specially imported food and expensive wine.

Several weeks later, Ellie-May had settled in her new home of Hornsmith Manor. It was time for her to visit Saville's cotton factory to overlook her new role. She was picked up from home by her driver and taken the ferry across the River Mersey to Liverpool and headed for the factory situated further behind the docks.

The dock area was lively with action, traders instructing their workers to load and unload their merchandise to and from the docked ships. It was a very vibrant city, much more pleasant than the dirty and murky looking area of London that she was used to. Workers sang and whistled as they carried out their duties. Even with her stern face, Ellie-May nearly smiled as she saw the happy spirit of the workers. This quickly vanished when a few young boys ran alongside the carriage, shouting through the window.

"Any spare change for two hungry boys?" a little boy called through the window.

"Blame your parents if you cannot eat! Tell them to work harder."

"But we have no parents," the boy shouted.

"Well, I suggest you get to work then," Ellie-May shouted back at the two boys who had given up chase of the carriage.

The carriage had made its way through the docklands and was pulling up to the gates of Saville's cotton factory. The factory was a large red brick building that stretched the length of the entire road. Iron railings surrounded it. It was clear to see that there was only one way in and one way out. This was to keep the workers from escaping. If overtime was needed the big iron gates would be closed and the workers would be kept there until they were no longer required. Ellie-May made her way out of the carriage door, helped down by the driver. She walked into the front of the building where several people awaited her arrival. Ellie-May headed straight to her office to check that all of her requirements had been met.

A couple of hours passed and Henry Saville arrived at the factory to ensure that all was alright. He made his way up to the offices overlooking the work floor to see Ellie-May looking out over all of the staff, keeping an eye on their performance.

"Ah, Miss Grangeworthy, I see you have already settled into my old office."

She had as well. All Henry's desk items had been removed and replaced by her own; pictures had been added to the wall, one of them being a personal portrait that had been painted in Venice.

"I think I'm going to settle in here quite nicely," she gloated as she walked back into the office.

"Glad to hear it. Have the lazy buggers been giving you any trouble?" Henry asked.

"Well, one lady was seen away from her workstation, so I went down to see what was going on. Her only excuse was that she was telling her friend about the illness that her husband had contracted so he was unable to leave the bed. I helped her with this solution, I fired her and told her to go and be with her husband if it was such a big deal." Henry gave a big gleaming smile at what he was hearing. "I then told the rest of the workers that if they would like to be at home with their loved ones to please leave, otherwise none shall speak to each other anymore." Ellie-May had already displayed her cruelty towards the workers and they were definitely too scared to put a foot out of place.

"Yes, they do tend to moan a bit," Henry commented.

"Well... They won't be moaning whilst I'm here. They are here to work, not to complain."

Henry was extremely happy; he had definitely found the right person for the job. "Well, it looks like I'm no longer needed here and all is in order. I shall collect my belongings and be on my way."

"All will be well here, no need to worry," Ellie-May said.

"I'm heading on a trip to the Americas with the family for some rest time; I hear the workers are even more desperate over there."

"Fabulous place it is, spent several years with Father in the south."

"Planning on travelling round, looking for an ideal spot for my new venture." Henry intended to purchase land to build a new factory. He had heard that the weather was extremely good all year round, but more importantly lots of money was to be made, and using cheap workers too.

"Before you leave, Mr Saville, I had an unfortunate run-in with a William Withens. Who is he and why was he in my house?" Ellie-May asked with a stern look upon her face.

"Ah, he is nothing to worry about. He is a madcap inventor. I believe he was the caretaker of the house before I purchased it," Henry said, picking up his box of items from off the chair.

"When he left, he seemed awfully careful to hold onto a collection of books. Was there anything of value within the house that he would be protecting, maybe a rare collection?"

Henry laughed in response. "I doubt there would be anything of significant value. Probably a book of science or some other nonsense."

"He just seemed so shifty and secretive," Ellie-May said.

"You see, Miss Grangeworthy, William Withens was a clever inventor, but he was never any good at hiding things. Can you see that machine down there, sorting the clothes into different boxes?"

"Ah yes, I see. The one there with all the smoke pouring out of it?"

The machine had never been perfected before it was stolen and plumes of smoke from the steam engine that powered the device poured out over the workers. It made them cough and gasp for air quite a lot, but they were not allowed to complain.

"Well, that belonged to dear Mr Withens, but he left it in the wide open of his workshop for all to see. It then found its way into my factory. Amazing how these things happen, isn't it?" Henry Saville laughed to himself, for it was his warehouse men, Jack and James, who went to the Withens workshop and stole the sorting machine. Just one of several items they had stolen from him over the years.

"Well, I've a feeling he is up to something. I'm sure I've seen him lurking around the back garden of a night time," Ellie-May said. She was right as well. Since her arrival at Hornsmith Manor, William had been worried that she would find the entrance to the tunnels in the garden. Of a night time he would leave his house and ride up to Hornsmith Manor to check that the doorway had not been breached.

"I'll put my men on the case to check it out, Miss Grangeworthy; I'll have them report back to you when I'm away."

"That will do just fine," she replied.

"I'll be on my way then. Goodbye, Miss Grangeworthy." Henry made his way out of the office.

As he walked through the building, people glanced up at the smiling Henry Saville and quickly looked back down at their work. The workers were on tenterhooks after what they had witnessed from Miss Grangeworthy that morning. Before he left the building, Henry stopped off in the warehouse, where Jack and James were curing their boredom by throwing knives into a piece of wood to see who could get it to stick in the furthest.

"Jack, James," Henry shouted.

The two men stopped what they were doing and turned to their boss, straightening their scruffy dirty clothes and standing up straight.

"Yes, Mr Saville, sir. It's a pleasure to see you, sir," Jack said as he straightened his hat on his head.

"It seems that our good friend Mr Withens is causing Miss Grangeworthy a few problems over at Hornsmith Manor. I want you to keep a close eye on him and see just exactly what he is up to."

"Shall we take some more of his toys?" James said, sniggering.

"No, I don't think he has anything of value to me anymore," Henry replied.

"How about we make him disappear?" John said as he ran his knife through his fingers.

"I don't think that will be required, thank you, John."

"Well, what would you like us to do with him, then?" James asked.

"I want you to follow him where ever he goes, see what he is doing and why he has been sniffing around Hornsmith Manor."

The two men looked excited at getting out of the warehouse; they had had nothing exciting to do for a long time.

"You will report your findings directly to Miss Grangeworthy. You will treat her with the respect that you treat me and do as she says."

"Yes, boss. As you say, boss."

"Go into the stables and fetch yourself a couple of horses. And here is ten pounds each for any expenses you require," Henry said, taking out a handful of notes from his pocket to give to the men. "Don't disappoint me now; you know how I don't like to be disappointed."

The men nodded. Henry left the warehouse and exited the factory premises, waving at a couple of workers, who hurried back in through the doors as he stepped into the waiting horse and carriage. He headed off home to instruct his servants to pack all of his essentials so he could go on his journey across the ocean.

Chapter Thirteen

William had gone to bed early the night before and he got out of bed at half past five in the morning, thirty minutes earlier than normal. William had a busy day ahead; he needed to get down to the cave as quickly as possible. He rushed downstairs and finished his breakfast faster than normal. The boys were not yet up and Grandma and Grandpa Withens were outside performing their daily duties.

"Thank you for breakfast, dear. I must rush. So much to do in so little time," William said to Melinda as he hurried out of the back door. He grabbed two of the sacks of coal out of the wooden coal store and dragged them across in his workshed. He fired up the furnace in

S.T.AN and rushed around collecting his tools until the transport device had reached optimal temperature. He checked that the water pipes were full, which they were, and then went down to the cave.

Once William had reached the end of the track into the cave, he hurried to collect all the items that he needed for his journey. Thankfully, when he returned from Mr Sprigg's hardware store, he had already packed his satchel so that it was prepared for when he was ready to leave on his quest. The satchel was filled with the most essential items such as a tent, fire preparation tools including matches and a flint, hunting equipment such as his knife, fishing line and hooks, and his rope. The latter were the three most important things he needed.

Because the horses were needed on the farm he would be unable to use one of them for his trip. Luckily he had been working on something new for several years and now was a good as time as any to test his new transport device. The transport device was a lot like S.T.A.N that ran the length of the tunnels via a track. However, instead of having to move on rail tracks, this transport device had rubber wheels. William had named the device "Free-

Way." This was because the device was able to move in every direction, forwards, backwards, left and right. The scientific name of the device was actually Free Moving Steam Operated Engine Transport Device. William found it easier to simply just call it Free-Way.

Just like a railway engine, it was powered by coal and water, but because there were no heavy carriages to pull like a train, it was able to reach quite reasonable speeds. William had tested the device out on many occasions, travelling around the cave, sometimes crashing into objects, getting too carried away. Free-Way was able to hold a passenger as well as the driver; it had leather covered seats with a soft cushiony finish to prevent getting a sore bottom from the terrible conditions of the road.

William collected all of his tools and essentials that he required and placed then within Free-Way, which was now attached to the front of S.T.A.N, ready to go up to the surface. He jumped in the machine which spluttering out steam and smoke as he prepared to leave. He drove just past the cave opening and closed the iron gates that he added for security, which he also bolted and secured with the giant padlock to prevent anyone from entering.

Once he had reached the workshed, he disconnected Free-Way from the front of S.T.A.N and reversed back down into the tunnel, but only enough so the transport device was hidden. He rushed back up and lifted the iron sheets to close over the opening. He locked them firmly with three iron bolts, dragging them into place one by one.

He then spread around handfuls of straw, so that the tracks and the iron sheets could no longer be seen.

"That's it, I'm done," he said to himself.

He stopped for a moment and had a look around the workshed to make sure that there was nothing he had forgotten. He admired all of the work he had completed since finding the tunnels; he was very proud of his achievements, great achievements that he could share with no other—well, apart from Melinda of course.

He returned to the house to retrieve the last of his warm clothing. He needed to wrap up as much as possible. Who knew what the weather will be like during his trip? It was still cold, although much of the snow had washed away with the rain during the night. William told the family to gather outside as he buttoned up his shaggy looking sheepskin coat. He then made his way back to the workshed.

The boys were chasing each other round in the yard Melinda, Grandma and Grandpa were talking amongst themselves about what they would do with the crops that had been damaged by the unusual snow. A series of splutters, hissing and chugging sounds were coming from the workshed. The gathered family all stopped to face the direction of the unusual sounds, as the workshed doors opened. The two boys' faces lit up as they saw their father's new transport machine for the very first time. The smoke spilled from a funnel situated at the back of the Free-Way and steam came out from the sides. Everybody was mesmerised by the sight of the machine. They had not seen anything like it before, apart from a train, of course. But they had not seen a machine that was not attached to a rail track, nor had they seen one with a shiny red colour that glistened in the sunlight that broke through the clouds.

"Well, boys, what do you think of this, then?" William said as the two boys circled the device, examining every inch.

"Father, she's beautiful. Can we have a go?" Mark asked. He opened the engine door to see the pistons working away in rhythmic motion.

"Close that over, will you, Mark? As soon as I return, I promise I'll take you both for a long trip somewhere." William jumped out of his driver's seat. Grandpa had come over for a closer look and was examining the large rubber coated wheels.

"We could use something like this in the field instead of the horses. It would get things done much faster," Grandpa said, as he ran his hand along the device.

"I'm already looking into it, Father, don't you worry."

Grandpa was examining the engine. "We could also use an engine like this as a milking device for the cows; I would no longer have to sit there for hours on end squeezing their teats."

William was surprised by his father's idea; it was actually a good one.

"I tell you what, Father, write down some of these ideas for me while I'm away and when I get back I can get to work on them straight away." Grandpa nodded and went off into the house to do just that.

"So this is goodbye for now, then," Melinda said as she placed her arms around William, not knowing when she would see her husband again.

"Keep an eye on you-know-what for me while I'm gone," William said as he winked at Melinda.

"Your secret is my secret," she said. They shared a kiss and William gave the boys a hug, and a kiss to Grandma, then jumped back aboard Free-Way.

"Until we see each other again! I love you all," William said.

Melinda had a few tears in her eyes as she watched her husband leave. William released the brake, pressed his right foot down on the accelerator pedal and pulled off down the path, giving a wave to his family, who stood together waving back.

It was a couple of miles from Montebello Manor to the Seacombe Ferry terminal, so with a high speed of forty miles per hour William needed to get a move on. The diary indicated that "You will not find what you seek before eight and you will not gain entrance without the three." The time was a little after seven in the morning, which meant time was tight and he could stop for no-one if he was to get there in due time, especially using roads that had been turned into pools of mud following the freak weather. William left the Manor House in the distance behind him and headed down the fence-lined country road towards the village. Farmers working in the fields put down their tools as they saw William passing on this very strange and unusual machine. William waved as he passed, with a smile on his face, proud of his new invention which was working well, spilling out smoke from behind with each revolution that the wheels would turn. He quickly passed through to the back of the village, only stopping when obstructed by carriages and people who had got in the way.

The Flynn ladies had come across to the Free-Way to grab William's attention.

"William, William; here now," Irene said in an excited voice.

William stopped as he saw the two ladies were in somewhat distress.

"Yes, ladies, how can I be of assistance?" he asked.

"The most peculiar thing happened the other day. We came home and our outhouse had exploded into pieces," Imelda said.

"That sounds quite a peculiar tale. May have been a pocket of gas from below the ground." William told a little white lie to the two ladies so that they would not worry.

"God must be testing us again," Irene said, looking up the heavens.

"Could you possibly come and fix it for us? We are having trouble having to go in a pot, and these old legs just won't bend anymore." Imelda pointed down to her knobby knees.

William tried not to laugh as he looked at the two giant kneecaps sticking out of her stockings, but he also knew that it was his boy's fault so should help them fix the problem.

"Alright then, Miss Flynn, I'll put it at the top of my list of jobs when I return."

"Thank you, William. What would we do without you? Bye for now." They waved at William as he pressed down on the accelerator and carried on out of the village.

William remembered some of the tricks that the boys had played on the Flynn sisters, such as removing the statue of the Virgin Mary from St Hilary's and placing it outside of the Flynn's kitchen window, which caused Imelda Flynn to faint when she glanced up from cleaning the dishes and saw the statue looking in at her. Also the time Irene Flynn was working out in the wheat field on the summer crops and the boys moved a tatty scarecrow and imitating a voice to make Irene think that it was waving and talking to her. "They really are mischievous sometimes," he said to himself.

William was on the direct road heading towards the ferry. Carriages ahead rushed for the eight o'clock ferry. William passed the old Littledale house which was now renamed Central Park, a large mansion with beautiful surrounding gardens. William had tried to purchase several years ago before the local board opened the grounds to the public. He planned on building a large workhouse within the grounds to hide his new inventions and even considered running a factory to give the locals work, following the closure of the nearby pottery factory. As luck would have it, if he had bought the land he might never have found the hidden tunnels that had sent him on this quest.

As William headed closer to the river, back-to-back houses lined either side of the road. Children were out playing in the street before school, dodging in and out between the carriages. That is until they saw William's machine, at which they just stopped and stared. Men and women were walking to and from the local shops. It was a lot like the village except there were fewer shops and more building yards and an iron works.

William quite often came down to Seacombe to get his mechanical parts from Spearing's Iron Works. In fact nearly every piece of metal on the Free-Way had been purchased from the large works owned by the Irishman Mr Spearing.

William had been so busy admiring all the different shops as he went by, he failed to notice that he was being followed. Jack and James from Henry Saville's cotton factory had arrived earlier that morning to keep an eye on William Withens' movements, as instructed.

"This horse is so irritating; every time we keep stopping he tries to throw me off the side. I'm sure he's doing it on purpose."

Jack shook his head in disbelief. "James, will you give it a rest? All you have done is moan all morning. Would you prefer it that we were walking instead? Be thankful Mr Saville has let us use them," Jack said as he kept two eyes focused on William Withens ahead.

"Keep back, James, we need to keep our distance. If he sees us we have had it." That's right as well; William Withens would recognise them since he had chased them away from his workshop in the village on several occasions. They both eased off so there was a fair distance in between them and William.

The time was coming up to eight o'clock and William arrived at Seacombe Ferry. The place was buzzing with excitement, it was a

Saturday morning and trading was at its peak. Many boats had been crossing from Liverpool all morning, unloading traders and their merchandise. Stalls were set out all round the area with just about everything on sale. William often came down with Melinda on a Saturday to look around the market, but today he had something more important to do.

William manoeuvred through the crowds and brought the Free-Way to a stop, parking it next to the horses and carts.

"So this is where it all starts," he said to himself as he stared at the tower. It was made completely out of red brick. As well as tower there was a large building that was the ferry boat terminal. Many people passed through the brick archways on a daily basis. In his excitement at looking up at the tower, he grabbed his satchel, forgetting to place the Hornsmith diary within it. He made his way into the clock tower, and opened a wooden door revealing a set of stairs which he started to climb. It was then that he remembered about the diary.

"The diary," he said to himself before quickly turning round and rushing back to the vehicle. As he returned to the Free-Way, Jack and James moved away. William saw them with something in their hands. He looked at their faces and it quickly dawned on him that he had seen them before.

"Stop, thieves!" he shouted as loud as he could.

It was no good. There was far too much noise and nobody could hear him. Jack and James were long gone as they had run back to the horses and ridden off as quick as possible.

"My diary! What am I going to do now?" William said frantically as he looked through his possessions. It was only the diary that had been taken. William paced backwards and forwards with his hands on his head.

"What will I do..?"

"I need the diary..." He stopped and remembered why he was there.

"What's the time?" he said as he turned to look at the clock tower. The time was coming up to twelve minutes past eight.

"My God, I'm in such a mess. I'm going to miss everything."

William ran as fast as he could. He would need to climb to the top of the tower within three minutes if he was going to catch the first marker. He ran up the wooden stairs as fast as he could. There were eight flights of stairs. His legs grew tighter as he ran up each flight of stairs, his breathing got faster and his heart thumped in his chest with each beat it took.

The chimes were starting to ring just as he got to the top of the second-to-last flight. He forced himself to get up the last flight despite the pains in his legs and serious lack of breath. He stood for a second to catch his breath but he could not risk missing the clue and so he stumbled across to the back of the clock face. The light shone through the clock face but there was nothing there.

"I'm too late," he said to himself.

"Maybe I've got it wrong. Maybe it's another building."

William was upset. He had lost the diary, and the marker was not here. He had failed on all accounts. Maybe he was not worthy of completing the quest after all.

"I've failed," he said to himself as he looked at the back of the clock face.

He looked closer and saw an opening slot in the clock face hand pointing to the number three. A small light beamed through.

"Surely it could not be?" he said as he peered closer.

He opened his satchel and took out his notebook. He held up the brown cover a couple of feet back behind the clock hands. Something shone on the cover of the notebook:

On the Hill we turn from the breath of God.
Not far from we you will see
Thirty paces forward
Then twenty to the right.
Come by day, not by night
Carefully through the Witches' door
You will find what you seek beneath the floor.

The writing disappeared as did the chimes; the tiny latch closed shut. William wrote the description in his notebook before he could forget. He had no idea what the riddle meant and without the Hornsmith diary would he ever be able to find out now? Things had become more difficult. William went back down the stairs of the clock tower, much easier going down than going up. He passed through the crowds making his way back out to Free-Way. He had no idea what he was going to do next. He sat for a moment to have a think about what to do.

"Why would somebody steal the diary and nothing else?" he thought to himself. "And those two men, I've seen them before."

After a few minutes of contemplating what to do, an idea came to him.

"Area maps," he said out loud. "Library. The library will have maps. I shall go there."

William was back in a positive mood again now. Despite losing the diary, he had gained the next clue. There was one person he knew who was great at reading maps.

"I'm going to have to speak to my father. He can read maps, he will know."

He was reluctant to involve anybody else in the quest but now the diary was gone he needed help. His father was a former navigator with the Royal Navy. Who better was there for the job? William started up Free-Way and headed back home to speak to his father.

All was not lost. The quest continued.

Chapter Fourteen

The last remains of the snow were melting and Mark and Michael Withens were outside the house, duelling with a pair of wooden swords. Puffs of smoke and the sound of a horn came up the lane. The two boys stopped as the nearing sounds became recognisable.

"It's Father! He's back," Mark shouted.

The two boys threw down their swords, with Michael getting in a sneaky last shot, as they both ran towards the oncoming vehicle.

"Hello, boys! Surprised to see me?" William smiled.

"We thought we would not see you again for ages," Michael said as the Free-Way pulled up beside him.

"There has been a slight change of plan, boys. Nothing to worry about, just a short delay."

The boys were not really listening to their father. They were more occupied by looking at the vehicle, which was hissing.

"Can we have a go on her now, father? You promised," Michael said.

"Unfortunately, she must be left to cool down now, but get in the seat whilst I push her back to the workshed and you can steer her for me." The two boys jumped into the front of Free-Way and fought for who got to sit in the driver's seat to steer.

"It's my turn, you always get to drive," Michael shouted, clinging onto the wheel with both hands as his brother tried to pull him out of the way.

"I'm the eldest. I should go first," Mark shouted.

"Mark, move off of there. Let your brother have his turn," William shouted as he pushed the vehicle towards the workshed. "Go and open the doors," William added. Mark jumped off the Free-Way and ran over to open the wooden doors before the vehicle got any closer.

"That's it, Michael, guide her in gently."

The vehicle slid in through the open doors, still puffing out clouds of smoke and steam.

"Thank you, boys. Let's get inside to see Mother."

"But mother's not here, father; she has gone to the market with Grandma," Michael said.

"Right, alright. Who's hungry? Because I am," William said as he rubbed his stomach.

They all went in through the back door to the kitchen where they were greeted by the smells of vegetables that were cooking on the stove.

After enjoying a bowl of soup and bread with the boys, William headed off to the living room where he found his father fast asleep with the newspaper covering his face.

"Pa, Pa wake up." William prodded his father.

"What, who in the..." Grandpa said as he broke out of a deep sleep.

"Hello Pa," William said as he pulled up a chair next to his father.

"What are you doing back? How long have I been asleep?" Grandpa said as he rubbed his eyes, then took out his pocket watch to check the time.

"Well, I've got a bit stuck and need your help," William said.

"Ah! The famous inventor who knows everything needs my help," Grandpa said sarcastically.

This was a perfect example of why William hardly ever asked for his father's help. He would always get some sarcastic comments which would usually end up in an argument when they disagreed over something silly. But William needed his father's help so he bit his lip and kept calm.

"Yes Pa, I really need your help."

"What trouble have you gotten yourself into this time?"

William frowned.

"I'm not in any trouble. Why do you always assume that I've done something wrong? You've been saying the same thing for the last thirty years, every time I ask for your help."

"Well, usually you have," Grandpa said.

"That was years ago and I only asked you for help one time, which wasn't my fault either," William said as he reminded his father of the time when he and his friend had been playing in the woods and accidently got old farmer McGregor caught in an animal trap trying to capture a bear—despite there not even being any wild bears in Wallasey.

"I would really appreciate it if you would accompany me to the library. There is something I need you to help me with."

"Alright, alright, I would be glad to accompany you to the library, but why do we need to go there?" Grandpa asked, getting out of his chair.

"What if I was to tell you that beneath this very house is a tunnel leading all the way to old Mother Redcap's Inn?" William said in an excited voice, trying to impress his father.

"I know there is. What do you think I did for entertainment when I was younger?"

William's face changed at his father's revelation.

"What do you mean? Do you mean to tell me you knew all along that there were tunnels under Wallasey?"

"Well, yes. I and my friends used to sneak into them and play hiding games all the time."

William was really getting angry.

"Why the bloody hell did you never tell me about them?" His face was bright red, looking like smoke was about to come out of his ears.

"Well, you never asked," Grandpa said simply.

"How could I ask you, if I never knew anything about them?"

"Well, you were young like I was, so I thought you would have found them. We grew up in the same house and area after all."

William had to bite his lip and calm down. He needed his father's help and at least he would not have to try and convince him that his story about the treasure was true.

"Right. Alright, forget about it now. I might as well tell you what I know and then you can tell me what you know." He sat back down in the chair next to Grandpa and explained what he had found from the beginning.

Meanwhile, following the retrieval of the diary earlier that day, John and Jack made their way to Ellie-May who sat behind her desk in the cotton factory.

"Hello, Miss Grangeworthy. I'm John and this is Jack. Mr Saville has asked us to help you," John said, standing in front of Ellie-May and taking his dirty brown hat off.

"Ah, yes. The warehouse boys. So what have you got for me?" Ellie-May said as she pointed to an item in John's left hand.

"We got this book for you; he seemed quite interested in it, despite leaving it in his strange looking vehicle." He passed it over to Ellie-May.

She was interested in the brown leather covered book.

"The diary of Hector Hornsmith, Volume V," she said out loud as she read the front cover.

"Why would an inventor be so interested in taking a book more than anything else when I asked him to leave?" she thought to herself as she opened the book. She scanned through the diary and dismissed most of the pages as nonsense, but one page particularly caught her attention.

"I had hidden the first key to the fortune within the new tower. The beginning starts with the ringing and the chimes of the singing. But you will not find what you seek before eight and you will not gain entrance without the three. On the tower you will find thee, where a vessel would transport me."

Oh no...She had found the start of the quest. But would she understand what it meant?

"Where did you say you were when you found this?" she asked.

"We were down at the ferry, Miss," Jack said, stepping closer to the desk.

She read the passage again from the book. "You will find thee, where a vessel would transport me. Hmm. So that's what he was doing at the ferry. He was looking for something. But what was it?" she said out loud as she thought to herself.

"Well, he was running up the stairs when we jumped in and took the book," John said, trying to answer Ellie-May's question.

"Hidden the key to the fortune?" Ellie-Mays eyes were lighted up and a big gleaming smile was emerging onto her face. The two men were getting excited too, just from hearing the word 'fortune.' They did not understand the rest, because they were not very bright.

"Alright, let's take a step back. When I arrived, he was in my house, and when he left, he took this book. Then this morning he was down at the ferry, inside a tower, a place where a vessel would transport thee." It was all making sense to Ellie-May now, she knew exactly what the inventor William Withens was up to.

"He is on a treasure hunt," she said out loud, excitedly.

She quickly got up out of her chair, knocking it over from behind the desk, and grabbed her priceless imported French coat from the stand. She was ready to leave instantly.

"I must return home; let's see what else is hiding there." She rushed out of the office and signalled her driver who sat in the waiting area, reading his newspaper.

"Giles, take me home," she shouted.

The driver got up out of his chair, grabbed his flat cap that he had hung on the back of the chair, and rushed in front of Ellie-May to have the carriage door open for when she arrived.

They hurried straight back to Hornsmith Manor, just catching the ferry boat before it left on its way across the river. Ellie-May was on the trail of the Hornsmith quest; she had the diary and knew where the first marker was. Just how prepared was she to join the quest? One little word had caught her eye and it was all she could think about: "Fortune."

After a good hour or two of talking, probably the longest chat that they had had in years, William looked at his watch and it was coming up to a quarter to six. It was too late to head to the library and Melinda and Grandma had just returned from a day of selling at the market.

"William, you're back," Melinda said, shocked as she walked into the living room, expecting to see Grandpa asleep in his chair by the fire.

"Hit a bit of a snag, will tell you about it later," William said.

The family had their evening meal and the evening was a quiet one which William and Melinda spent together, chatting about the day's events.

Chapter Fifteen

The next morning, William skipped breakfast and headed out to check the tunnels, fearing that the stolen diary had already alerted the thieves to their existence. Thankfully, there was no sign of entry at any of the doors. But when he was down there, Ellie-May was already in the garden of Hornsmith Manor.

"I want you to search every inch of the garden until you find what that William Withens was looking for."

"Yes, Miss Grangeworthy. Come on Jack, you heard the lady," John said.

John and Jack had been summoned to Hornsmith Manor by Ellie-May. She wanted answers and wanted them fast. She was never one for much patience.

"You take the right side and I shall take the left."

The two men began by pulling flowers from their beds, uprooting small trees, giving everywhere a right thorough look. They shook the hedges until they revealed nothing more than a few birds that had been nesting in them. Frogs scattered off the lilies on the pond as Jack's huge feet pounded through several feet of water.

"Let's try the trees," John shouted as he pointed to the back of the large garden.

"There is nothing here, John. Have you got anything?

"Not a dickybird. Come on, let's go back up to the house."

The two men found nothing; the wooden doors had been perfectly covered with old leaves and soil by William earlier in the week.

"Nothing to be seen, Miss Grangeworthy."

Ellie-May was reading more of the diary and had not heard a word that John had said.

"Miss Grangeworthy, there was nothing we could find in the garden," he said a bit louder.

"Sorry, you were saying?" she said as she looked up from the diary.

"Nothing to report, Miss. The area is clear."

"Forget the garden; we have a trail to follow. Tomorrow morning we go to the clock tower and find out just what Mr Withens found."

"What about the factory, Miss?"

"Never mind about the factory, this is much more fun. Besides, Mr Saville has already left for America. We will leave Jack in charge."

"Jack!" John shouted.

"Me?" Jack panicked.

Jack could not even tie his own shoelaces properly. How was he expected to run a whole factory on his own? Mr Saville would not agree to it either.

"Yes. Jack will go to the factory and we shall go the clock tower."

Ellie-May closed the diary and went back inside the house. The two men followed, with Jack looking worried.

"Suppose it's just like looking after my kitten, isn't it, John?"

"Oh, shut up, Jack. All you have to do is sit down at a desk and pretend you're busy."

"Oh yeah. A bit like Mr Saville does when he reads his newspaper with his feet up."

"Exactly," John said as he closed the doors behind them.

Ellie-May and the men had been busy in the Hornsmith garden; William went to the library with his father. He had the clue for the next part of the quest; he just needed Grandpa Withens to help him find it.

"So you're sure you will be able to locate the next destination from the area map?" he asked.

"I've been reading maps for years, my boy. I once navigated my captain and crew from Australia all the way back home. I'm sure I'll be able to navigate us to a location not so far." That's true, William thought to himself. His father had been as far as the other side of the world, when taking passengers to the Antipodes. The horse and cart pulled up outside the sandstone building. It was particularly large due to the fact it had previously been the home of a wealthy merchant, who had donated the premises for public use.

"The doors are closed," William said, indicating the two large oak doors.

"Don't worry; it's to prevent the dogs from getting in again," Grandpa said as he pointed to the sign stating "No Dogs Allowed."

"Dogs? What dogs?"

"Do you not read the paper? It made the national news."

He was right as well. Poor old Mr Norman the Librarian had been pestered by a roaming pack of dogs that had caused damage and upset as they ran amuck around the three floors of the building.

Mr Norman was busy stamping a collection of returned books, focusing down through his thick rimmed glasses, ensuring that he was as professional as ever.

"Morning, Mr Norman," Grandpa said as they walked to the main desk.

"Ah, good morning, Mr Withens, and young Mr Withens is with you as well! Good to see you, William, it has been a long time."

"Hello, Robert. Yes, it has been a while. Pa said you have been having some trouble with dogs?"

"Those wretched things... They have caused me nothing but trouble. Scaring all the customers... one even ripped out several pages of Chaucer's wonderful tales. Absolute mockery it was." Robert Norman was irate; nothing upset him more than the desecration of a book.

"I may have just the device to help you with your problem. Leave it with me."

"William! That would be wonderful. There is nothing worse than a closed door to a library." Robert Norman looked a sense relieved.

"We are here to see area maps of Wirral, preferably late eighteenth to mid nineteenth century," William said.

"Very well, come with me. Second floor is where you should go," Robert Norman said as he put down his ink marker and pottered from behind the desk.

William admired the walls of the stairwell as they travelled up the two flights of steps. Some were portraits and several were of iconic buildings from Wallasey, but one picture was all too familiar. It was, of course, a portrait of Hector Hornsmith. William smiled as he walked by.

"So, David. I've not seen you down the Cheese recently," Robert said, referring to the Cheshire Cheese Inn.

"Bit of an extra walk since we have moved. Have been busy with the cows a lot as well," Grandpa said.

"Surprised you don't come down with your boys. They are always in, playing cards. Getting quite good at it, I believe. As you know, I'm not one to gamble, I just sit and watch.

William's face frowned as he knew his two brothers were no good at poker. They lost the cottage and he was now lumbered with them in the manor house.

"Ah, here we go," Robert said as they approached the map drawers on the second floor of the library. "I believe what you seek is in the third drawer down. If you have any problems just give me a shout. Well, not a shout. Come and see me." Robert quietly laughed.

"Thank you, we will do that," William said as he opened the drawer.

He took out several maps and placed them on the table nearby where Grandpa was already sitting.

"Here you go, Pa. Scan through these and remember the riddle:

On the Hill we turn from the breath of God.
Not far from we you will see,
Thirty paces forward
Then twenty to the right;
Come by day, not by night;
Carefully through the Witch's door.
You will find what you seek beneath the floor.

"Right, find me every hill in Cheshire; I'll decode the rest of the riddle."

"What...? Every hill? Are you joking, there are hundreds of them," Grandpa said.

"Here is a pencil and paper, write them down. You said you would help, so help me."

"Hmm, alright," Grandpa mumbled.

Grandpa got to work on the list, William thought about the riddle.

"The breath of God. What is the breath of God?" he thought to himself.

After a good ten to fifteen minutes of thinking in silence, his thoughts were broken as several sheets of paper floated around the table. He quickly collected the papers and the thought he had been looking for crept into his mind.

"Wind!" he shouted as he stood up.

"Pardon you," Grandpa replied.

"No, no! That wind," he told his father, who peered at him over his glasses. "The breath of God is wind... I should have known this. What is wrong with me?"

"Do you really want me to answer that?" Grandpa replied.

"Quiet, Pa. I'm thinking."

"Alright. So we have determined it's something to do with wind. "*On the Hill we turn from the breath of God.*" It mentions hill and wind. Is it a tall hill where the wind would blow strong?" He sat back down to think.

"What in Cheshire would use wind as a power source? Maybe a weather vane, but there would be too many to choose from. It can't be that. Pa, back when you were younger, what used wind as a source of power?" he asked.

"Well, that would be easy; the mill of course!" Grandpa said.

"That's right; Wallasey Mill, but it was demolished in 1887. It's flattened. Nothing left to be seen." William sank back into the cushioned chair as if all his hopes had perished.

"My boy, why the long face? You're forgetting one thing," Grandpa said.

"What's that? I didn't stand a hope of completing the quest in the first place? Go on, Pa; rub it in. Have your laugh at me."

"No, silly, the mill may have been knocked down. But think about it. The mill never stood on a hill, and anyway, I have your answer right here," Grandpa said, pointing to the map.

William rose from his chair in excitement as he looked over to the area his father had circled on the map.

"My God, Pa, you're right. It was staring us in the face all along.

> On the Hill we turn from the breath of God.
> Not far from we you will see,
> Thirty paces forward
> Then twenty to the right;

Come by day, not by night;
Carefully through the Witch's door.
You will find what you seek beneath the
floor.

"It's Bidston Hill. I even know where the marker is placed."

William collected up the items off the table, put them in his satchel and returned the maps back to their rightful place.

"Come on, Pa. We have a quest to continue."

"Right you are, boy," Grandpa replied as he leapt out of his seat, falling straight back down. Grandpa escaped the chair on his second attempt and followed the determined William.

They were back on the trail of the quest; they had successfully found the location of the next clue.

Chapter Sixteen

The 12.15 arrival at New Brighton Pier was on time as always. Holiday makers had flocked to the little seaside town, hurrying their children, hoping to take advantage of the horses and carts available at the end of the terminal. One man was in no hurry at all. He slowly fastened the buttons of his jacket and stepped onto the wooden platform carrying only a small brown suitcase as his personal luggage. Being over six feet tall, he was able to peer over the railings of the pier with ease. Fishermen lined the way in front of him, casting lines in search of their evening meal. He filled his lungs with deep breaths, taking advantage of the fresh sea air with its occasional waft of fish guts; this was much more delightful than the smog ridden air he'd suffered in Manchester.

He reached the end of the pier where a driver held open the door to an available carriage.

"Good afternoon, sir. What's your destination?"

"Hornsmith Manor," he replied.

"Right you are," the driver said and closed the door.

After a short ride along the Cheshire coastline, the carriage arrived at Hornsmith Manor. Having paid the driver, the man went to the front door, using the large knocker to bang on the wooden door.

Bang, Bang, Bang...

The door opened. Ellie-May's butler adjusted his spectacles to see if he could recognise the unexpected guest.

"Hello. Can I help you?" he asked.

"I'm here to see Miss Grangeworthy."

"Ah, I see. And who may I say is calling?"

"The name is Brown, Professor Brown. She is expecting me."

"You had best come and wait inside. Miss Grangeworthy is due back shortly."

The butler directed Professor Brown to the lounge, where he offered tea and refreshments. Professor Brown was more interested in the book that lay on the table.

"Ah, the Hornsmith diary. Let's see what you are hiding in there." The Professor opened the diary to see what all the fuss was about.

Several hours passed and the house began to bustle. Ellie-May entered and was informed of the Professor's arrival.

"Ah, Marcus. I trust you got my letter in good speed."

"Hello, my dear Ellie-May. I came as soon as I received your news."

"I see you have found the diary; very enlightening, isn't it?"

"There are some passages that have caught my attention. Some very interesting things indeed. Have you any plans for this evening, my dear lady?"

"Nothing in particular, as of yet. Why?"

"I have read something rather interesting that I would like to investigate."

"Oh, really. And what would that be?"

The Professor opened the diary and turned to the page dated 13th April 1837.

Today I continued work with one of my friends, Richard Leay. I used this opportunity to place my next marker, on the wall it rests. The hill of Bidston is a very peculiar place indeed, something that Richard has been awfully quiet about. I sometimes wonder if he has been as untruthful to me as I have to him, not that I can complain of course. I find it odd that a man would build a cottage as beautiful as this, but on the wrong side of the hill. Surely a man would prefer to look at the beautiful landscape across the way that would glisten in the sunshine, rather than a treeline of darkness and a working mill. When I asked, he explained that he was merely a guardian over the hill and by placing the cottage here he was able to keep a fruitful eye at all times. What he meant by this, I am unsure.

"I don't understand. What has this got to do with the quest?" Ellie-May asked.

"In your letter, you spoke of the importance of the diary that possibly contained clues. Well, this sounds like one of Hornsmith's clues. Why start at the beginning, when you can join the fun from further on? The diary is the key to the quest."

"That's all good and well, Professor, but where exactly is the place he is speaking of?"

The Professor turned further into the diary until he came to the entry marked 31st October 1837.

"Here, my dear Ellie-May. It is right here."

Today we witnessed the completion of Richard's cottage. We held a small gathering to mark the occasion, with family and friends invited. Richard has named the cottage Tam O'Shanter. A fitting name for the completion date of Hallows Eve. Robert Burns would be honoured indeed. Richard has now left his temporary home in the village of Wallasey and is re-acclimatising to his former surroundings following the fire at his former residence. They never did catch the culprits. Why he returned to the hill of Bidston, I do not know. Rather him than me as I would not like to live alone in the strange area around the hill of Bidston, it is a most eerie place indeed. But Richard is a peculiar man indeed. Some would say he was allergic to the sun. He was not very fond of it at all.

"So you see, my dear Ellie-May, if what you have said in your letter is true, we can join the quest ourselves this very evening. That is, if you have nothing else better to do, of course."

"Marcus, you're the best. This is why I knew you would be the right man for the job." Ellie-May threw her arms around the Professor ecstatically. "Treasure! I get to play with all my treasure!"

"I trust I shall be receiving my usual fee?" he asked.

"Fifty-fifty as always, my dear Professor. Now let's go and find my treasure."

"First things first, my dear Ellie-May. We must make a stop and get some supplies; we cannot go searching empty handed. I trust you know of a local trader?"

"I know just the place, Phillpotts. Ready our carriage, we're heading to the village," Ellie-May instructed the butler.

John was already waiting in the carriage when Ellie-May and the Professor exited the manor doors.

"It's a rather nice place you have here, Ellie-May. I trust you plan on staying for a while?" the Professor said as he admired the beautiful building and gardens of Hornsmith Manor.

"I have a new factory and I have these premises to reside in. That is just the beginning, and I have many plans for the area. Exploitation will be the key. Their sweat and tears will bring me money and cheers. But that's for another day."

"Just let me know if you require a permanent guest. You are always the object of my desires, my sweet Ellie-May," the professor said, taking hold of Ellie-May's hand and giving it a gentle kiss.

"Of course, Marcus, you shall be the first to be informed of my situation."

The Professor helped Ellie-May into the carriage and they set off for Sprigg's hardware store.

Chapter Seventeen

After an unexpected stop, thanks to a fault with the vehicle, William and Grandpa had reached the hill at Bidston. The time had just turned seven in the evening and the sun was near setting.

"Come on, Pa, we have to go the rest of the journey by foot."

"What...over the hill?" he replied unhappily.

"It's too dark and I can't see the road any longer. We will be fine using the lanterns."

"But it's Hallow's Eve... Who knows what may be up there?"

"They are just ghost tales, Pa, nothing more. Now come on, let's get moving."

William grabbed his satchel and the lanterns, ready to assault the hill that was engulfed by darkness.

William and his father began making their way up the dark dirt path. Trees lined either side with a glimpse of moonlight breaking through each time they passed an opening. It was completely silent and Grandpa held his lantern out ahead of him, turning each time in a panic at the sound of a twig snapping or the rustling of leaves.

"It's just animals running around. Probably a fox chasing a rabbit," William said, trying to reassure his father.

"Must be a big sized fox. It sounds like it's got hooves," he replied.

The path went round in a circular motion around the hill; it had to be as gradual-sloping as possible to make it easier for the horses and carts to get to and from the factory based at the top of the hill next to the observatory.

They carried on upwards for several minutes, with more strange sounds in the distance growing louder with each step they took. There was light up ahead of the summit of the hill.

"Witches...!" Grandpa shouted at the top of his voice in a panic.

William quickly put his hand over Grandpa's mouth, and pulled him into safety behind some rocks.

They both peered through the rocks in the area filled by firelight; four figures could be seen circling a fire. Grandpa turned to William in a sense of confusement.

"These can't be witches; they're young and dressed in white robes. I thought witches dressed in black and were old and haggard."

"Shush, Pa. Listen to what they are saying," William replied.

A banging of drums could be heard, thumping in a rhythmic fashion. The four women moved to the sound of the music, slowly moving in a clockwise rotation. This lasted for nearly ten minutes by the count on William's pocket watch.

Silence suddenly fell on the hilltop; the four females positioned themselves back into a circle and extended their arms into the air as if to catch something from above.

"Hail to the guardians of the North, mighty earth who feeds us, our home and mother, welcome to the circle," a lady shouted.

"Hail to the guardians of the East, blessed air who cools us, the breath of life in all, welcome to the circle," the second lady shouted.

"Hail to the guardians of the South, sacred flame that sparks life in all, our protection and father, welcome to the circle," the next lady shouted.

It was starting to make some sort of sense to William; the four females were positioned in North, East, South and West positions around the fire and it sounded as if they were chanting some sort of spell.

"Hail to the guardians of the West, waters of life, where all are cleansed and reborn, welcome to the circle," the last lady cried out.

The drums beat again and the females began dancing round the fire again chanting, "Belisama, Belisama, Belisama."

"What is Belisama?" Grandpa whispered to William.

"I don't think it's a what; more of a who," he replied.

The fire grew in height, flickering brighter with ashes swirling in a circular motion. The burning embers changed from red to orange then brighter to yellow. Then suddenly a flashing bolt of green light shot into the air, reaching heights of up to thirty feet. The whole area was illuminated and the four women shook their arms as if they were in some sort of trance.

The area grew darker as the fire ebbed and the figure of a woman could be seen standing in the middle of the four ladies who no longer danced but were graciously bowing down.

"I don't like the looks of this, William," Grandpa said as he clung to the back of the rocks, peering through the gap at the figure dressed in black.

"Right, Pa. What we need is at the bottom of the hill. We can sneak around behind the factory without them seeing us," William whispered.

"Witches see everything! They have eyes in the back of their head! They will smell us! And they will try and eat us!"

"Pa, control yourself," William said, trying to calm his father down who was walking round in circles mumbling.

"Come on an adventure, he said; come and find some lost treasure; it will be fun, he said. He never mentioned witches, though; nothing at all about witches and glowing women walking out of a raging fire."

"Pa, get down! They will hear you," William whispered as he pulled his father behind the rocks.

"How're we going to get past them William?"

William peered out the side of the rocks, scanning the area and hoping for an escape route. To the left, there were more rocks, which made it impossible to reach unnoticed. In front the witches continued their ritual, and to the right was the plantation of oak trees.

"The trees are the only option, Pa. We'll have to head for the trees."

"But we can't make it to the trees without crossing the open pathway. They'll see us."

Grandpa was right. The access path to the top of the hill was several yards wide. William had to think quickly what to do. He closed his eyes and cleared his mind.

"Trees and opening, rocks and darkness, witches and burning," he said to himself as his mind filled with ideas.

"We already know this," Grandpa said interrupting him.

"Shush, Pa. I need silence."

"Be thankful you're with me and not your mother," he replied.

William continued with ideas flashing through his mind, but each one resulted in being captured. The witches' chant got closer and louder. He would have to think quickly or they would be caught for sure.

"I've got it!" William said as he opened his eyes. "Follow me," he added, heading down from the rocks and back into the trees which they first arrived.

"Are we going home, William?" Grandpa asked.

"No, Pa. We are Withenses, we don't quit."

"Well, why have we turned round?"

"You'll see. Just follow me."

William guided his father through the treeline heading down, then left to where the path became closer. Towards the top of the pathway was the only available option. The embankment was too steep for them both to embark, especially since it was pitch black. But how would they cross the path without coming into the direct view of the five witches, who were now embroiled in what seemed to be a deep satanic ritual?

William and his father navigated the steep hill as quietly as possible, using tree branches to guide them through the darkness. Heading crosswards they finally reached the open path.

"How has our situation improved, William? We're now right behind them," Grandpa whispered as he pointed to the witches several yards in front.

"As quietly as you can, I need you to grab me as many fallen branches as possible and bring them to me."

Grandpa nodded and scouted the area for anything he could find. William opened his satchel, removed his trusty carpenter's knife, and began cutting away at the thick branches directly above his head as quietly as he possible could. William's plan was to combine as many branches and leaves as possible to make a camouflaged covering to shield them as they passed from one side of the path to the other. If they could reach the other side without capture, they could indeed reach the cottage they sought.

William made good progress on the camouflaged shield. The base was now in place, and he had stepped down the leaves from the branches and tied them together using the rope acquired from Sprigg's hardware store. All he needed was the remaining branches and leaves from Grandpa to complete the process, but where was he?

"Pa, Pa, where are you?" William whispered to no response. "Pa, we need to hurry. What are you doing?" Again there was no response.

William became worried and put down his tools and set off down the embankment to find his father. He had not been heard from for fifteen minutes.

William guided his way down the hillside, taking each step with care as it was getting steeper. It worried him that his father might have fallen and hurt himself.

"Pa, Pa! Can you hear me?" he whispered. With each time he got increasingly louder with worry. There was still no response.

"Where has the old fool got to?" he said to himself.

It was now completely pitch black. The light from the fire had disappeared, the moon was struggling to break through the canopy of trees.

"William, over here." He heard a distant voice.

"Pa, where are you?" he shouted back. He no longer cared if the witches could hear him. He was several yards down the hillside and his only concern was for his father. He looked round and could not see any sign of him.

"William, I'm down here. Look for the light."

William looked through the trees from right to left, but there was no light.

"Pa, I can't. No light. It's pitch black; you'll have to guide me."

"I'm here, waving the lantern. Look to your left. No; my left, your right."

William peered through the trees and saw a faint light through an opening of rocks. He gave a sigh of relief that his father was alright and continued down the hillside, crossing a small stream to the rocks where Grandpa stood.

"What are you doing all the way down here? I've been worried sick."

"Well, my boy. To put it shortly, I kind of got lost in the dark."

"Speaking of dark, where did you find that lantern?"

"What lantern?" Grandpa replied

"The one you're holding."

"Ah, yes. This lantern, of course. Well, that's quite a funny story. As I was minding my own business, looking for the branches as you asked, I lost my bearings. You know my eyesight isn't the best at times, even with my spectacles."

"Yes, Pa. Just get to the point."

"As I said, I headed down the hillside as there were hardly any branches at all, then I lost my footing and fell down into that little stream over there."

"But where was the lantern?"

"I am coming to that, William, give me a chance," Grandpa said.

"I pulled myself up and dusted myself down, removing the leaves and soil from my hair. My backside was wet, as I'd landed directly in the stream; most uncomfortable it was indeed. I walked over to these rocks to catch my breath and get my bearings. My shoes were also filled with soil, so I leant against the rock wall so I could empty its contents. To my surprise the wall made a clicking noise and started rumbling."

"The wall began rumbling?" William had now become more interested in his father's story.

"Yes. I was most surprised. I could hear a clicking noise, so I walked around the corner and a doorway had appeared in the rocks. So I peered in and saw the lantern. Only problem was I stepped back out to find my matches holding the lantern and the doorway disappeared."

"Then what happened?" William asked.

"Well, that's when you started shouting me so I came looking for you."

"Show me exactly what happened."

"From the beginning?" Grandpa said.

"No, Pa. Just the bit where you leaned on the rocks."

Grandpa showed William the rock wall which he had been leaning against. William took the lantern and examined the area. Using his hands he pressed against the wall. The rock was bitterly cold and his hands soon became numb. He found a slit in the rock wall. Holding the lantern closer, he peered at the small crevice. Taking out his carpenter's knife he stabbed away at the opening, increasing its width and revealing a square pattern.

"Well, this is it, Pa. This is the way forward. Are you still willing to continue the quest?"

"We've come this far. We'd be fools to stop now."

William smiled, patting Grandpa on the shoulder as a sign of his delight. He pressed hard on the stone and it retracted, emitting a rumbling sound. They stepped around the corner to the opening which had appeared in the rock face. Both took a deep breath and in they stepped.

Chapter Eighteen

Whilst William and Grandpa had made fantastic strides into the quest, Ellie-May, John and the Professor, had arrived at the summit of Bidston Hill.

"Witches...! Professor, are those really witches I see before my eyes?" Ellie-May asked.

"The diary warned us of this. Have no fear. It is all going to plan; I have prepared for this moment," the Professor said reassuringly.

"But how shall we pass?"

"Don't worry, my dear Ellie-May. This is not my first encounter with those who summon the spirits."

The Professor walked up the path directly to the coven of witches.

"Who goes there?" a voice roared.

"We mean you no harm. We come in search of enlightenment from those blessed with truth and spirit," the Professor said as he kneeled courteously before the glowing figure in front of him.

"You come with knowledge, son of Adam. What do you seek?"

"We seek nothing but safe passage to the other side of this summit."

"Others before you have not been so gracious. Your forefathers were not so gracious."

"May I ask to whom am I speaking?"

The white witch glowed from the embers of the fire from which her ghostly figure had departed.

"My name is Maryanne. I was born to the earth in the 15th Century." The white witch spoke in a softer voice as she stood before the Professor and the trembling Ellie-May and John, who remained silent.

"I too am a seeker of wisdom," the Professor replied. "I come in search of knowledge preserved on this very hill. I am humbled to be in your presence."

"Many before you have sought the truth of this blessed place. Sons and daughters of Adam and Eve have inflicted their wrath on many like myself," Maryanne replied.

"We seek revenge on those who have wronged you. Your enemy is our enemy. We search for the hidden truths of Richard Leay the witch slayer."

The four other black dressed witches surrounded Maryanne upon hearing the name "Leay."

Maryanne's eyes glowed with fire and she hovered above the ground. Clouds had formed, with bolts of lightning flashing in the sky as the sound of thunder shook the ground.

"The descendant of Leay, you say. I have not heard that name in many years."

"How has this man wronged you?" the Professor asked.

"Like his father before him and his father before him and so on, they have burned innocent witches who were guardians of the sacred hill of Bidston. I myself was a protector against bringers of evil and Satanists. I was wrongly accused of sorcery and burned at the stake for my crimes, on this very summit."

"We condemn those that have wronged you," the Professor shouted as more gusts of wind engulfed the area.

"Upon my last words before my death, I cursed Richard Leay. He shall never walk in daylight, nor shall he ever grow old. His curse is to experience lifetime after lifetime of the death of those that he may love. He will never bear the fruits of the Son of Adam nor the daughter of Eve. A guardian of the Realm."

"Richard Leay guards the secret which we desire. Will you let us pass?" the Professor asked. "We search for only the answers to the quest and nothing more."

"I don't know of any such quest. You have a heart of truth, yet you have a mind of despair. For the other two I cannot say the same, your hearts are black with greed, power and hate. This will lead to your own demise," Maryanne said as she turned and pointed to Ellie-May and John. They remained silent in fear, not knowing what could happen.

"I foresee you will one day be given a choice which will have serious consequences in your life, one way or another. It is then that you must decide your destiny. Are you a servant of God or a servant of Satan?"

Professor Brown was clueless as to what Maryanne was referring to, but he agreed with her for the good of the quest.

"I trust I shall make the right choice when it presents itself," the Professor said as he rose up from one knee, bowing before her.

"Very well. You may pass and continue your journey. But mark my word of warning, the answers you seek may not be the answers that you find."

The professor ordered Ellie-May and John to move forward. They walked the path across the summit and through the black dressed witches who had created an opening allowing them to pass.

The Professor, Ellie-May and John thanked Maryanne and hurried on through before the witches could change their minds.

"How did you know what to say?" Ellie-May asked

"I have done some research into witchcraft. I used to think that witches were all worshippers of the devil and brought destruction and misery upon the world. But not all witches were seekers of evil. Many witches were good people and sought connections to the divine as guardians to the earth. Many of these were exposed and burned at the stake by village people and witch hunters, who thought witches were out to send curses against the Church and its people. In reality most witches were mere guardians of something more powerful, stopping the underworld from roaming the earth once again. But most of these tales are just myths and legends. How much of it is true I don't know."

"Well, I seen with my very own eyes, which was no myth," John said in a trembling voice.

"Let us no longer worry, John. What we seek is down this pathway and in the cottage of Richard Leay. We are on the quest and nothing can stop us now. We shall not worry about anything else this strange hill of Bidston holds."

The Professor pointed to the building in the distance. They gathered their speed as they approached Tam O'Shanter's the cottage of Richard Leay.

William and Grandpa felt like they had been walking for several miles and should have reached the cottage long ago, but in fact they were lost in the maze of tunnels beneath the hill of Bidston and had not travelled far at all.

"I told you it was the tunnel leading to the right, William. Look! We are back where we started," Grandpa moaned as he sat down to relieve the pain from his aching feet.

"Alright Pa! But we never take the right tunnel. History tells us that is always the easiest answer. Obviously not on this occasion. Let's rest for a minute. I'll make a map and get us out of here."

"Could have told you this earlier and saved all this unnecessary walking. My feet are going to fall off. You forget that I'm old."

"Alright, alright. I'll take more notice in future. You know best," William mumbled under his breath.

"Anyhow, I thought you said these tunnels were built long ago? They could run anywhere. How do we know it will lead us to the cottage?"

"It was in the diary, Pa. If I had it, I would show you what it said. That darn Grangeworthy lady has got it. It would not surprise me if she has already been and gone," William said.

"Don't worry about it, William. Women like that have no understanding for historical details. She will more than likely read the entire book looking for words such as: money, gold, treasure, silver..."

"I hope you're right, Pa."

"Get on with the map, and let's get out of here."

Grandpa was doing his best to lift William's spirit. Not having the Hornsmith diary was a huge loss, but he knew where Ellie-May Grangeworthy had the diary. William had the advantage and skills to complete the quest. Little did they know about Professor Brown. That really would dampen spirits, but for now,

Grandpa believed they held the tactical advantage.

"Alright, so I have looked at the layout of the hill and I position the opening here within the rocks," William said, pointing to the map.

"Then we headed in a straight line to here before we got lost," Grandpa added, running his finger along the map.

"We then took a left."

"When I told you we should have gone right," Grandpa shouted.

William looked up and glared at his father.

"Alright! As I said before I was interrupted..."

"Don't you use that tone of voice with me, young man," Grandpa shouted.

William did not respond and took a deep breath.

"We took a left turn and that led us on to a circular path, all the way back to this point. So, if I remember correctly there was a selection of tunnels at this point." William pointed on the map. "So if we take the right tunnel first, we should lead back to that point and we know it's not straight on, so again we'll have a choice of right and left. So in order to move forward we need to return to that point." William was feeling positive again.

"Right. Well, the circulation has returned in my feet. Ready when you are. We have a quest to complete," Grandpa said.

"I couldn't do this without you, Pa," William said as he helped his father to his feet.

Continuing onwards they found themselves back where they had made a wrong turn.

"Alright, so here we are. This time, Pa, I will let you make the decision. Left or right?"

"Easy, I told you; we shall head to the right. The right way is always the right way," Grandpa said confidently as he led them down the passageway.

William shook his head and carried on behind his father.

After walking down the passageway for a further nine to ten minutes, William felt that this time they were back on the right path.

"By my calculations we should be not far from the cottage of Richard Leay."

"But most of all, my dear William, we are a safe distance from the witches," Grandpa said with a smile on his face.

The passageways sloped downwards for a good fifty yards or more. They had made it out of the maze of tunnels and they should be reaching their destination anytime soon and indeed they did. They finally reached the end of the passageway and met a wooden door.

Just as William and Grandpa arrived beneath the cottage, the Professor, Ellie-May and John reached the front of the cottage. Little did either party know of the other's location.

The chase was on.

Chapter Nineteen

Standing outside the cottage, the Professor read the rest of the Hornsmith diary page, dated 13th April 1837.

Today I continued work with one of my friends, Richard Leay. I used this opportunity to place my next marker; on the wall it rests. The hill of Bidston is a very peculiar place indeed, something that Richard has been awfully quiet about. I sometimes wonder if he has been as untruthful to me as I have to him, not that I can complain of course. I find it odd that a man would build a cottage as beautiful as this, but on the wrong side of the hill. Surely a man would prefer to look at the beautiful landscape across the way that would glisten in the sunshine, rather than a treeline of darkness and a working mill. When I asked, he explained that he was merely a guardian over the hill and by placing the cottage here he was able to keep a fruitful eye at all times. What he meant by this, I am unsure.

"According to this, the item we are looking for will be found attached to a wall. Surely it can't be that simple," the Professor said out loud.

"Well, what are we waiting for? Let's go and find it," John said eagerly.

"We can't just barge in, John, it's somebody's home," the Professor said.

Ellie-May was not one to wait round. She had already walked up the garden path and was knocking loudly on the door.

"Well, looks like no one is home. Let's invite ourselves in shall we?" Ellie-May turned the door handle and the door slowly creaked open.

Richard Leay had been startled by the sound of movement. Arming himself with his sword, he went to investigate. But it was not the movement from the front of the cottage, it was from below that had caught his attention. Going down the stone steps into the cellar, he saw the wooden door in the far corner was rattling. Drawing his sword, he positioned himself against the wall, ready to strike anything that came through the door.

On the other side of the door was William and Grandpa.

"I thought you said you could open any locked door, William," Grandpa said as William prodded small iron rods into the lock.

"Patience, Pa. I cannot concentrate with all this commotion. Please keep quiet."

"Oh, I see. It's my fault now, is it? I will just go and sit down and keep my mouth closed," Grandpa said sarcastically.

"Nearly there, just one more turn to the right."

The lock on the door clicked and unlocked.

"Right, Pa, are you ready? Let's see what lies behind it."

Grandpa returned to the door with William and they both prepared to go through.

They walked into the light.

"Who are you?" Richard Leay shouted. He leapt out in front of William and Grandpa waving his sword. William and Grandpa screamed as they jumped out of their skin.

"Answer me or I'll remove your limbs one by one."

"Please, please. We are just simple explorers. We are on a quest, we mean you no harm," William shouted in panic, pleading for his and Grandpa's life.

"A quest, you say?" Richard said as he lowered his sword.

"Yes, we are in search of something that has led us here. Is this the Tam O'Shanter Cottage?" William asked.

"Indeed it is. Hector said you would come one day."

"You knew Hector Hornsmith?" William asked.

"Why, yes. He was a good friend of mine, he built my home."

William and Grandpa grew more settled as Richard grew calmer and more welcoming.

"But you must be over a hundred years old. How can this be?" William was puzzled.

"Indeed I am, I am older than you think. My name is Richard Leay and I am the guardian of the Hill at Bidston."

"Pleased to meet you. My name is William Withens and this is my father," William replied as he shook hands with Richard.

"How can you be so old, yet so young?" Grandpa asked.

"I have been cursed. I trespassed against a guardian of the hill. I live forever in sin for my grave error. I will never grow old and I will never die; this is the debt that I must pay. The tunnel to Tam O'Shanter's was built by my good friend Hector Hornsmith for me to navigate the hill during sunlight. You'd best tell me what you have been doing and how you got here," Richard said.

They sat at the wooden table situated in the cellar. William told Richard what had happened and how they had ended up at his cottage. Richard also informed them about his encounter with the witches of Bidston Hill.

"Hector Hornsmith entrusted me with the secret of Mother Redcap's treasure and said one day the righteous man shall seek the treasure of all treasures. This was my payment in return for the tunnel and cottage. It was an easy trade to make."

"Can we see the stone marker?" William asked.

"I believe that this was indeed left for you. Wait while I remove something." Richard rose from the table and headed across the cellar to where a painting was hanging on the wall.

"I often look at these ships in the painting and wonder what connection they have to the stone behind." He removed the painting from the wall. Before Richard could continue, he was interrupted by the sound of footsteps coming down the stone step into the cellar.

"Well, well, well, what do we have down here, then?" Ellie-May laughed as she entered into the cellar.

Richard drew his sword once more.

"Who are you and what are you doing in my home?" he said.

"My dear man, what do you expect to do with that old piece of tin?" Ellie-May laughed. John and the Professor joined in the laughter.

"I am a trained swordsman. Do not underestimate the power of the sword," Richard replied as he stood with his weapon ready to strike.

"What good is a sword if you are already dead?" Ellie-May replied as she pulled a pistol out of her undergarments. The Professor and John were just as shocked as Grandpa and William.

Richard smiled. "Your bullets will not harm me."

"Oh, I know all about your immortality, but it will harm them," she said as she pointed the gun at William and Grandpa who panicked, looking down the barrel of a loaded gun.

"John, remove that stone. We'll take it with us," Ellie-May added.

John took out his knife from his pocket and carved away at the stone that contained the written words.

"Clever thinking, Ellie-May; leave no traces behind." The Professor smiled.

"It's more for you to figure out. You can solve it back in the carriage," she replied.

"Indeed. A good idea." The Professor nodded.

"Now, all of you, walk through that door," Ellie-May shouted as she waved the pistol at William and Grandpa who were frozen still as if their feet were set in stone.

"Do as she says, Pa," William whispered.

"I'd do so, William, but I can't move," Grandpa whispered back.

Ellie-May moved forward, pointing the pistol even closer at William and Grandpa, who moved backwards with their hands in the air.

"And you as well! Put your sword on the ground and walk through that door," Ellie-May ordered.

Richard Leay did so, joining William and Grandpa who stood inside the tunnel.

"John, close that door and make sure nothing can come through it," Ellie-May said. She turned to walk back to the steps.

John closed over the door. He then used the key to ensure it was locked then added the extra wooden bolts, which had not been used in a very long time.

Ellie-May, John and the Professor, along with the stone tablet, headed out of the cottage and back to their carriage.

William, Grandpa and Richard Leay were trapped in the tunnel. The only way out was to head back the way they came, but this time they had Richard with them who had navigated the tunnels for many years.

"We didn't solve the riddle, William. What are we going to do?" Grandpa expressed his frustration.

"I know, Pa. We have sure blown it this time. This looks like the end. Let's just get out of here and go home. Every tale has a villain and this time the villain has won," William said as they walked up the tunnel.

"Are you both going to give up that easily?" Richard asked.

"But without the stone marker we cannot find the next part of the quest," Grandpa said.

Richard laughed.

"Begin West of Kirby. You'll travel by day. Take a right and a left, don't get led astray.

Wait till you gaze at the haze of this isle
You'll find it in three, in half of a mile.

The sunlight will guide you. Stay on the right path,
But be wary of Poseidon, you'll soon feel his wrath.
The journey you'll take, you're halfway here.
Wait for the tide, but don't wait all year.
Over the isle and on to the Dee
You shall travel by boat, must head to the trees.
Beware of the silt, don't travel too far,
No large vessels, or you'll stick like a jar.

Keep out of the water, if you travel by night
The mermaids below, they sure do bite.
Arrive on the shore, stick close to the trail
Look during daylight, or you will fail.

Inside the forest, it gets very much darker
Travel by foot, till you see the stone marker
Beware of the Bandas, they're hiding in here.
What you seek is not far, but yet also not near.

William stopped walking and turned to look at Richard.

"What did you say?" he asked.

Richard repeated what he said.

"How can you remember that?" William smiled.

"I've been living in that cottage for many years, remember. Not much to do when you cannot go out during the day. I often whistle the words when walking the tunnels. It keeps me focused."

William was overcome with excitement and found himself throwing his arms around Richard, giving him a grateful hug. Richard was surprised by this emotion and showed no response.

"I'm sorry, Richard. I do apologise. You see, I was just so excited that we can now carry on the quest. Please forgive me," William said as he removed himself from around Richard.

"I have not felt human contact in a very long time. Let us carry on, I'll take you to the exit," Richard replied.

"Can you tell me one more time, please, so I can write the words into my journal?" William asked as he opened his satchel.

"Very well," Richard replied as he recited the words once more.

William and Grandpa smiled all the way to the end of the tunnel and silence remained.

Richard took William and Grandpa back to the other side of the hill to where Free-Way was waiting. He opened the door, which was hidden within trees, but William knew exactly where he was as he looked through the darkness.

"I trust my secret remains with you," Richard said.

"Your secret is safe with us, Richard. Thank you for your help," William replied as he shook Richard's hand.

"Good luck on your quest. Be sure to let me know what happened on your return."

William and Grandpa waved goodbye and walked across the bottom of the hill back to Free-Way.

Sitting in the vehicle, William decided that it would be a good idea to take the opportunity to get some much needed rest. He set up then attached the tent-like roof structure of Free-Way and they settled down for a night's sleep.

Chapter Twenty

William and Grandpa awoke the next morning. The sun was shining but the ground was wet as it thawed out from an overnight frost. They both stepped out of the vehicle to stretch their legs, taking in their surroundings.

"The hill certainly looks less scary in the day, doesn't it, William?" Grandpa said as he looked around at the beautiful wildlife in the autumn sun.

"It certainly does, Pa. We'll have to bring the boys up for overnight camp sometime." William laughed.

"I'll stick to the day walks, thank you very much," Grandpa said as he remembered the witches from the night before.

"Remember what Richard said, Pa. The witches only come to the hill on All Hallows Eve."

"I've had quite enough excitement and frights to last the rest of my life. I will be happy when the quest is over and I'm back home. Your mother is enough to put up with as it is."

Both William and his father laughed.

"I can't remember the last time we actually spent this much time together, William. You're always hiding away fiddling with things."

"Inventing, Pa," William quickly corrected his father.

"Even so, whatever it is you do, you should spend more time with the boys. Watch them grow up, teach them things."

"Like you did with me? You were always away at sea. I have barely seen you most of my childhood," William replied.

"Exactly, and now you are doing the same with Mark and Michael. You are always working."

William stopped and paused before he said anything else. He knew his father was right.

"Maybe when we get home, things can be different. I will show them the tunnels and caves. They could even help me. There's plenty of room down there, after all."

"Right, William; enough chitter chatter for one day. Get your journal and let's figure out where the next destination is."

William grabbed his journal.

"Begin West of Kirby. You'll travel by day.
Take a right and a left, don't get led astray.
Wait till you gaze at the haze of this isle
You'll find it in three, in half of a mile.

The sunlight will guide you. Stay on the right path
But be wary of Poseidon, you'll soon feel his wrath.
The journey you'll take, you're halfway here.
Wait for the tide, but don't wait all year.
Over the isle and on to the Dee
You shall travel by boat, must head to the trees.
Beware of the silt, don't travel too far,
No large vessels, or you'll stick like a jar.

Keep out of the water, if you travel by night
The mermaids below, they sure do bite
Arrive on the shore, stick close to the trail
Look during daylight, or you will fail.

Inside the forest, it gets very much darker
Travel by foot, till you see the stone marker

Beware of the Bandas, they're hiding in here

What you seek, is not far, but yet also not near.

"West of Kirby? Wasn't Wallasey called Kirby in days gone by, William?" Grandpa asked.

"I believe it was, Pa. But we can assume that West Kirby, situated around the coastline is where we need to start," William replied as he took out his map.

"What about the rest of the riddle?" Grandpa asked.

"We have a good few hours travel ahead of us, so we can work it out on the way. We really could do with finding some more coal, we're running low already."

Grandpa took the map off William, checking the route to West Kirby.

"I know just the place. We can stop for a bite to eat too."

"Where do you have in mind, Pa?" William asked.

"Your Uncle Winston lives not far from here, in Moreton."

"But you haven't spoken to him in over twenty years."

"Well, now is a good of time as any. I am sure he will pleased to see us. That's if the old bugger is still alive." Grandpa smiled.

"Well, alright. Seems the only option we have. We will replenish our stock and move on. Remember, don't mention anything at all. I remember the last time I stepped inside the Farmers' Arms," William replied.

Grandpa nodded in agreement as William fired the engine of Free-Way and they set off down the Hoylake road.

Gliding through the horses and carriages that occupied the road, William and Grandpa's trip did not go unnoticed. People stopped and stared in amazement as they saw the unusual machine driving along. Grandpa felt like royalty, giving the odd wave as they passed by the crossroads.

"Just up the road now, William," Grandpa said.

"I remember, Pa. Keep your eyes open for a coal merchant. We are down to the last half a sack," William replied.

The Free-Way pulled up outside the Farmers' Arms. The daily bout of fist fighting had already broken out and it was not even midday.

"See? This is why I didn't think it was a good idea," William shouted.

The men broke apart, dusting themselves down as they stopped and stared at the strange machine that had appeared. They slowly walked over to the Free-Way, admiring it and surrounding the trapped William and Grandpa.

There was a loud bang and everybody scattered away from the vehicle, running in all directions.

"That's right! Get out of here, you good-for-nothing scoundrels," a man shouted, waving a pistol in the air. Just as he turned to go back inside, he looked at William and Grandpa who were sinking into their seats. He adjusted his spectacles and squinted for a better view.

"Warwick, is that you?" he shouted.

"Oh, good lord, it's Uncle Winston," William said to his father

"It is you! How in the devil are you, old boy?" the man said as he approached Free-Way.

"Haven't changed, I see. Hey, Winston?" Grandpa said as he exited the vehicle.

The two brothers hugged.

"Been about twenty years, hasn't it, hey, Warwick? It is good to see you again, little brother," Winston said.

"Yes, about that," Grandpa replied.

"And you must be little William. Not so little anymore, are you?" Winston laughed.

"Hello, Uncle Winston. Good to see you again," William said as he stepped out of the vehicle to give his uncle a hug.

"Well, come in and let's talk all about what brings you here on this day, after so long," Winston said as he walked back inside the Inn.

William and Grandpa followed.

Winston was the eldest of the two brothers, but he was very different to Warwick Withens, who we know as Grandpa. Winston was not a lover of the sea and when Grandpa Withens chose to sail on the seas, he preferred to stay on dry land. Living in Moreton he has spent most of his life working at his beloved inn "The Farmers' Arms," which he now owned. Having been a skilled card player, he had won the ownership in a game of poker. This was the first time he had ever struck lucky playing cards, nearly twenty years ago. He borrowed money from his brother and lost it all. A debt that was still to be paid.

"What can I get you both?" Winston asked as he stood behind his bar.

"Food would be great. I am famished," William said

"Me too," Grandpa added.

"Go and take the weight off your feet, Warwick. I'll bring over some drinks." Winston pointed them to a table near the fire.

Grandpa and William used this time to think about the clue. William took out his map and placed it across the table.

"So we know we have to start West of Kirby, which as we know is West Kirby. It then states we must travel to the isle. Looking at the map it must be this here," William said as he pointed at the map.

"Ah, the isle of Hilbre," Winston interrupted as he placed two glasses of ale on the table.

"You know of this place, Uncle Winston?" William asked.

"Yes, why do you ask?" he replied.

"Tell him, William, he might be able to help," Grandpa added.

William was at first reluctant to include Winston in his business, but it made sense to ask somebody who knew that side of the island. He was family, after all. He recited the clue.

"What did you say this was for again?" Winston asked.

"Oh it's...erm, just a game me and my friend are playing," William replied.

"Strange type of games you seem to be playing, William."

"It's an inventor's thing," he replied.

"Well, you will be pleased to know the clues are quite clear, but I don't see why you need to go to Hilbre Island," Winston said as he pointed on the map.

William and Grandpa peered down.

"The end destination is over here in Wales. There is no point going via Hilbre Island, you can travel straight across from here to here. Using a small steam boat, you can travel around the Isle of Hilbre, up the River Dee to here." He prodded on the map.

William looked at Grandpa and they both smiled.

"What are you two really up to?" Winston said quizzingly as he walked away.

There was no answer from William who folded away the map, placing it back in his satchel. Winston went to the kitchen and soon returned with two plates of food in his hands.

"Here you go, boys, tuck in."

William and Grandpa's eyes lit up as they stared down at two large pieces of pork, carved straight from the spit, with eggs and mushrooms, served with a cob of bread.

"Looks wonderful, Uncle Winston. Thank you," William praised him.

"Indeed, brother, this looks and smells delightful," Grandpa added.

"Is there anything else I can get you? Free of charge, of course," Winston asked.

"How about two sacks of coal?" Grandpa laughed.

Winston disappeared back to the kitchen. William and Grandpa filled their empty stomachs as fast as they could.

Not one to enjoy sleeping outdoors, Ellie-May demanded she was returned to her home following the night on Bidston Hill. Ellie-May, John and the Professor sat around the dining table of Hornsmith Manor enjoying a selection of the finest imported food. Only the most luxurious of cuisines would do for Ellie-May. John and the Professor did not complain.

"Have you figured it out yet, hey, Professor?" John asked as he gnawed down on a plump pheasant.

"Seems like we have to find an island of some sort, West of Kirby, wherever that is," the Professor replied as he held the stone tablet in his hands.

"It says:

"Begin West of Kirby, You'll travel by day
Take a right and a left, don't get led astray
Wait till you gaze, at the haze of this isle
You'll find it in three, in half of a mile

The sunlight will guide you, stay on the right path
But be wary of Poseidon, you'll soon feel his wrath
The journey you'll take, your half way here.
Wait for the tide, but don't wait all year.
Over the isle and on to the Dee
You shall travel by boat, must head to the trees
Beware of the silt, don't travel too far
No large vessels, or you'll stick like a jar

Keep out of the water, if you travel by night
The mermaids below, they sure do bite
Arrive on the shore, stick close to the trail
Look during daylight, or you will fail.

Inside the forest, it gets very much darker
Travel by foot, till you see the stone marker
Beware of the Banda's, they're hiding in here
What you seek, is not far, but yet also not near.

"I know...of a Kirby," John answered in between bites of the succulent meat.

The Professor looked up, quite surprised if anything.

"You know of this place and you have let me sit here for several hours staring at this piece of stone?" he said.

"Yeah, well, you're the Professor. I thought you would know these things," John replied as he picked up several quails' eggs, and swallowed them whole, one by one.

"Where is it then?" the Professor replied.

"Well, it's across the water in Liverpool, I'll show you." He smiled.

"Ah, good. Liverpool. We'd best pop into see how Jack is getting on at the factory. Who knows what is happening over there? But first, we must continue with this delightful food."

Talking about food...

William and Grandpa had finished their meals, rubbing their stomachs that were full to the brim.

"We needed that I think. Burp..." Grandpa said happily.

"We must thank Uncle Winston and be on our way," William replied.

Winston Withens returned through the doors of the inn carrying two large sacks of coal on his back. Despite his age he was still as strong as ever.

"Here you go, boys," Winston said as he slammed down the bags beside the table.

"What do we owe you?" William asked.

"It's on the house. Everything is free for family. Oh, and by the way, I have set you up with a boat leaving from West Kirby. He is a friend of mine, spotted him in the village before. He's ridden on ahead to prepare the boat. He owes me several favours. Now is a good of time than any to start cashing them in."

"Are you sure there isn't anything we can do for you?" William asked.

"An invite to Christmas dinner would be nice. Been a long time since I have seen all the family, and you are all that I have left," he replied.

William looked at Grandpa to see what his reaction would be. Grandma Withens still had not forgiven Winston and still spoke of him with ill feelings.

"Done, I will speak with the family. You will be welcome to join us, brother. A clean slate from now on," Grandpa replied as he stood up to shake his brother's hand.

William smiled and was glad to see that his father had finally made peace with his brother.

"Uncle Winston, I must say it has been good to see you again and I look forward to seeing you in December." William gave his uncle a hug.

"When you get to West Kirby, look for a short man with a beard named Pippin. Oh, and he has a missing hand. Don't ask him how it happened, though, or you will never get rid of him. A long story indeed." Winston laughed.

William and Grandpa said their goodbyes and returned outside to the Free-Way where a young boy was polishing down the last of the vehicle frame. He had also filled the tank with water and it was stocked with plenty of coal ready to depart. Another gift from Winston.

"Moreton isn't bad after all, hey Pa?" William chuckled

"Indeed not, my boy, indeed not."

They set out on their journey to West Kirby, excited to be once again on the trail of the quest.

Ellie-May, John and the Professor made way to the horse and carriage, setting off for Henry Saville's cotton factory.

The carriage arrived at the factory to a scene of chaos. People were everywhere chanting and screaming.

"What in the hell is going on here?" Ellie-May shouted.

John and the Professor looked at each other and had nothing to say, more not knowing what to say in fear of retaliation. There was one thought in John's mind and that was "Poor Jack."

"You two, go and find me my next clue. I will sort this lot out," Ellie-May shouted with a face of thunder as she opened the door of the carriage. She slammed it shut behind her.

Barging her way through the protesters she entered the building. Anger was really setting upon her. Ellie-May's face was getting redder by the second. It would not be long before steam started escaping from her ears.

The office door swung open. Jack looked up from his chair.

"Jack! What the hell is going on?"

"They just all walked out and wouldn't come back," he whimpered.

"You fool! Do you realise what would have happened had Henry come home? You count your blessings that it's me who is here," Ellie-May said as she stormed over to the window.

243

Jack did not move from his chair.

Standing on the balcony overlooking the protesters Ellie-May began shouting. "Everyone back to work immediately or you will all be sacked without pay."

The protest went silent.

"We want more money; less hours more pay," a man shouted.

The crowd cheered.

"I will give you all less hours if you don't return to your stations immediately," Ellie-May roared back with a smile on her face.

The crowd booed.

"We are human beings; we are not slaves, we have rights," the man shouted back again.

The crowd cheered once more.

"You can all easily be replaced. Many people will be happy to do your jobs. If you want to keep them, get back inside. Whoever is not back within those doors in the next five minutes will no longer have a job here nor will you receive any pay. The time is ticking, I suggest you start moving." Ellie-May returned inside her office, shutting the balcony doors.

The workers were left with no option and returned inside the building.

"Maybe one day we will have a voice," a worker said to another as they walked back in through the doors.

A few hours passed and John and the Professor had returned from Kirby and were entering the office.

"So, what did you find?" Ellie-May asked with a smile on her face.

"Well, it was the wrong place. I asked a local and he said we were on the wrong side of the River Mersey. There is no island off the coast of Kirby and we should be looking further afield," the Professor said.

"Are you two both as stupid as each other?" Ellie-May screamed as she looked at John and then Jack.

They looked at each other without reply. Ellie-May looked like she was about to explode.

"Right. Jack, your work in this factory is done for now. You and John, go and find me a boat. I and the Professor will fix this mess you have made. Go on, both of you, get out of my sight!" Ellie-May screamed as she sat behind her desk.

John and Jack went in search of a boat to hire, blaming each other on the way for the troubles that had occurred that day. The

Professor joined Ellie-May and they worked out the rest of the clue from the stone tablet.

Chapter Twenty-One

William and Grandpa arrived at West Kirby, where a brand new modern walkway was under construction. Men were hard at work; many others dressed in their best attire were out for a leisurely stroll. Unable to navigate the Free-Way upon the sand, William parked as close as possible to the nearby Marine Lake and then they continued the journey on foot. Boats were everywhere. It would take them a while to find Pippin. They passed several boats whose crews had all gone ashore.

"Can't be many more to pass now," William said as he looked round in all directions. "He must be here somewhere."

"We don't even know what his boat looks like. I didn't think there would be so many; there are small ones and large ones everywhere, even bloody rowing boats. It'd better not be a rowing boat, I hate rowing boats," Grandpa moaned.

They circled the lakeside and finally came across a man standing on a small tugboat, scratching his beard with an iron hook.

"This has to be him," William muttered.

"Ahoy there!" Grandpa shouted.

"Ahoy there, you must be the Withens boys," Pippin shouted back as he lowered a wooden gangplank.

"Permission to come aboard, Captain?" Grandpa shouted.

"Permission granted," came the reply. They both walked across to the boat.

"Welcome aboard."

They greeted each other and shook hands—well, a hook and a hand.

"What time can we set sail? It would be good to leave as soon as it looks like it's high tide," William said.

"You can leave right now if you like. She's all set to sail," Pippin replied.

"Wonderful! Raise the anchor," Grandpa shouted in delight.

"Did Winston not tell you? I'm not going with you; you shall be travelling alone."

"I am afraid he didn't," William said with a confused look.

"I won't travel across the Dee anymore," Pippin said, shaking his head.

"He just said that there would be a boat waiting for us. What will we do if you can't come? We will not be able to go," William pleaded, hoping for Pippin to change his mind.

There was a moment of silence and thinking.

"I can sail the boat," Grandpa said as he stood up with a smile on his face, standing to attention, saluting the British flag.

Pippin joined him in the salute.

"Of course you can, Pa. How could I forget?"

"Right you are, then. I've mapped your course of direction. Follow the route and you will find what you are looking for. But remember to avoid the rocks," Pippin said.

"We shall return your boat when we have finished our task. Are you sure you don't require any type of payment?" William asked.

"Just bring her back in one piece and most of all, don't bring anything back with you that does not belong here. I tried once and look at me now," Pippin said as he raised his hook.

William agreed. He had no idea what Pippin meant, but a boat for free? Who can argue with that?

"Been a long time since I've done this, hey, William?" Grandpa said as he spun the wooden wheel of the boat.

"Yes. Let's hope this does not end the same as your last voyage, hey, Pa?" William said sarcastically.

"I told you, that was not my fault."

"Yes, that's what the Navy thought, too."

"Hold tight. It may take us an hour or two."

With Grandpa already at the helm, William waved goodbye to Pippin as he raised the anchor and they set sail. They soon left the Marine Lake and headed out into the River Dee. The destination set out by Pippin was Mostyn, across the other side of the river in Wales. William had never been to Wales. He was unsure what to expect.

Meanwhile, back at William's home, "Montebello," in New Brighton, there was a loud knock on the door.

BANG BANG.

Melinda opened the door.

A gentleman stood before her, surrounded by several suitcases.

"Hello. Can I help you?" she asked, looking confused as she assessed the gentleman who wore in a long black cape, a tall hat and waistcoat.

The gentleman removed his hat.

"Good afternoon, madam. My name is Abraham, Abraham Stoker."

"Good afternoon indeed, sir. How may I help you?"

"I wondered if you would be able to help. You see, I'm on my travels, looking for a couple of lost relatives, and I have been informed that they may be living close by. It is my great aunts, Irene and Imelda. Do you know them?"

"Ah yes. Yes, I do, and funnily enough, they are due here any minute now! Please, come in. The kettle has just been placed on the fire."

"You are too kind! Much obliged, madam."

Abraham Stoker looked relieved and picked up his luggage. Melinda opened the door wide, giving a helping hand with the suitcases. They both went into the house.

"Here, take a seat. It looks like you could use one. Have you travelled far?"

"Thank you. That is most kind of you. Yes, I've just travelled up from London. It has been quite an experience, you could say."

"You travelled all this way to find your aunts?"

"Yes, amongst a few other things."

Melinda set out two cups and then placed several leaves inside a ceramic pot, then retrieved the iron kettle from off the fire and poured hot water into the pot.

"Best let that settle for a minute or two. So, how long has it been since you last saw Irene and Imelda?"

"Well, I have never actually met them. They were my late father's younger sisters. When the great famine hit our lands, they left. My father and mother stayed and I was born several years later."

"What is it that you do, Mr Stoker?"

"I am a man of several talents, but would like to be known as a writer. It has been my dream for many years."

"A writer, hey? My husband William likes to read many books. What is yours about?"

"I have written several pieces through my life, but something I am soon to finish, I feel and hope will do well. The main character is a Vampyre from a place called Transylvania, a somewhat horrid character, yet also somebody looking for love." Abraham spoke highly of his character.

"Round here we have a few horrid characters. No one worse than one man."

Melinda shuddered as she thought of the name.

"Is he of evil supernatural identity?" Abraham laughed.

"No, he is just a rich, spoilt, money-loving greedy tyrant. He is like his father before him and his children will be like him. A horrid family."

Melinda picked up the ceramic pot and removed the lid, inhaling the rising fumes she knew that the tea was now prepared.

"Would you be so kind to pass me the Tea-Bag behind you?"

"The what-you-say?" Abraham said in total confusement.

"Oh, I do apologise. My husband is an inventor, I forget we talk in riddles to the outside world in this house. It is that little item there."

She pointed to a little piece of round cloth, surrounded by a brass ring.

Abraham picked it up, looking at it extensively.

"Fascinating item, what is it?"

"We use it to keep the leaves out of the cups and save the leaves for a second helping. Here, let me show you."

Melinda placed the item on top of the first cup, securing it in place using the copper band and began pouring the hot water infused with tea leaves. The water filtered through and the bits of leaves were caught in the fabric.

"What a wonderful idea! He must be very talented," he said in amazement.

Melinda passed over the cup of tea to Abraham and sure enough, when he drank it, there were no leaves in the cup.

"William is also working on another idea, Tea-Bag2, but he has not quite perfected it yet. This one will hold the leaves in a ball-like shape. You will be able to pour in the water and stir it without worry and it can be used several times over. That may take another few years, yet."

"I certainly would like to meet your husband. Is he about?"

"No, he is away on a quest at the moment.... Erm, I mean he is away on business." Melinda stopped herself short before she said too much. She quickly changed the subject. "Anyway, Mr Stoker, have you somewhere to reside for the evening?"

"A friend of mine got in touch with one of his friends who is allowing me to use their house whilst they are away travelling."

"Oh, wonderful news. That is really kind of them. This time of year, hotels can be hard to come by."

"I am very lucky. They have even got servants for me. It is quite an interesting little resort up here. I am interested to see more of it." Abraham smiled.

"Are you planning on staying here long? If so, we would be honoured to show you round the area. There is a wonderful showing of *Antony and Cleopatra* currently at the Palace Theatre," Melinda said with excitement. She had seen the show several times and was mesmerised by the performance of the star of the show, Molly Maquire. So much she was looking forward to enjoying it again.

"I would be delighted to accompany you to the show," Abraham replied.

"Would you care for another cup of tea? I am sure your aunts won't be long now."

"Yes, please," he replied.

An hour or so passed and Irene and Imelda had not arrived as expected.

"How about we take in that performance you mentioned? And I am famished. I am not sure about you, but I would be delighted if you would join me for the evening," Abraham asked.

"My boys Mark and Michael are currently out with their Grandma, so I am free for the evening. I would love to join you. I'll get my coat."

Melinda and Abraham set out to New Brighton Resort.

Chapter Twenty-Two

A man sat alone at his desk writing his memoirs. He lived in a house made almost entirely from wood, but that was normal for a house that was situated amongst trees. The man gazed out from his window that overlooked the River Dee and even though land was not far away, it was far enough. It wasn't that he didn't like having companionship, he was just far too busy to spend time interacting with the outside world. The area was pretty much deserted apart from the man, the trees and his home, just how he liked it. He had spent many happy years alone and was more than happy to spend many more years the same.

Looking in the distance of the river, he saw something heading directly towards him. He produced his spyglass to take a closer look. Two men were sailing in a small boat.

"I wonder where they are heading?" he said to himself as he watched them draw closer to the shoreline. He decided to go down and greet them and see what business they had in this part of the land, a place where not many people tended to travel. He released the rope that was tied securely next to the window which closed the hatch, specially crafted with twigs and leaves. The home was now secure.

The boat edged towards the shore where the man stood.

"Ahoy there," Grandpa shouted.

"Hello there, chuck me the rope," he shouted.

"Hold it steady, Pa, and I'll throw it over," William said as he steadied himself on the end of the boat, lassoed the rope and tossed it over to the hands of the waiting man. He caught it with ease and pulled the boat ashore. When it had come to a complete stop, he secured the rope to a pole of the small wooden landing stage.

"Greetings! What brings you to these parts of the river?" the man asked.

"Greetings, my good man. We seek to explore the dark forest. Is it nearby?" William replied.

The man paused. Nobody had come looking for the dark forest; not since he had been here, anyway.

"Yes... it's not far from here. But can I ask, what are you looking for? Not many come to venture into the dark forest."

William didn't know how to reply. He simply couldn't say he was on a quest and that he sought words written on a stone tablet hidden somewhere inside the dark forest. The man would think he was two shillings short of a pound.

"We are simple explorers. We come to investigate new surroundings. We are from Wallasey. Across the other side of the coast. You may have heard of it."

"No, I can't say I have," the man replied.

"We live on a farm with a manor house. I am an inventor. I invent things to help grow our crops and tend our livestock."

The man was feeling more at ease; he liked the idea of speaking to an inventor. These men didn't seem so bad after all, he thought to himself; maybe they were just simple explorers, but why the dark forest?

"Where do you live, may I ask? Is it far from here?" William asked.

"I live here," the man said.

"Where, exactly?" Grandpa asked as he looked up and down the coastline with no house, hut or shack to be seen.

"Look above you," the man said, pointing.

Both William and Grandpa looked up and saw the outline of a large hut hiding up in the branches of the trees.

"I see you have used your surroundings very well," William said to the man. He admired the work that had been put into the disguise of the home, for he understood better than most the hard work undertaken when inventing.

"Thank you," he replied. 'I am currently working on a new supply room. I don't tend to go across river much, so it is handy to be able to store as much as possible.'

William and Grandpa looked up and saw a base of wooden planks perfectly suspended between several branches of the thick oak trees.

"How many rooms do you have here? It's bigger than our old house; hey, William? I bet you have a great view across the river," Grandpa said as he stood in admiration.

"Come with me and I'll show you. You're going to like this," the man replied as he signalled them to follow him.

"This is magnificent, but how do we get up there?" William asked as they walked into the trees with no doorway or ladder to be seen.

"Cleverly hidden, isn't it?" The man chuckled to himself with delight at being able to finally show somebody his work.

"I am very impressed. It is marvellous work indeed. You would not even know that the place was here," William replied.

"The lower branches of the trees have been removed, making ascending to the higher levels impossible unless you know how, of course. Security is the key factor of any home and here I feel very secure. Nobody ever comes here. They just sail on past as if there was nothing here at all. In fact, you are the first people I have seen in many months."

William understood the importance of security all too well.

"Come over to this tree. Looks normal doesn't it?" the man said.

"It's just a large oak, but its trunk's much wider than the others. Must be thousands of years old," William said as he looked the tree up and down.

"It is indeed, but this tree is like no other tree; it holds secrets that only a few shall know. I trust you will keep this to yourselves?" the man asked, feeling that he could trust them both despite only just meeting.

"Of course, William is good at keeping secrets. Aren't you, William?" Grandpa said sarcastically.

"Your secret will be safe with us," William replied, frowning at his father.

The man approached the rear of the tree and called William and Grandpa to follow him. He lifted off a piece of bark. Behind it were carved symbols showing in a pattern of three high and three wide.

"Gentleman, I introduce you to the Gablestop Lock," the man said with pride.

"A code lock! Wonderful. I do like codes," William said as he studied the symbols thoroughly.

The man smiled.

"A simple lock. By entering the correct four digit sequence, the door will unlock. Enter the wrong code and you may be in for a nasty surprise," he said as he peered down at the floor.

William and Grandpa got the idea and dreaded to think what may be waiting beneath their feet, they took a step back.

The symbols were numbered 1, 2, 3 on the top row, followed by 4, 5, 6 on the middle row, and 7, 8, 9 on the bottom row.

He stepped up and entered the sequence. 1 was the first number, a sound clicked. Next was number 8, again there was a click. 3 was the next and third number of the four digit sequence.

"May I press the next number?" William interrupted, he knew the answer after the second digit.

"Be sure you get it right; otherwise we go below."

"You think like me. I also find this a very important year. A year when things changed and the world became how we know it today."

"Very well, please be my guest." The man stepped back allowing William to step up to the symbols.

"I hope you know what you're doing, William," Grandpa said worryingly.

He reached out and pressed in the number 7. He stood back quickly in case he had got it wrong, but the floor did not give way. A clicking sound could be heard, followed by the sound of a chain moving. The nine symbols disappeared and the bottom of the tree trunk opened up.

William smiled. "1837. The year Queen Victoria came to the throne, a glorious year."

"Actually, I picked that number because it was the year the SS Great Eastern was launched, not far from my home," the man said. "It's my favourite childhood memory."

William stopped and paused for a moment.

"Good job it was the same year, then, hey?" William laughed.

The man stepped inside the opening and advised William and Grandpa to follow him.

"Quickly! Huddle round! We are about to go up," the man said.

They huddled together as the opening closed. At the same time they ascended inside the trunk of the tree.

"Marvellous, isn't it?" the man said.

"I've never seen anything like it! Simply fascinating," William replied as he looked upwards.

They reached an opening and came to a stop. After shuffling off the ledge that had clearly been designed for only one person, William straightened his clothes and glasses. Upon doing so he was greeted by a sight that was greater than he imagined.

"It's beautiful," William said as he looked at everything before his eyes. Balconies running in all directions, some heading up and some heading down, all connecting to wooden huts perfectly designed to fit within and around the branches of the trees. William was truly impressed.

"But how do you manage to get everything up here?" William asked.

"That's the easy part. Come this way," the man said as they walked across the drawbridge to one of the huts. They entered the room. There was a large pulley connecting the wooden floor to a collection of iron chains running to a large wheel in the corner. This was fascinating to William; Grandpa was not so enthusiastic.

"This is one of my favourite inventions. Watch as I turn this wheel! I got this idea from a castle I once visited. Not only does it lower the platform but it also activates the drawbridge to disconnect from the main building at the same time. Watch this."

And sure enough the man was right. As the platform lowered to the ground, the drawbridge ascended into an upright position on the far side, making it impossible to reach any other part of the structure when the platform had descended.

William was fascinated by this device. He was already thinking about how he could use something similar back home in the cave, but then he thought he had found a flaw in the plan.

"It's all very well the drawbridge being unscalable when the platform is down, but my dear man, how indeed do you get down and then back up?" William thought he had a valid point.

The man laughed.

"It's quite simple really. I'll show you." The man turned the wheel in an anti-clockwise manner until the platform had returned back to hut level. "You and your father get on there and I'll wheel you down."

William and Grandpa stepped on to the platform and were lowered down to the ground.

"This should be interesting," Grandpa said to William.

"Indeed, I have no idea how he'll do it," William replied.

"The famous inventor has no idea. That's a first," Grandpa said as he smiled at William, who frowned back.

The hatch doors closed with the sound of clicking and the platform remained on the ground. Another large click sounded and another followed each time in coordination, with a small stone ledge that appeared around the tree in a spiral fashion.

"Amazing! Absolutely amazing!" William shouted with delight, watching the stones come out in a rhythmic fashion all the way to the bottom of the trunk.

Even Grandpa was impressed. "Well! Never in my life have I seen anything like this before. A staircase on the outside rather than the inside. This could be a good way for me to avoid one of those unavoidable confrontation with your mother, William."

The man descended down to the ground with ease, each stone was, as they say, solid as a rock.

"Well, what do you think?" the man asked.

"It's fantastic. Did you do this all by yourself?"

"Well, yes. I have had plenty of time on my hands to—let's say—perfect things. Oh, I nearly forgot; watch this."

The man took out a key from beneath his shirt, and held it up showing it to William and Grandpa.

"This is where the fun begins," he said.

He removed the key chain from around his neck and walked over to the tree trunk.

Removing a piece of bark, he exposed a keyhole. Placing the key in the hole, he gave it a turn to the right. The clicking sound returned and one by one the stones disappeared.

"Simply remarkable. I really could use something like this back home in the cave. It would be very secure," William said.

"What cave?" the man replied.

"Oh... it's nothing too important. I'll tell you about it later," William replied, having nearly let the cat out of the bag.

"I would like that. You must be hungry. Come upstairs and join me for some supper. I would like to hear some more about your inventions and what life is like living on your farm."

The man used the key once more to return the stones, and they all went back up the spiral staircase.

Grandpa was at the window, looking out across the river. He took in several deep breaths, remembering his time sailing on the seas.

"It's a wonderful view, isn't it? I didn't quite catch your name," the man said to Grandpa.

"Warwick, Warwick Withens is the name. And that's my son William."

"And my name is Gerald. It's a pleasure to meet you," he replied as they shook hands.

"William, come here and greet Gerald. William... William. Where are you?" Grandpa shouted.

William was not answering.

"Where has he got to?" Grandpa wondered

William was outside on the balcony, crouching down in a hidden position.

"William, what are you doing out here?"

"Ssshhh, you'll scare them away."

"Scare what away?" Grandpa replied, looking confused as he could see nothing.

William waved his father over.

"Come here and look! Down there." He pointed.

Grandpa's eyes adjusted as the sunset crept through the trees. He saw something moving, but he had no idea what it was.

"What is it, William?"

"I don't know, Pa. I really have no idea what it is."

The creature disappeared into the woodland and could no longer be seen. William stood up, wondering just what it was that he had seen. Maybe he was just seeing things and tiredness was affecting his judgement.

Gerald walked outside to see where his guests had got to.

"Ah, Gerald! Hello, my name is William, William Withens. It's a pleasure to make your acquaintance." They shook hands briefly.

"What seems to have caught your attention?" Gerald asked as he stared over the balcony in the direction William was looking.

"I think I have just seen the strangest thing. A small animal walking on two feet. I am getting tired, though, so it could just be my imagination. It was too big to be a squirrel and too small to be a deer. Then again, they do not walk on two feet, so I don't have the foggiest what it could be."

The man stopped and paused, but was not fazed at all.

"That's unusual. It's a bit early for them to be out yet."

"Early for what?" both William and Grandpa asked.

"Come inside and sit down. I will prepare some food and we can drink some tea or something stronger. This may take a while."

Gerald escorted William and Grandpa back into the main room and he served up a delicious meal of salmon and mushrooms that had been caught and freshly picked earlier that day.

Chapter Twenty-Three

The evening back in New Brighton was currently mild with a light sea breeze. The stars shone brightly in the cloudless sky. It was unusual weather for England in December. Melinda and Abraham made their way along the front of the resort. Living in London, it was not often that Abraham got to enjoy an evening beside the seaside, especially this time of year.

"What a remarkable place it is here. Everywhere I look, there is something being created. A wonderful and innovative era in time," Abraham said as he looked up above to a huge iron structure being constructed upon the hill.

"Yes, this one is going to be bigger than the one that has been opened in Blackpool. They say it's to be the Eiffel tower of the British Empire."

"We are indeed living in interesting times. Anything is possible. Everybody is in a magical state of creativeness in Britain. It is truly fascinating to watch. From the wonderful inventions of your husband that you have shown me, to the new buildings all around us; I am really enjoying my time in New Brighton. I'm glad that I came. I can tell that everybody who has a dream would want to be around here right now."

"Funny you should say, Abraham. There is an interesting story behind the lady who plays Cleopatra. Let me tell you."

Abraham Stoker was intrigued and yet already enlightened by what he could see around him. His head was thumping with ideas; he was being truly inspired and was mesmerised by New Brighton. He listened with open ears.

"Molly Maquire was a young nineteen year old actress from Liverpool. Having played several small roles in theatre productions, she was seeking to further her career. Unfortunately, she did not get this opportunity in Liverpool. Major theatrical roles were always being handed to the regular stars of the show. There was no hope for new and rising stars, they had to look elsewhere. In the last ten years, New Brighton became a major venue for pleasure and entertainment seekers. Molly Maquire said goodbye to her parents, packed one suitcase containing everything that she owned and used some of the money she had saved to cross the river.

"'You'll never make it!' her father shouted as she exited the front door. 'Don't come crying back to us! Once you leave that door, you are not to return. The workhouse will have you,' Michael Maquire shouted as his daughter left without looking back.

"Molly was full of excitement. She had waited for this moment for several years. She was aged twenty three and was ready to take on the world. Well, the first step was to venture to a place she had never been before. A place that she had only read about in newspapers, a place that she could only see through the thick smoggy air of the city. A place that held all the answers to her prayers. The new resort upon the Cheshire coastline, a place for all to enjoy.

"On arriving at the New Brighton Pier, Molly's eyes were greeted by an array of many colours. Somewhat different to the dirty black and white, smog filled clothing that she seen on a daily basis back home. There was men and women in their best attire strolling along the decks of the pier, some heading for a day beside the seaside and some back to Liverpool. Already Molly had a warm glow sense of prosperity inside of her. Opening up today's edition of the Liverpool Daily Post, she was greeted by a page full of advertisements featuring New Brighton. She did not have much money, but she had enough to purchase a room for a week in one of the local hotels. Searching the page for the cheapest but most cheerful properties, she came across one place in particular in Wellington Road that she instantly took a liking to. Getting directions from a local shop owner on Victoria Road, she made her way to her destination.

"Having secured a place to stay the night before, there was only one thing left that Molly needed to do and that was to get an audition at the local theatre. Leaving the hotel, she followed the crowds who were making their way to the theatre. Everybody was dressed in the most fashionable clothes. Men in their best suits, normally saved for church of a Sunday. Women dressed in the latest designer dresses, which have been imported to Liverpool via the French capital. Molly arrived in front of the building and there it was in big letters 'Tonight's show— Antony and Cleopatra. Starring Louis Calvert as Antony and Janet Achurch as Cleopatra.' Molly envisaged her own name upon the board, but Janet Achurch! What an actress she was. Molly could only dream to have the following and respect that Janet Achurch had. Janet had worked all over the world, she was the number one sought after star in the whole of England. Molly stood there staring up at the board, the lights flashing at her. A commotion could be heard from behind her as the crowds formed a circle, getting louder, with camera flashes engulfing the area. It was Janet Achurch herself walking through the crowds directly towards Molly. Molly stood there in awe, her jaw had dropped, standing frozen unable to move. She was completely star struck.

"'Miss, Miss, Miss,' Molly mumbled

"'Yes, my dear, go on, spit it out,' Janet Achurch replied

"This was Molly's chance, a chance she had been waiting for years. There she stood in front one of the biggest stars in the theatre, all she had to do was ask for an audition. Her moment was then and there.

"'Well, I haven't got all day. What is it?' Janet asked again.

"'I, I, I...' Molly mumbled again. She could not bring herself to say the words.

"Janet Achurch carried on walking into the theatre as Molly looked on behind with tears beginning to form in her eyes. Her moment had gone, the doors had closed firmly behind Janet Achurch, and the audience was a sell out for that evening's performance. Molly walked away.

"'What have I done, what have I done?' she said to herself.

"She sat outside the New Brighton Pier as crowds disembarked from the Ferries, which had special double service from Liverpool.

"'Molly Maquire, just a girl from Liverpool. That's all I'll ever be.'

Molly wept heavily into her hands, becoming more inconsolable by the moment. She had no job, she had very little money, she was too ashamed to go back home. She had told her mother and father she was to be a big star. They told her she was living in a dream world.

They were right and she was wrong. She continued to cry.

"'Don't worry girl, it can't be that bad,' a voice said as a hand was placed on Molly's shoulder.

"Molly looked up, wiping the tears from her eyes, to see a middle aged lady standing and smiling down at her.

"'Who are you?' Molly asked.

"'My name is Vivienne Vixon.'

"'What a beautiful name.' Molly sniffled.

"'Come over to my shop just over there. You look like you could do with a nice cup of tea or maybe something stronger.'

"'I would certainly appreciate that, please,' Molly replied.

Vivienne took Molly by the arm and together they walked across the road as for the first time Molly entered the Ham and Egg Parade and the darkness in her life really began..."

Melinda was parched after speaking of the story of Molly Maquire; she would really prefer to call it "The Ballad of the Ham and Egg Parade."

Pulling out his pocket watch, Abraham indicated to Melinda that there was still time for more of the story to be told. Abraham pointed at a building across from the pier. For of course, Molly was to be the star of the show tonight, Abraham wanted to hear more.

"How about here? Could we gain refreshments from this establishment?" Abraham pointed to a large white building situated across from the pier.

"Gets a tad crowded in the Ferry Hotel, it does," Melinda replied.

"Let's stop in there, then," Abraham pointed again to another building, which was this time across the bottom of Victoria Road.

"That's just a café. It's closed during the evening," she replied.

They continued on a bit further.

Abraham's senses were becoming enriched. They were approaching outside a continuation of window fronted shop after shop within one large building. He took a small step back to look up; it was three stories tall. People pushed past as he gazed above. The walkway narrowed and everybody was walking in line; the finely dressed were forced to walk with the less desirably dressed. The atmosphere changed in an instant. The building sat neatly on the edge of the shoreline. Various renditions of music had filled the air, piano keys ringing out, and strings of what Abraham thought to be violins being plucked in the background.

"Well, surely this sounds like the place to be," Abraham said as he passed each shop front, looking into gain a closer look.

Melinda tried to encourage Abraham to keep walking, giving him a gentle nudge here and there, but Abraham's curiosity got the better of her.

The first window they passed was filled with bright light and floral decorations. Indeed he could see a quartet in one corner of the room, returning a beautiful sound of violin strings being played out and a small wooden stage was being used by a couple of performers to a room filled with men and women seated around circular clothed tables. Abraham was familiar with this kind of setting; he knew it very well from back in London. The second window, what was left of it, was boarded up with wood. As he stopped and peered through the cracks of the wood, it reminded him of a Wild West saloon. It was mayhem. In one corner, a table was filled with men holding cards in their hand as smoke billowed out of their mouths above them. Wooden stairs in another corner leading up to a balcony filled with women dancing away, trying to attract the attentions of the many men who stood with drinks in hand gazing up at them. Some tables had been overturned, bodies of men slumped against walls and some were lying down from either too much ale, or possibly something worse. Abraham did not stop to decrypt the scene any further and continued on his way. The third and final window was more confusing than the second to Abraham, a room full of people sitting around, no music, no tables and just one door at the back of the room. Sitting in silence, not one person acknowledged any other, as if they were waiting for something, but waiting for what? It made no sense to Abraham.

He could not work out how a variety of establishments can vary so much in one tiny area. The building in no way fitted in with the New Brighton scene that he had come to learn that day. Maybe the first window he passed did but definitely not two and three. He scratched his head in confusement.

"A very odd place indeed," he said to himself.

Melinda showed a sense of relief when they moved away from the shops and back on to a wider pathway. She took a deep breath, exhaled and thanked God doing so.

"Quite an eerie atmosphere I could feel there, something very odd about that place. Feels like it is mispositioned," Abraham said.

Melinda lowered her voice and whispered in Abraham's ear.

"That's what we know as The Ham and Egg Parade. We never stop there."

"The Ham and Eggs Parade? What an unusual name," he replied.

"Well, let's just say, they sell ham and eggs, but they also sell a little bit more," she whispered again.

It took Abraham a few moments to think about it, but he got Melinda's message.

"Ah, I see. Yes, maybe it is best if we try elsewhere."

There was still an hour to go before the performance was due to start. Melinda and Abraham enjoyed a three course meal. After hearing the rest of the tale of Molly Maquire, Abraham insisted that he must pay for the meal. Melinda was only too happy to accept. It had been a while since she had accompanied anybody out of an evening; not that she blamed William of course. His work was very important and she understood that, but Abraham's company has been fascinating. Little did she know that he was from the performing world himself. As an added bonus, she was thankful that she could even introduce him to her friend Molly Maquire after the show if he enjoyed her performance. As expected, her performance as Cleopatra that evening was as good as ever, captivating him enough to return to London with Molly Maquire the following morning, without waiting to meet his long lost aunts as he first intended. He left Melinda in possession of a note for them both and returned to the Lyceum Theatre of London to inform his friend Henry Irving of a new talented main star for his theatre

Chapter Twenty-Four

William and Grandpa enjoyed a thoroughly delightful meal. Gerald poured out three glasses of rum and returned to the dining area. He also decided to bring the bottle. It was going to be a long conversation, something that he had not undertaken in a very long time.

"Right, so here we go. What you saw before was very real."

William and Grandpa sat forward in anticipation.

"My name is Gerald Gablestop and I come from a place called Bath in Somerset. You may have heard of it. I have lived with the Kiccabanda for several years now after finding myself shipwrecked during a terrifying storm. It was a night like no other. I escaped the perils of the stormy seas and flashes of lightning which guided me to the treeline up on the beach. Injured from my struggles, I tore strips of clothing to bind my wounds. I walked for many paces through the wood, which became darker with each step, and still the rain fell but the thunder and lightning did not pass. With my body shivering it was vital that I made camp as soon as possible. My first thought was to use my carpentry skills and build a small hut, but my hands were too badly damaged. I walked into what was a very dark forest, the one you have also come here looking for. Believe me, this forest has a feeling like no other. I constantly felt like I was being watched, but I did not care at the time because I was desperately in need of shelter. I navigated my way through the trees while hearing noises around me, but it was so dark I could not see what made them. Finding myself coming to a small embankment, I managed to scale down the bank by grabbing branches exposed out of the earth. On several occasions I lost my balance. Resting for a while to catch my breath, I continued my journey, and it was not long until I came across shelter. Deep in the middle of the forest in front of me was an unusual stone cave, which at the time I did not find odd. In need of warmth I entered without hesitation. Guiding my way using the brief sparks from the lightning that broke through the trees, I hobbled up the passageway searching for the warmest spot possible. I gathered a couple of loose twigs that had blown into the cave and positioned them ready to make a fire. The only problem was my clothes were soaked through and the chances of my matchsticks being usable were slim. Luckily, I always kept some spare in case of emergency. I took out my silver tobacco tin. Thankfully no water had got in. I struggled to light the sticks due to my damaged hands and the matchsticks were becoming fewer and fewer. I tried again and finally it ignited. The warmth from the fire was immediate and I felt a sense of relief.

"Whilst sitting down and catching my breath, I noticed a doorway just across from me. Again, not finding this odd at the time, I struggled my way over to it and when I pulled the handle, it was unlocked. I opened it and I was greeted by light and a warm breeze, but it was the faint sound of music echoing in the distance that caught my attention and made me really wonder about my surroundings and where the hell I could be. Suffering from my wounds each time I moved, I had to crawl on my hands and knees through the passageway, which was only four feet high and six feet wide. I felt increasing pain, but the warm breeze kept my hopes up and I managed to struggle on.

"I carried on bravely till at last the small passageway opened into a cavern. I pulled myself up and briefly enjoyed the ability of being able to move freely once again, until the aches and pains returned.

"The sound of drums was clearer and I could hear chanting of some fashion. The cavern was fully illuminated, thanks to several lit torches on the wall. Again, I was not fazed by this, but more intrigued, I wanted to see more. I continued and everything became closer, I travelled down a passageway and came to a wooden door. Strange symbols were carved around the doorway, ones I had never seen before. I did not pay them much attention. I was fully focused on the door itself. I opened it.

"I was greeted with a scene of sheer excitement. The sound of drums beat loudly and I looked out over a large cave, one like I had never seen before. I could see crevices in walls, like sleeping quarters with rope ladders leading to each one. I moved forward and it was then that I saw something that I thought I would never see in my life. Creatures were dancing round happily. I rubbed my eyes, thinking maybe I was suffering from the storm. There was no confusion, what I was seeing was real. There was a hundreds of them, at first I thought of Leprechauns or maybe fairies, but no, these creatures were nothing like anything heard of before. All of a sudden the drums stopped and silence followed. Several hundred sets of eyes were looking at me. I was too weak to run away and literally too scared to move. It dawned on me, what if they want to eat me? The silence continued. I decided they were as frightened as me, so I picked myself up and hobbled down the pathway that circled the cavern.

"As I walked round, I started to notice things, things that looked completely out of place, things that looked manmade such as wooden benches, tables. There was even a water supply like a beautiful waterfall, glistening in the light."

William thought that this was starting to sound very familiar.

"I had reached the floor level and was just about to say hello and introduce myself, but the room went black. I had fainted from the result of my wounds and exhaustion.

"I opened my eyes and I could hear the sound of drums and commotion. My wounds had been bandaged up and despite feeling quite dizzy, I was feeling less pain than I had earlier. Somebody or something had treated me. I found myself in a small wooden hut with paintings hanging up and even a dressing table. I was really confused. What was all this doing down here in a cave in the middle of a forest?

"Then the cloth curtain on the far side of the hut opened and in stepped a creature, a creature like nothing I had ever seen before."

Gerald stopped to take a sip of his drink. All the talking had made him thirsty. William and Grandpa remained silent, amazed by what they were hearing and desperate to hear more. Gerald continued.

"To cut a long story short, I will give you the outline of our conversation. Let's just say the Kiccabanda don't speak very well. We communicated by drawing lines and pictures in the sand on the floor of the hut. I could tell that they were friendly creatures, but when I made sudden movements they reacted in a defensive way, so I acted more calmly. They were called Kiccabandas.

"A Kiccabanda is a small creature that stands on two feet. It has four toes on each foot containing long claws. Unlike most animals and creatures, the Kiccabanda uses the claws on its feet to open fruits and nuts for eating. The horse chestnut is a popular food and we shared some when eating together. The Kiccabanda are two feet tall in height and have sandstone coloured skin with brown hair all over their bodies, especially their backsides.

"The Kiccabanda are originally from Africa, but they were more than often eaten by lions and other large animals so they decided to leave their underground habitats and head for pastures new. It took nearly ten years to find their perfect place, but they finally made their new home here in Wales. They told me that they found this cave already made and with nobody living here, they decided to make it their new home.

"The Kiccabandas are naturally friendly, but stroking them without permission will cause them to bite. They enjoy eating wild nuts and shelled fruits of the forest, but their favourite food is the sacred Yugogo plants which they brought with them from Africa. The Yugogo grows in the dark and produces fruit like the coconut only smaller in size. The cave was a perfect place for the Yugogo to grow. The Kiccabanda use their sharp claws on their feet to prise open the fruit. I stayed with them for several days while my wounds healed. The more time I spent with them, the more I understood them. When I was fit to leave, they helped me back to the surface as I had completely forgotten which direction I had come. They guided me back through the dark forest. The boat was destroyed; there was no way of me getting back across the river unless I built a small vessel or raft. However, I began to enjoy my surroundings and it was then I began to get to work on where I live today.

"As you can see, I live near the river's edge. I keep myself to myself and the Kiccabanda come and visit me during the evening when they are sure nobody is about. Not that we see many people around here anyway, but they prefer to keep out of sight. You may even meet some later this evening.

"So that is my story and how I got here. Now tell me why is it you have come to explore in these parts, then?"

Grandpa and William were both stuck for words of how to respond after what they had just heard.

"Kiccabanda, you say?" William said.

"Two feet tall you say," Grandpa added.

"Tunnels and caves," William said as well.

"Yes," Gerald replied calmly.

"My dear man, how long did you say you have been living alone for?" Grandpa said.

"I know what you are thinking, but I tell you, I'm really not going crazy. They do exist. You have seen them for yourself."

Grandpa shook his head and decided to have a sleep.

William told Gerald his story from the beginning, while Grandpa had a nap. William and Gerald had a lot in common and they enjoyed each other's stories. They spoke for several hours.

"And so you see, Gerald, this is how we came to meet you today," William said as he took a drink of tea after bringing Gerald up to date with the quest.

"You really are an interesting man, William. Sounds like you've had quite an adventure. I will help you on your quest," Gerald replied.

"So you see why I must finish the quest before Ellie-May Grangeworthy," William said.

"Indeed, she does sound like a nasty piece of work. She quite reminds me of my old wife. It's so much easier living alone," Gerald said, shaking his head with anguish.

"Ah, I see now why you enjoy living here."

They both remained silent and finished off their glasses of rum as they simply stared into the fire, reflecting on what had come to pass that day. Grandpa's snoring did not disturb them for the rest of the evening.

Chapter Twenty-Five

The next morning, William woke to the smell of something delicious. Gerald and Grandpa had been out since early searching the forest and picked a basket of wild mushrooms and fresh herbs. The cuckoo was out of his clock on schedule as usual.

"Ah, good morning William," Gerald said.

"Good morning indeed! What time is it?" William asked as he searched for his glasses.

"7 o'clock precisely. Big journey ahead today, William. Come and get some food," Gerald said as he placed the hot plate of food on the table.

Grandpa had already eaten and was now engaged in a copy of Jules Verne's *Around the World in Eighty Days*.

"Morning, Pa. Ah! *Around the World in Eighty Days*. Good book, isn't it?" William smiled.

Grandpa looked up from the book.

"Well, it's not that bad actually, William, it is quite enjoyable. One of his more believable works."

William was surprised by his father's response. He had actually paid a compliment to a fictional writer of the scientific genre.

"That's one of my all-time favourite books," Gerald said as he joined them at the table.

"You could build us something to take us round the world in less than eighty days, couldn't you, William?" Grandpa asked.

William was put on the spot with a very good question.

"Well.... I suppose it's possible. Technology and science improves every day. Who knows what we will be able to do in the next ten years?

That is the beauty of innovation, Pa," William replied.

"Well, as soon as you've built it, we shall go," Grandpa continued to read his book.

William actually thought it was a good idea. He could better the route taken from the book by Phileas Fogg and often imagined the idea if he could complete it in a shorter time. He began thinking about the possibilities again, but he quickly snapped out of it; he had more important things to do first. He was certain the stone tablet must be hidden in the cave with the Kiccabandas. Their tunnels and caves were all too similar to the work of Hector Hornsmith and his fellow pirates.

"So, Gerald, you said that you will take us to the cave. We need to find the stone tablet. It is important we find it as soon as possible, as you well know."

"What makes you think it's in that particular cave, then, William? I have been there several times and never seen anything."

"It has to be there, I just have a feeling."

"If what you say is true about this Hector Hornsmith character, it does sound rather like the place it could be residing," Gerald said with confidence.

"I am certain it must be there. From your description of the hidden tunnels and the cave, it all sounds about right. This is definitely the work of Hornsmith and his crew."

"We'll leave after breakfast, William," Gerald replied. "Best to go whilst the Kiccabandas are sleeping, and if what you have said is correct, Miss Grangeworthy and her men cannot be far behind either. We will secure my home to disguise it from intruders and hopefully they will have no idea where we are."

Grandpa was already up at the window with the spyglass, searching the river for a sign of any boats that might be heading this way. There were none.

William nodded in agreement. He must find the next clue first and stay ahead of the other search party. They finished breakfast and prepared to leave on the voyage into the forest.

Meanwhile, Ellie-May and her men had finally got the destination right—the right river at least—and were currently travelling around the coast. John and Jack found a boat along with a captain and they set sail at six in the morning. Jack had, unfortunately for him, returned to his factory duties. Ellie-May, the Professor and John were aboard the vessel.

"What's up with you?" Ellie-May shouted at John, who had his head over the side of the ship and was slowly turning a pale green colour.

"Nothing, Miss Grangeworthy, not been on many ships in my life, not when they rock up and down so much," John replied.

Ellie-May and the Professor laughed as John began having convulsions again. The mere thought of going up and down and up and down made his stomach churn.

"Well, my dear Ellie-May, we saw a most beautiful sunset this morning," the professor said as he attempted to capture a moment of romance.

Ellie-May was certainly not in the mood. All she could think about was finding her prize.

"How long till we reach the shore, Captain?" she asked.

"Just another hour or so and we should be in the Dee," the captain replied.

"You best get reading that diary, my dear Professor. Your work is not completed yet. We have to know exactly where it is we need to go." Ellie-May headed back to inside the cabin.

The Professor sat down. He took out his notepad and pieced together the clues left in the diary of Hector Hornsmith.

Land could not come soon enough for John. He remained with his head over the side for the rest of the journey.

William, Grandpa and Gerald had secured the home and it was once again in its full disguise. They prepared to set off on their journey into the dark forest.

"I must warn you that things get very creepy in here. Whatever you do, don't go wandering off on your own," Gerald said.

William and Grandpa agreed.

"Oh, and one last thing, put these in your pockets." Gerald placed a bag in William's hand and one in Grandpa's. They put them in their pockets without asking why.

The forest was just as Gerald has described; the thickness of the trees ensured it was truly dark. William and Grandpa were on edge. Every sound such as a twig breaking had them skipping a heartbeat. Owls could be heard hooting; flutters of wings and other rustles of woodland activity were never far behind. One thing was for certain, they were definitely not alone in the dark forest.

"I much preferred the witches to this," Grandpa whispered.

"It can't be much further now, Pa. Stop worrying," William said, trying to calm his father down despite his heartbeat going twice as fast as it should do.

"Alright, here is the embankment. Mind your step as you go down. Use the roots to guide your way," Gerald said as he descended the side taking each step as carefully as possible. William and Grandpa followed.

The darkness had become increasingly worse and William decided enough was enough and opened his satchel to get his lantern. Gerald did the same and led the way.

"Won't be much further up here now. A few hundred yards and the rocks should become visible."

They carried on until they had reached their destination. The cave opening was just how William imagined and they prepared themselves before they entered.

"One minute, William. Before we go in, I just need to check something," Gerald said as he opened his rucksack.

He pulled out a tin pot and picked up a wooden stick and banged them together vigorously with the sound echoing through the cave.

William and Grandpa looked at each other with slight amusement, but also with concern, wondering what Gerald was doing. The sound of running could be heard and the vibrations became stronger as each second passed.

"Quick, out of the way," Gerald shouted.

William and Grandpa did not hesitate and they all scattered to the sides just as a large colony of bats engulfed the cave opening, bursting out from all angles. The noise was deafening. Hundreds of high pitch squeaks were joined by flapping of wings, until the last bat had exited the cave.

"You get used to it after the first few times," Gerald said as he picked himself up off the floor.

"You can get up now, Pa," William said.

Grandpa was still face down on the ground with his hands covering his ears. William gave him a slight nudge with his foot.

"I hate bats, I hate bats...I really hate bats," Grandpa muttered.

William helped Grandpa to his feet and dusted him down, removing the dry leaves and twigs that had become attached to his clothes.

"Why did it have to be bats, William?" Grandpa moaned.

"It's a cave, Pa. Bats live in caves. Be thankful it wasn't a pack of bears, or we would really be done for."

"No bats at sea, no bears at sea, this is why I liked the sea. The only thing we had to worry about was the weather."

William spent several moments calming down his father, who had become quite erratic. A few soothing thoughts and he began to relax. Rum would have done a quicker job.

"Alright men, it's safe to move on, nothing else to fear," Gerald interrupted as he pointed the way inside the cave. They picked up their lanterns and moved inside.

Meanwhile, another boat a0rrived on the Mostyn shoreline.

"Are you sure this is the place?" Ellie-May asked the Professor. "It looks uninhabited."

"It has to be the place." The professor looked up and down the shoreline. There was nowhere else that fitted the description.

"Look! Footprints!" John pointed as he jumped out of the boat.

Ellie-May and the Professor followed and moved into take a closer look.

"Not so dim after all, are you?" Ellie-May said.

"They're heading that way." He pointed at the trees.

"He is right, we have a match. This is where the diary and the stone marker has instructed us to come," the Professor said as he looked at the drawing and the passage that Hector Hornsmith had written in his diary entry of January 7th 1839.

"If the last clue has been adhered to correctly those seeking the fortunes of Captain Bones and Mother Redcap will find themselves in an unusual place. Situated deep within the heart of the forest is a cave and in this cave, I have placed the next marker. Upon my travels here, I have encountered an unusual species and they have been interesting at the least."

"Alright, you two, I am trusting you not to let me down and go into those woods without returning with either the treasure or the next clue. Remember you will both be handsomely rewarded. I shall wait here, as I am by no means dressed for the occasion. Here, take this with you. Do whatever it takes."

Ellie-May opened the slit on her long Parisian dress, revealing a garter around her leg. Holstered inside was a small pistol which she pulled out and threw over to the Professor.

"Whatever it takes, Professor," she said once again.

The Professor nodded and he and John headed off into the woods hot on the trail of William, Grandpa and Gerald.

Still aware that they had others not far behind, William needed to focus and get things done as quickly as possible.

"Alright, Gerald, you say that you have never come across a stone tablet. Where have you not been in the cave and tunnels?" William asked.

"Well, come to think of it," Gerald replied, "there was always one room that they have never allowed me to enter. They say that it is cursed and I should never enter. Not even they enter."

This could be the answer William was looking for.

"We must gain access to that room," he said swiftly.

"You'll need permission from the chief Kiccabanda," Gerald replied. "It will be the only way."

"To the chief we go, then," Grandpa said as he moved forward.

"I'll lead the way," Gerald said, grabbing Grandpa's shoulder.

Just as Gerald had described to them earlier, the tunnel passages got smaller the further they reached into the cave. They then approached a closed door.

"Alright, this is it. What you see behind this door, you must never repeat, as I have said before. The Kiccabandas have trusted me in guarding their secrets and their safety," Gerald said

"You have our word; you can trust us, we promise," William replied.

"Yes, I won't tell a soul," Grandpa said.

"Alright then, here we go."

Gerald gave out three large bangs on the wooden door.

A few seconds passed with no response.

"Maybe nobody is home," Grandpa said.

"Trust me, they are here," Gerald replied.

A click was then heard and then the door creaked open.

What greeted William and Grandpa was something they had never seen anything like it before. Stood in front of them was a real live Kiccabanda.

As Gerald described to them the night before, he was two feet tall in height and had sandstone coloured skin with brown hair all over his body, especially his backside. This William noticed as they were ordered to follow in through the door.

"Yugogo," was the word shouted.

William gazed round at the manmade objects that, Gerald had described. Running water was also present, with a waterwheel.

There was further evidence of Hector Hornsmith and his fellow pirates. Mirrors similar to those that had been placed inside the hidden tunnels beneath Montebello were also present, giving light to the Kiccabandas during the day time.

"So this is what was given in return," William said to himself.

"What was that, William?" Grandpa replied.

William pointed around at the objects. Grandpa got the message. Well, at least he thought he did.

"We'd like you to take us to the Chief himself," Gerald told the Kiccabanda. The Kiccabanda stood looking at the men directly, not understanding. Gerald used his hands to describe the Chief.

"Yugogo, Yugogo," the Kiccabanda replied. He turned and walked off. The men followed.

They stopped in front of a door.

"I have only been given the right to enter the Chief's quarters once. This is truly an honour. Not even the Kiccabandas themselves see much of the Chief, unless summoned," Gerald said to William and Grandpa, who both understood the importance of the occasion.

"One thing I must say, you shall bow in his presence at all times. He does not take kindly to those that stand above him. Trust me, I learned on a couple of occasions." William and Grandpa nodded in agreement.

The Kiccabanda opened the small door, only three feet high. Using his golden spear, the Kiccabanda ordered the men to get on their knees, which they did, and then crawled through.

Gathering his momentum and rising to his feet, William fixed his glasses and was greeted by a room full of many treasures.

"Hector has really looked after you," he thought to himself.

He then made eye contact with the Chief, and quickly fell to his knees. The Chief was a Kiccabanda dressed in several golden necklaces and a head crown fit only for a king, somewhat like an Egyptian pharaoh. William believed that much of Redcap's treasure could very well be within the room.

Gerald thought it would only be fitting for himself to greet the Chief.

"We bring you the fruits of the forest in return for your help. Can you help us?" Gerald said, lowering his head in respect to the Chief. "I bring to you these men, who are on an important quest."

The Chief looked on in silence.

"We must visit the sacred room. It was left for these men as part of the trail. With your blessing only we can enter. With my trust, you can also trust these men. Will you let us pass?"

Gerald returned to his kneeling position.

For a minute or two the Chief looked on at the three men kneeling before him without responding. He looked across to the door and the two guards standing either side of him. Then he rose from his throne-like chair.

"Yugogo," was his reply.

William and Grandpa looked at each other, unsure of the outcome. But his nod of the head was a signal of yes. He raised his arm and pointed in the direction of the closed wooden door.

"We have been granted passage," Gerald whispered as they all rose to their feet.

They bowed as a thank you and walked to the door.

"Yugogo," the chief shouted loudly.

The men stopped.

"Quick, empty your pockets, I nearly forgot," Gerald ordered.

William and Grandpa emptied their pockets. Earlier on when leaving, they were given items, which happened to be chestnuts. The Kiccabandas loved them, especially the Chief.

They placed the items in a golden bowl situated before the Chief, who then sat down upon receiving his goods. They could now proceed. And that they did.

Walking across to the locked wooden door, they were greeted by another puzzle key, very similar to the one they had seen before.

"Yugogo," the Chief shouted out to Gerald. He signalled a few instructions that only Gerald could understand.

"What did he say?" William whispered.

"This time you cannot remove the Sacred Stone Tablet, as the Kiccabanda fear a curse will follow. They fear it so much that they have never set foot in the room, nor do they know what it looks like or what it contains. You must leave the room with only that which you entered."

William understood he would need to memorise the contents. That is, if they could get through the puzzle door itself, which he began to decipher.

William stood in front of a locked door made from oak. There was no keyhole; there was only one way through the door and that was by solving the puzzle. The puzzle consisted of nine letters, again three rows of three high and three wide.

On the first row were the letters S, N, R. On the second row were H, H, T. The final row consisted of O, M, I. William was baffled by this one.

"What is it then, William?" Grandpa asked.

"Not sure on this one, Pa," he replied.

He spent several minutes staring at the device, running the letters over and over in his head. Reading the letters out in every row one by one, they were all mumbo jumbo.

"It can't be Latin," he said.

"It's not Greek," Gerald added.

They thought in silence and Grandpa paced up and down, repeating the letters over and over in his head. He stopped.

"William, I think I've got it," he shouted with excitement.

"Shush, Pa, I'm trying to think," he replied.

Grandpa was certain he was correct. He pushed William out of the way of the door.

"Look, it's an anagram, just like I do in my newspaper."

He pressed the first letter H. The stone moved backwards.

William watched on as his father worked on the puzzle.

Grandpa pressed the second letter "O" the stone moved backward.

"Keep going, Pa, you're doing it," William said with excitement.

Grandpa pressed the third letter "R," followed by the fourth "N". The stones moved backwards. The fifth letter "S". The sixth letter "M". The seventh letter "I". They all fitted.

"Just two to go, Pa, and you have done it."

Grandpa stepped up and pressed the letter "T" and finally the letter "H". They all clicked into place. Everyone stepped back.

"The answer was Hornsmith," Grandpa said.

"Well done, Pa. well done indeed." William patted his father on the shoulder. He had been on the complete wrong path; he would never have thought of an anagram. And an anagram of Hector Hornsmith himself a simple yet cryptic answer.

The door unlocked and William, Grandpa and Gerald looked on as it edged further open, creaking like a door that has not been opened in a very long time.

"Well, in we go, gentlemen," Gerald said as he stepped forward. William and Grandpa followed.

They all stood in amazement as they looked around the room, which glistened in the light that followed them from the doorway.

"William, take out your lantern," Grandpa said.

William removed his lantern and box of matches from his satchel and soon there was further light.

"Wow," is all William could say as he held up the lantern.

Grandpa and Gerald could not speak.

In front of them were several wooden chests filled with gold and silver coins.

The men edged closer to the boxes, wanting a closer look. Gerald stopped them immediately.

"Remember the agreement. We must leave only with what we entered with."

"Indeed, we must focus and find the tablet," William replied.

Grandpa smiled and the coins, unaware of what had been said.

"Pa, Pa. Snap out of it! Come on, remember why we are here."

"But William, the treasure is here! We have found it," Grandpa said, continuing to smile, rubbing his hands.

"Trust me, Pa. What we expect to find is much bigger than this. Now get your act together, help me find the tablet…"

Grandpa snapped out of it and searched the room.

"It could be anywhere. There is nothing on the walls except pictures," Gerald replied

They searched the pictures on the wall and nothing depicted a riddle. They depicted golden objects, but nothing of an unusual nature.

"I've seen these objects before somewhere," Grandpa thought to himself, but he could not think where.

William looked around. There was definitely no stone tablet on the wall.

"It's not here. Maybe it was never here and this is indeed the end of the quest and we have agreed we must not take it," William said out loud.

They all stood around in silence. Maybe this was it, they all thought together.

There was silence for several minutes, minutes of disappointment for them all.

William placed his lantern on the floor.

"Never mind, Pa. Maybe this was it. Hector Hornsmith led us on a trail and we won, we finished the quest. Maybe the missing treasure of Mother Redcap was never to be enjoyed and must forever remain here locked away for eternity."

He walked over and gave his father a hug.

"Maybe you're right, William, maybe you're right." He patted William on the back.

Gerald shared their moment with a smile, then looked round the room at the paintings that flickered in the low light. Wanting to take a further look, he bent down to pick up the lantern. But as he bent down, he noticed something etched into the stone floor. Kneeling down, he gave a big blow, removing dust and dirt, revealing more etchings.

"William, would you happen to have some sort of brush in your bag?" he asked.

"Yes, sure, why?" he replied, removing himself from his father's grasp and opening his satchel.

"Look here, there is something marked on the floor."

William bent down for a closer look.

Taking out a small hairbrush he used it to remove the remaining dust and dirt particles.

309

Moving the lantern into a closer position, he saw clearly. The quest might not be over at all.

"It's a skull and crossbones," Grandpa shouted.

"One of you help me!" William said as he started looking for cracks to grab hold of. "There must be something beneath it. We need to prise it out."

Using the other end of the hairbrush he dug out around the edges of the stone. It was brittle and just crumbled like it was supposed to be removed.

"You're on to something here, William." Grandpa clapped his hands with excitement.

He forced a few more items besides the stone from his satchel and they used them as levers. After a few strong pushes, the stone broke free and on turning over it revealed the clue.

To De Gruchy's Palace, you shall sail
Reverse the last steps, or you shall fail
Make way to the Village, West Kirby
De Gruchy's walls, you sure shall see

It was a horse that he loved, once so much
All will be revealed, with just one touch
Down through the tunnels, one, two, three

The entrance to the Abbey, not one can see

That was it, the clue had been found. All was not lost. The trail continued.

"Pa, Gerald, I already know the answer. Let's go," William said.

They quickly gathered their belongings and thanked the Chief for his hospitality, vowing to keep the silence about their secrets.

As they left the cave, William, Grandpa and Gerald were excited by what they had found. Honouring the deal with the Chief Kiccabanda, they left with only what they entered with, minus the chestnuts that they gave as gifts in return for learning the next location in the quest. But all was not well, upon leaving the cave, they did not anticipate what was to happen next.

A smile from the Professor and John greeted the three men as they moved out of the cave.

"Good afternoon, gentlemen," the Professor said.

"Uh oh," Grandpa replied

"We got em, we got em good," John laughed.

"Your orders are to come with us. Miss Grangeworthy has requested your presence and you gentlemen shall adhere to her wishes."

William looked round and there was no escape. He could make a run for it, but Grandpa and Gerald would not.

"Do as he says. This was going to happen sooner or later."

"But William, we have friends who could help us right now," Gerald whispered.

"Not worth the risk, Gerald," William replied.

Gerald nodded in agreement.

"Move, now," John ordered.

"Come on, gentlemen, back to the boat," the Professor added.

They both waved their weapons to strengthen the statement. William, Grandpa and Gerald had no option. They held up their hands and were marched out of the dark forest, back to the shoreline.

Chapter Twenty-Six

Everybody arrived back at the shoreline. Ellie-May was quite pleased, as the creepy smile on her face indicated.

"Well, well, well. What do we have here, then? If it isn't the famous inventor from New Brighton, William Withens." She laughed.

"He will be more remembered for good than you will ever be," Grandpa said, jumping to the defence of his son.

"Ooh, and who might you be then? Surely you must be Grandpa Withens, the sailor who could get lost in his own lake," she responded, to loud laughter from the Professor and John.

"Now listen here, lady, we have never done you any harm. All we ask is that you let us be on our way," William pleaded.

"Never done me any harm? Never done me any harm, you say? Was it not you that I caught stealing from my house?" Ellie-May's eyes became bloodshot as she shouted angrily.

"Well, erm, what can I say... The diary was left for me to decipher. I was given permission to go in the house, I truly was not aware that the house had been purchased by Saville."

"Don't apologise to this vile lady, William. You have nothing to be sorry for. It is she who has been the intruder, sticking her nose into places where she should not be," Grandpa said valiantly.

"Treasure of any nature is my right. I shall take what is mine and mark my words, it will all be mine. Not yours, mine. You will give me the next location and sooner or later, I shall have my treasure. My treasure." Ellie-May began romancing her dreams; she would wear as much jewellery as physically possible; she would wear a golden crown coated in diamonds,

314

emerald necklaces, and a ring on each finger. Her dresses would be laced with leftover gold and precious stones. She would show off her wealth and everybody would stop and stare at her; she would be the richest woman alive.

The Professor could imagine it too; she would be his queen.

John was also thinking of the prize and he envisioned himself aboard a ship sailing the seas, his crew tending to all his needs he ran his hands through piles of gold and silver coins in wooden chests. They were sure that soon enough their dreams would become reality.

William, Grandpa and Gerald could only think of something more important to them than the treasure itself. Escape.

"So, where is the next location? I know you have found the stone tablet. Give me it, give me it now," Ellie-May ordered.

"We'll never tell," William shouted back. "The treasure is not for you, it is for the people of Wallasey to enjoy."

"Yes, yes. I have heard this all before. I am quite sure you would keep it all for yourself given the option, William," Ellie-May replied.

"I have all the wealth I need in my family. As soon as I finish the quest, the treasure will be donated to the local museum for everybody to see," William said.

Grandpa patted William on the back, Gerald nodded in agreement.

"Tie them up, Professor, tie them up now."

Ellie-May had waited long enough and her patience was wearing thin; she was going to do something about it. She had no time to waste, only the next clue stood in the way of her and her treasure.

The Professor did as he was told and the men were securely tied up to a tree.

"Pass me those matches, John."

"What for?" he replied

"Why do you think? If they won't tell me willingly, we will smoke the truth out of them."

"My dear Ellie-May, I don't think there is any need to do that," the Professor said, trying to stop her.

"Out of my way," she said as she barged her way past.

Ellie-May gathered a collection of dry leaves and placed them by the tree behind the men. Little did she know that Gerald's home was above and all around them.

"You'll tell us, you'll tell us what the riddle said, right now," Ellie-May screamed angrily.

She lit the match, it blew out.

"By Jove, she has gone mad," Grandpa said in disbelief.

"Ha, ha, ha! I'm not mad, old man. I want my treasure and I want it now," she replied as she pointed her knife at William, Grandpa and Gerald, who were helpless to defend themselves.

"Give me the location, or I will burn you all alive."

She lit another match, again it blew out.

"Just tell her, William. No secret is worth more than your life. Look around us! If that match lights, we are done for," Gerald pleaded.

William paused for a moment, thinking about his wife and children. Gerald was right, no treasure was worth more than spending time with them.

"It's De Gruchy, De Gruchy's Stone. That is where you need to go." William was trembling more than ever, Ellie-May had overpowered him. Grandpa and Gerald remained silent.

"And where would I find this De Gruchy's Stone?" she replied.

"West Kirby, it's back in West Kirby. That's all I know. Now please let us go, we just want to go home to our families."

Ellie-May glared at William. He saw the thunder in her eyes. She had become overthrown by envy. He saw that she was willing to do anything to get her hands on her prize.

"I am afraid, William, that this will be the last time we meet. Your quest ends here, along with your life. Goodbye, Mr Withens."

The Professor looked cautious too at what he had just heard. Surely Ellie-May was just scaring them off the trail. She could never commit such a thing as murder, could she? He remained silent.

"John, go and get the boat ready." Ellie-May struck several matches which lit without problems.

"Don't do anything stupid now, my dear Ellie-May," the Professor said, concerned.

"Don't be so stupid, Miss Grangeworthy. This is not a game," William pleaded.

"I like games and I play them, the best of all." Ellie-May looked up, winked at William, and threw the burning matches onto the floor. She laughed with pleasure.

The flames were engulfed by clouds of smoke and it was not long until the twigs, kindling and planks around the tree followed. William, Grandpa and Gerald would be done for in no time, if the wind changed its course.

The Professor ensured that all three men were securely tied up to one of the remaining trees that was yet to catch fire.

"I'm sorry about this, old boy," the Professor whispered into Gerald's ear, patting him on the head, "but love makes us do curious things." He went to join Ellie-May and John in the boat.

"So long, gentlemen, it was a pleasure knowing you," Ellie-May shouted as the boat pulled away.

"Oh no, dear, the pleasure was all ours," Gerald shouted.

"Ellie-May, it's not too late to fix this," William called. "Just untie us and let us go. We won't cause you any harm, we promise."

"That's a risk I shall not be taking. Good day, Mr Withens."

The Professor shrugged at the men, offering some form of apology. Ellie-May was not going to change her mind. Nobody was going to stop her from gaining her treasure.

They set sail for West Kirby.

The flames had extended, the fire became widespread. "What am I going to do?" Gerald cried as he looked in desperation.

William looked up in disbelief at what he was witnessing.

"Barney Browne said we would find trouble. I just never imagined it to be like this," he said to himself.

"We're sorry, Gerald, it's all our fault," Grandpa said as he watched the flames increase. "Your wonderful home is ruined. So, so, sorry."

"Forget the house! Look over there! We need to get out of here and out of here quick." Gerald nodded in the direction of the trail of leaves and twigs that had ignited from falling flames.

"I don't wish to alarm you, but we are in serious trouble," he added as he looked up.

"What are we going to do?" William shouted as the roar of the fire grew louder.

"Oh my lord," Grandpa said as he saw what was happening.

All the rooms above were on fire, objects fell around them by the minute. Flames jumped from one tree to another, it became ferocious.

"We need a miracle," William thought to himself.

"Maybe someone will see the smoke and come and help us?" Grandpa said.

"I highly doubt it. You are the first people I have seen in months. Nobody ever comes here," Gerald reminded them.

But the trouble on the shoreline had been noticed far away. Back in the Marine Lake Pippin had been worried.

"They best not have ruined my boat," he said to himself. He commandeered a vessel and forgetting his fears of the River Dee, made haste across the water.

As he grew closer to the Mostyn shoreline, Pippin knew something was not right. As he drew closer he could hear the cries for help coming through the smoke.

"That's not my boat," he said to himself.

"Help, help us," William shouted.

"Where are you?" Pippin shouted back through the crackles of wood popping and spitting as it burned furiously, unable to see anything.

"We're tied to the tree! We can't breathe much longer! You must hurry."

"That's Pippin," Grandpa shouted.

"Is this the man who would not set sail across the Dee?" Gerald asked.

"That's him, alright! He has come to save us." Grandpa was jubilant.

"I can't get close enough, the boat won't make it," Pippin shouted back.

"You're going to have to jump, Pippin, swim ashore and un-tie us," William shouted back.

"But, but...I can't come in the water. I just can't do it."

"Pippin, listen to me. You don't have a choice. You'll have to," William responded.

Pippin moored as close as he could. The heat of the flames was too hot to handle; he could not move in any closer. He vowed never to enter the waters that cost him his hand, but he could not ignore the cries for help. Dropping the anchor, the boat was secured and he dived into the waters, thinking only of those in need.

Pippin made it safely onto the shore. He used his shirt to prevent breathing in too much smoke. Moving forward, he saw the three bodies tied to the tree.

"I'm here, I'm here," he said as he crawled over beneath the smoke.

"The knot is behind Gerald. You need to break it," William shouted.

The crackling of the fire was louder than ever. Pieces fell from the trees above, crashing sounds were heard as Gerald's possessions smashed to the floor.

"I can't budge it! It's too tight," Pippin shouted as he struggled with the knot.

"Use your hook, Pippin, it's the only way," Grandpa shouted.

Pippin looked at his hook, a hook that he had never found useful since losing his hand that dreadful day.

"Maybe you'll finally be of some use."

Using all of his power he held the hook tightly with his remaining hand and pulled as hard as he could. But still the ropes would not move.

"Harder," Grandpa shouted.

Pippin again pulled as hard as he could and still nothing happened.

Several more crashes followed as more of the hidden tree home fell. Fire roared all around them; there was only one more floor left to fall and that was situated directly above William, Grandpa and Gerald. They looked above and saw the fire beginning to burn through, the floor had been compromised and it would not be long till that floor would come down. William paused to calm himself.

"Pippin, this is our last chance."

Pippin looked up as he panicked. He saw what was going to happen soon enough.

"Pippin," William shouted. Pippin focused on William. "This is our last chance. You have got to give it your all."

"Alright, I know what I need to do," he replied.

Jumping up he ran into the areas of fire that he could manoeuvre. He searched as quickly as possible for something that could be of use. Fire was melting his hair and eyebrows as he searched wherever he could.

"Come on, come on," he shouted.

The sound of splitting could be heard above the three men. They all closed their eyes as they knew it would be any moment now. Grandpa recited the Lord's Prayer, William thought of Melinda, Mark and Michael. Gerald simply closed his eyes.

Pippin was running out of ideas. There was nowhere left to look. Then, suddenly:

"I've got it, I've got it," he shouted.

"Hurry," William shouted back.

"There is a broken piece of glass on some sort of metal object, but I can't reach it; the flames are too great."

"My spyglass," Gerald shouted as he opened his eyes.

"Use your hook, Pippin, you can do it," William shouted.

Pippin raised his arm and the hairs on what remained were singed from the heat. The hood remained intact. He knew what had to be done.

"Here goes nothing," he shouted.

Plunging his hook into the burning hot flames, he reached and hooked onto the spyglass, dragging it back towards him. Then he smashed the remaining part of the glass using his hook. He then used his hand to pick up a shard of glass and ran back to the three men as quickly as possible.

Using the glass he hacked away at the rope, with each layer breaking free one by one. Finally the fourth and final layer snapped free.

"Run men, run," Pippin shouted as he removed the rope.

William, Grandpa and Gerald broke free and made a run for it just as the floor broke through. The remainder of Gerald's possessions smashed to the floor, missing them only by inches.

All of the men spent the next few minutes gathering their breath and thinking of what might have happened only seconds later, had Pippin have been unsuccessful. It was a very close call indeed.

Pippin was down by the water's edge, cooling off his hook in the river. "I will never be afraid to enter the water again. This affliction happened for a reason. Without it, I would have been unable to save your life."

"And for that, I shall be forever in your debt," Gerald replied.

Pippin jumped back into the water to prepare the boat ready to sail. His fears were long gone.

"Come on, Gerald. We are going to head back to the mainland. You must join us," William said.

"I am afraid my quest must continue here." He smiled.

"But what about your home, Gerald? It has been destroyed! Where will you live?" William replied.

"Oh, I have a place in mind where I can stay for a while." He smiled again.

"I will send help if you need it," William offered.

"I will be fine," Gerald replied. "I can rebuild it. The Kiccabandas will look after me. I shall stay with them like I did when I first arrived. You get going and complete the quest. Do not be beaten by that vile lady. Greed has got the better of her and it will be her downfall one day soon."

"Here is my address. If you need anything you come and visit me. There's plenty of room for you," William said as he slipped a piece of paper into Gerald's hand.

"I'll do just that. Now, go both of you. Go and complete your quest."

William and Grandpa shook hands with Gerald and returned to the boat with Pippin, ready to head back to the other side of the river. They knew that the quest was nearly over, but there was still so much to do. Ellie-May's behaviour had become increasingly violent and erratic and William was worried, not knowing what she might do next in order to get her hands on the prize. As they pulled away, the flames died out but the smoke still continued. Several faces appeared on the shoreline. It was the Kiccabandas. Gerald waved and turned and left the shoreline with the Kiccabandas, ready to rebuild his life.

Chapter Twenty-Seven

Ellie-May, the Professor and John had already crossed the River Dee and acquired horses for the next part of the journey. For the first time in a long time, they were ahead in the quest. Ellie-May had her mind firmly fixed on her prize and gave no further thought to the men she had left across the water.

"Get that diary out and find me every reference to this Philip De Gruchy fellow," she told the Professor as they moved along in the carriage being driven by John. They had asked for directions to his home, but nobody had heard of Philip De Gruchy and where he lived. "I want to know everything," Ellie-May shouted erratically.

The Professor did as he was told.

"It says here Hector Hornsmith first came into contact with De Gruchy after seeing him constructing strange looking walls for his friend John Robin," the Professor said as he flicked through the pages to find more. "He got speaking to De Gruchy, who told him that he had been brought over from Jersey to build walls for Robin, a man from his home town. It was his style of work that interested Hector Hornsmith the most. The ecclesiastical stone masonry was unique to this land and could be used on a grander scale. It says that Hector knew De Gruchy would become a useful asset and would do his utmost to acquire his services from his friend John Robin, but it may come at a price."

"But does it actually say where he lived or built these walls?" Ellie-May said in an impatient voice.

"Patience, my dear, patience," he replied.

The Professor could see a change in Ellie-May. She had become overwhelmed by the thirst for the treasure.

"We must find it, I want it, I need it, it will be mine," she shouted.

Ellie-May spoke under her breath as she looked out the window. The Professor looked up from the diary at her without saying a word. He wanted to help her. She was losing her mind. If he found the treasure for her, she would love him forever.

"Stop...Stop the horses at once," the Professor shouted.

John pulled on the horse reins immediately and the horses came to a halt.

"What is it, Professor? What have you found?" Ellie-May asked.

The Professor turned back several pages in the diary.

"I've found it, it's right here!" The Professor pointed into the book.

Ellie-May switched seats in the carriage and sat next to the Professor.

"Listen to this," the Professor said as he read out a passage from the diary.

"The Diary of Hector Hornsmith, entry date 29th November 1841. Today I travelled back across to the Village of West Kirby, I had finalised my plans and was now ready for Mr De Gruchy to begin his work. Having become acquainted with Mr John Robin some time ago, he was most interested in our tunnels and requested that we would create the same for him. And so we did, for personal safety reasons, of course. We also added a bit extra for ourselves. In return, John Robin offered us anything we require, and this is why I am travelling today to claim my return. The man himself, Philip De Gruchy..."

Ellie-May's eyes were brighter than ever.

"So where is it, where did he go?" she asked.

The Professor turned a few more pages.

"Ah, here we go," he said.

"The Diary of Hector Hornsmith, entry date 1st December 1841. I am on my travels today to check on the progress of Philip De Gruchy. A man who is now working under my command, thanks to my friend John Robin. I have great plans for Philip De Gruchy and he has already begun the

important work to which he has been entrusted. This was to be the ending of endings"

Ellie-May became enraged with impatience.

"This has got to be the end. It says so. You have just said it yourself."

The Professor closed his ears to the noise and searched the diary, skipping forward many pages.

"The Diary of Hector Hornsmith, entry date 7th February 1842. Today marked a very important day indeed. Philip has now finished his first important task and has made way for other important matters that need his attention beneath. That I will be discussing later, but for now, I am very excited to see my grandest idea yet. The De Gruchy Stone. The entrance to the ending of endings. Situated on the outskirts of the Village, one of my many homes, and this one is thanks to John Robin, of course. A man with much wealth kindly built me this home situated at the end of his wonderful walls. And in these grounds lies the De Gruchy Stone, the stone that will conceal all."

The Professor closed the diary.

"I know what we need to do, but what we need is not here. This diary has served its purpose; it has indeed led us to the end of the trail. It shall be of no use anymore. What we seek is finally within our grasp." He smiled and closed the diary.

"Well, if that's the case, Professor, our journey awaits us. John, drive on."

John signalled the horses with a tug of the reins.

"Where are we headed then, Professor?" she asked.

"The library, my dear, they have all we need further," he replied.

"My-my, my Professor, you have been true to your word."

Ellie-May grabbed the Professor by his coat and passionately stared into his eyes, before taking the diary out of his hands. She wound down the window of the carriage.

William and Grandpa had travelled into town on Free-Way and were sitting on a bench eating pots of the best local shrimps money could buy. They did not care what was happening around them as locals and carriages rushed by. They were talking together of their despair and how they would be returning empty handed from their quest. What would they tell

Barney? Should they warn him of Ellie-May? What would Melinda say? What should they tell the children? Their heads were thumping, they had just about had enough. It was time to return home.

"Well, we'd best be on our way, hey William?" Grandpa said.

"Yes... I have missed being home. I suppose it's time to cut our losses and get back to reality," William replied.

"My boy, you have not lost anything. You cannot lose something that you never had." He patted William on the back.

"You're right, Pa, you are right indeed."

They both stood up. Cold and tired, they were ready to return home, but then a carriage rushed past. William looked up and a lady threw something out of the window. Their eyes met as the item hurdled its way through the air. It was Ellie-May. She screeched as she realised what she had done too late.

William looked down at the item as it hit the ground.

"It's the diary," he shouted.

He quickly retrieved it.

"Quick, Pa—run!"

They both ran as fast as they could into the crowds of people, out of the sight of the carriage that had now stopped. John was ordered to follow them, but it was too late. They were already long gone.

"What did you do that for?" the Professor asked.

"You said we no longer needed it," Ellie-May replied.

"Yes, but I never said throw it out of the window."

"Well, we know what we are looking for, don't we? You said you know what to do. I command you to do so. My treasure awaits!"

Ellie-May pulled aside her dress and removed her pistol, pointing it at the Professor.

"Now what are you doing, woman? You've lost your mind, you really have." The Professor had become fed up with Ellie-May's antics.

"Business is business, Professor." She laughed and put away the pistol.

The Professor joined in the laughter, but secretly wondered what was going on. Ellie-May continued to baffle him. She was not to be trusted.

"John, John. Stop here and ask for directions to the local library, will you?" he asked.

"My-my, Professor. See? You can think for yourself when ordered to. Maybe I should do this more often."

Ellie-May moved over and forced herself onto the Professor's lap, offering a kiss, followed by a bite of the lip. She had him hook, line and sinker.

Having made their way through the crowds, William and Grandpa stopped to catch their breath.

"I think we've lost them," William gasped.

"I've definitely lost something, my health," Grandpa said. His heart was beating twice as fast as it should do, his lungs felt like they had been lodged up near his ears. It had been a long time since he had run that fast.

"Get some water. You'll do well to take a sip."

William took out his water canister from his satchel for Grandpa to refuel, which he did with several big gulps.

"Ahh... That's much better," he replied as he felt the water running through his body.

"Look Pa, we should head in there." William pointed across the road to a public house.

"Now is not the time for drinking, William," Grandpa replied.

"No, no, it will give me a chance to look at the diary. I know we need to get to the Abbey, which is just up that road there. But remember what the riddle said:

To De Gruchy's temple, you shall sail
Reverse the last steps, or you shall fail
Make way to the Village, West Kirby
De Gruchy's walls, you sure shall see

It was a horse, he loved once so much
All will be revealed, with just one touch
Down through the tunnels, one, two, three
The entrance to the Abbey, not one can see

"This speaks of the Abbey, but is that De Gruchy's temple? I must read the diary thoroughly, the answers must be in here, Hector will have concealed the answers for us to find."

William and Grandpa crossed the road and entered The White Lion Inn, where they further investigated the diary.

Ellie-May, the Professor and John had been to the library and acquired the plans for John Robin's estate.

"We must follow the walls to find the stone," the Professor said as they left.

"But what about this Abbey? Surely it must be some sort of temple. We must go there," Ellie-May said.

"If only it was that simple, Ellie-May, my dear. It's holy land, the monks will be guarding the perimeter. We must find the back door," he replied.

"I don't care how we get in there, but we must do it and do it now," she ordered.

The Professor held out the parchment containing the layout of the walls. He took out his compass and indicated the direction of the area they must explore. The De Gruchy Stone must be here somewhere.

"Maybe we should ask someone who will know all things holy. Follow me."

The Professor signalled the way forward.

Back in the White Lion Inn, William and Grandpa had recaptured their breath and enjoyed a swift drink for their troubles. William had been reading the diary extensively.

"It says here that De Gruchy was to build a network of tunnels leading to a holy temple, but it does not say exactly where. Maybe it is not a temple that we know, maybe it's just a reference to De Gruchy? This is confusing," William said as he flicked through the pages of the diary.

"You know, William, a temple is a great place to store treasure," Grandpa said rubbing his hands.

"This must be it; the final journey, surely," William said. The final resting place of the treasure of Mother Redcap. We just need to find the way in." But he could not figure out where to start.

"Well, I have an idea who could help us. Most probably the man who will know of the holiest of holiness in the area," Grandpa said confidently.

"The Reverend," William shouted.

The White Lion quickly became silent as William stood with his hand in the air. People took one look at William and then carried on as they were.

"We must go to St Bridget's," William whispered.

"Yes, I know," Grandpa whispered back.

They both finished their drinks and made an exit from the premises.

William and Grandpa walked for several minutes along the lane towards the old village of West Kirby. Arriving at the church, William and Grandpa tidied up their appearance before knocking on the door.

Knock, knock, knock. William pulled the iron handle of the wooden door and they entered.

"Hello, hello. Is anybody here?" William shouted.

He could hear a moaning sound, so he shouted again as he walked further inside the church.

"Hello, Reverend. Are you here?"

The moaning got louder.

"William, look!" Grandpa pointed.

The Reverend was right before their eyes, but he was all tied up. William and Grandpa ran to his aid.

"Reverend, Reverend, are you alright?" William asked as he untied the gag from around the mouth of the Reverend.

"Thank God you came! I have been attacked, attacked by the work of the devil himself." The Reverend was shaken.

"Don't tell me! Was she blonde, very pretty, well dressed and a mouth like the whore of Babylon?" William described.

"William... Not in the house of God," Grandpa shouted and clipped him around the ear.

William apologised to Grandpa and the Reverend.

"Not the best choice of words, my son," the Reverend said, "but yes, that was her. She was accompanied by two men."

"Reverend, we need your help. We must find a holy temple here in West Kirby. Do you know of it?" William asked.

"And do you know of a Philip De Gruchy?" Grandpa added

"Yes, yes I do, but I am sorry, gentlemen, those questions have already been asked. I am afraid they got the answers they were looking for. They know everything. I had to tell them."

"Go on, Reverend, it's alright, it couldn't be helped," Grandpa said as he helped the Reverend to his feet.

"You see, they threatened to set the church on fire. This is holy land, who would do such a thing?" The Reverend was ever so upset.

"Come now, let's get you a nice cup of tea and all will be alright," William said as he and Grandpa consoled the Reverend.

"I may be in need of something stronger right now. Come and join me in the rectory. I will tell you everything I know about Mr De Gruchy and the holy temple."

They retired for drinks and discussion back at the rectory across the village.

Chapter Twenty-Eight

The Reverend was now feeling much better, warmed by a roaring log fire and a glass of rum. William and Grandpa had enjoyed some too, but it was time to speak about important things.

"Reverend, as we were saying, it is vitally important that you tell us everything that you told the others," William said as he sat down in the chair opposite the Reverend.

"I was minding my own business when I heard a loud bang. I rushed out into the church to see what the commotion was. Three people were heading towards me. The lady, if I can call her that, ordered me to tell her about a man named Philip De Gruchy. That is a name I have not heard mentioned for many years. I asked if she was a relative, and she replied that she was his long lost daughter. I thought this was strange to begin with as, in his younger years, Philip disappeared for over twenty years."

William and Grandpa looked at each other without response. The Reverend took another sip of rum and carried on.

"I was then asked if I knew of his home. I advised her that he was a resident in Jersey Street." The Reverend took another sip of rum.

"Do you know, gentlemen, what is significant about Jersey Street?" he added.

William and Grandpa had not a clue and shrugged their shoulders.

"It is the only street in West Kirby," he replied.

William and Grandpa thanked him for this piece of knowledge.

"Anyway, as I said, they then proceeded to ask directions to his home. Further to that, I was then asked about a holy temple. This question seemed absurd to myself, as the only holy places I knew of that still existed were the church and the Abbey, but neither was a temple. It was then that I was accused of holding secrets and telling lies. The woman became quickly angered."

"She does that quite a lot," Grandpa replied.

"I told her that this was the house of God and anything that is told within these walls is spoken in confidence and never spoken of again. But still I explained that there was no temple that I know of in West Kirby and that I was sorry I could not help more. Out of nowhere, I was suddenly grabbed and ordered to reveal the truth. I refused. I did not have the answers they sought, I did not know of any temple. They threatened me, then they threatened the church. This I will never allow, I am sworn to protect it."

The Reverend made the sign of the cross with his hand.

"But what else did you tell them? You said earlier you had revealed all to them," William said.

The Reverend paused, then he took a long swig of rum.

"I am afraid I revealed the secret of De Gruchy. It was against my nature to do so, but I had to, for the church's protection."

"What was his secret?" William asked as he leaned forward.

There was a moment of silence.

"De Gruchy had a second home," the Reverend whispered.

"A second home?" Grandpa replied.

"Yes, a second home. He disappeared for nearly twenty years. Nobody knew where he had gone, he was never seen by any of his friends. It was in this home that I think he hid away. For what reason I do not know, I just know it was most likely in this place."

The Reverend made the crucifix gesture once again and took in a larger quantity of rum. The bottle was near half empty.

"Can you tell us about the location?" William asked.

YAWN.

The Reverend seemed to be in need of sleep.

"You will find what you seek at Darmond's Green." The Reverend closed his eyes and did not say another word.

William and Grandpa left the rectory and went in search of Darmond's Green.

After an hour or so, Ellie-May had decided enough was enough looking for De Gruchy's Stone and she would make her way to the Abbey instead.

"Are you sure you want to do this?" the Professor asked.

"You've made me wait long enough. You're never going to find this stone. Now we are going to do things my way," Ellie-May replied as they entered through the Abbey gates.

"There is no way back from this, Ellie-May," the Professor said.

"All we are going to do is knock politely and ask if we can look around the Abbey. We shall stick to the story that I am De Gruchy's long lost daughter."

They exited the carriage and made their way to the front door. Several monks, who were tending to their duties in the garden, turned to look at the unexpected visitors. Ellie-May just frowned back and they soon returned to what they were doing.

"Oh look, the door is open," Ellie-May said as she invited herself inside the Abbey. The Professor and John followed.

A monk rushed towards them.

"Can I help you, madam?" he asked.

"Hello, yes, my name is Ellie-May. I have come in search of my father, they say he once lived here," she replied.

The monk was confused. No man of the order could bear children. It was strictly forbidden.

"I think you may be mistaken. This is a place of worship. We are humble monks who have taken a vow of celibacy," he said.

"His name was Philip De Gruchy," she said sternly.

The monk froze at the sound of the name. A name that he had not heard mentioned for many years.

"De Gruchy, you say..." the monk replied.

"You know of this man De Gruchy, don't you?" Ellie-May glanced at the monk who was dressed only in a long brown robe, with leather sandals on his feet.

"I can't say I do," he replied.

"He's lying to me, I can tell he is," Ellie-May shouted. "Seize him at once! I will get the truth out of him."

"But, but, I am just a monk, I am a man of God, I mean you no harm," the monk pleaded.

John and the Professor took hold of the monk and escorted him inside. The monks around the grounds of the Abbey looked on in disbelief. What were they to do?

As they sat the man down in one of the chairs in the dining room, his robe revealed something around his neck that had been concealed.

Ellie-May snatched it.

"And what do we have here?" she said as she took a closer look.

"It's a key, Miss Grangeworthy, look," John said, quite excited.

"I know what it is, you buffoon, I was not asking you," she replied sarcastically. "I shall ask you once again. What do we have here?" she asked the monk.

"Oh, it's nothing, just the key to our wine cellar. You see, we are just monks and we make wine to raise funds for the order and to help the sick and needing," he said.

But Ellie-May was not convinced.

"John, keep him secure while the Professor and I take a walk. We shall go and see this so called wine cellar," she ordered.

Ellie-May and the Professor made their way downstairs to the cellar. Ellie-May inserted the key and indeed, the key was for that door.

The door opened.

"Come on, in we go," Ellie-May said to the Professor.

"After you, my dear." The Professor smiled.

They both went in.

Inside was as the monk had described, a room full of wine bottles and barrels.

"He wasn't lying after all," Ellie-May said. They looked round, picking up bottles, removing the cork and tasting the several selections.

"There has to be something more here, I just know it," Ellie-May said abruptly.

"Years ago, many religious places would have secret passageways," the Professor said, "ways for in need of a quick escape. The diary spoke of John Robin wanting tunnels. There must be a secret door here somewhere."

He began taking a closer look around the room, feeling each wall with his hands, inch by inch. All that remained were a few walls occupied by wine racks. He searched them too. Removing bottles one by one, he finally found something that he had not expected to be there.

"Ellie-May, I think I've found it," he said.

She moved into take a look.

A wooden lever was attached to the wall. Ellie-May pulled it impatiently.

The stone wall moved sideways, scraping as the wall moved behind another. An entrance was revealed.

Immediately beside them was a wooden torch. The Professor took out his matches and lit it.

"Your treasure awaits," the Professor said as he signalled Ellie-May to move forward with his hand.

They descended down a spiral staircase where they then reached a long, dark, tunnel. They walked on.

Finally, they came to a large wooden door. It was locked.

Still holding the monk's key, Ellie-May tried the lock. It unlocked.

The Professor paused for a moment. He had something to say.

"Behind this door, my dear sweet Ellie-May, is everything you have dreamed of, the treasure you have so valiantly striven for. Everything is for you." He placed his hand softly on her face, following up with a sensual kiss on the lips.

He pushed the door. It creaked open ever so slowly.

They walked through. It was pitch black.

"I can hear running water, but I can't see anything," Ellie-May shouted.

"Stand there one moment. It's not safe," the Professor replied as he looked round for a solution. And a solution he found.

Light suddenly engulfed the area. Ellie-May's eyes were strained as they had adjusted to the darkness. Again, there was another flash of light. The Professor had found two large objects that contained what smelt like oil.

The room lit up. More containers could be seen. The Professor lit those too.

"Ellie-May, Ellie-May, are you alright?" the Professor asked.

Ellie-May stood still, silent, just gazing at what was in front of her. The Professor followed her gaze.

"Wow," was all the Professor could say

"It's beautiful," Ellie-May replied.

Before their very eyes was the largest cross you have ever seen. But this was no ordinary cross. It was golden and sparkled in the glistening of the light.

"It's magnificent," the Professor said as he looked at the cross more and more.

"It's mine, it's all mine," Ellie-May said, her eyes firmly fixed on the greatest thing she had ever seen.

The Professor changed his glance to take a further look around the room. There was a fountain in the corner of the room with running water gushing out, directing itself surrounding a large circular shaped stone floor, which connected to where they were standing only via a stone pathway. He looked up and around. It did in fact resemble a temple. Symbols decorated the stone monuments and columns that supported the roof of the very room they were stood in.

"De Gruchy's Temple," the Professor said to himself.

Ellie-May crossed the stone bridge and stared at the golden cross. She had found Redcap's treasure; it was magnificent. A huge golden cross, filled with diamonds, rubies, and emeralds. There had never been anything like it. She stood in awe of the cross, not noticing the several wooden chests surrounding it. The Professor noticed, though.

"It shall all be mine," she said as she rubbed her hands with glee.

The Professor walked across the bridge to take a closer look at the wooden chests. Upon opening the third chest he found papyrus, a thin form of paper used many years ago. Gently lifting one out, he took a closer look at it.

"Biblical texts! They must be nearly two thousand years old," he said as he carefully opened one.

Ellie-May looked round to see what he was doing but she had no time for the old bits of paper, her fortune stood right in front of her.

"Now, how do I get you home?" she said to herself. The cross would take at least seven to ten men to carry it, if she was lucky.

"The final resting place of the ark of the covenant," the Professor shouted. He picked up another scroll.

"The Lost City of Atlantis," he cried with joy.

He quickly looked at one after the other, shouting more and more.

"The spear of destiny, Heracleion!" The list went on and the Professor grew more and more excited.

Ellie-May was becoming very disgruntled.

"Put them down at once!" she ordered. "We have more important issues to attend to first. You can read your books later."

"But don't you know what these are?" he said in surprise.

"I don't care what it is. What I care about is my golden cross and how we get it out of here."

"But..." The Professor had an idea. Ellie-May did not know what was held in these chests. He would take them for himself.

Ellie-May tried to give the cross a shake. It would not budge. It was solid gold. She wrapped her arms around it.

"My dear Ellie-May, would you mind if I have these for myself?" he asked.

"Take what you like. I have no need for old pieces of paper containing mumbo-jumbo." Ellie-May was enthralled by her newfound fortune. She had no care for anything else in the world.

The Professor smiled as he looked down at what he considered to be a richer treasure than the golden cross.

"We are going to need more manpower," Ellie-May said. They needed to come up with a plan.

"The monks! We will use the monks," Ellie-May shouted.

"No man of god will participate in such an act, my dear Ellie-May. What we need is something with wheels. We can cart it out of here," the Professor added.

"But how are we going to lift it?" Ellie-May asked.

"That's the easy part, we will make a pulley. But we are going to need supplies," the Professor replied.

Ellie-May agreed with the idea and they decided to return to the Abbey where John remained with the monks.

Meanwhile, William and Grandpa had found their way to Darmond's Green. They were approaching a noisy scene of men laughing and singing. Now they found themselves standing outside The Mill Inn.

"Look, William! It's Jersey Street." Grandpa pointed up at the sign at the side of the pub.

They looked down the street. It was not very long, but it was lined with several shops and cottages and seemed sufficient.

"So that's where the Reverend said De Gruchy once lived," William said, but he was more interested in looking at The Mill Inn. "I've heard of this place before, I'm sure I have."

"Can't say I have," Grandpa replied.

"Yes, I'm sure Hector Hornsmith spoke in his diary of how he helped build The Mill Inn. If I am right, it was made from the timber of the old mill, from up the hill, which was destroyed during the great storm of 1839."

"Why does that not surprise me? The man seemed to be everywhere at that time," Grandpa said.

"Come on, let's keep walking. We can't be far away now," William said, and they walked along Darmond's Green. It was not long until they reached the end, what they sought was now before their very eyes.

"The house of De Gruchy," William said.

"It's got to be, look at it," Grandpa replied.

At the bottom of the road stood a house like no other; it was enormous. But most interesting was its design. It resembled a palace, and it was surrounded by large stone walls. They walked a little faster to reach the gates.

They were locked.

"What are we going to do, William? There is no way in except for over the walls," Grandpa said.

William stopped for a moment to think. He repeated the riddle once again.

To De Gruchy's temple, you shall sail
Reverse the last steps, or you shall fail
Make way to the Village, West Kirby
De Gruchy's walls, you sure shall see

It was a horse that he loved, once so much

All will be revealed, with just one touch
Down through the tunnels, one, two, three
The entrance to the Abbey, not one can see

"The walls. There is something here hidden in the walls. I will start from this side, you start from that side. Look for something to do with a horse. Maybe a horseshoe or even a symbol. Just look for anything," William said.

Upon searching for several minutes, carefully looking at each stone in detail, they found nothing.

"It's not here, William, it must be somewhere else," Grandpa said.

"Keep looking. I know it is here. It has got to be," William said hopefully.

They were nearing each other and not much of the walls remained unsearched. Then there it was, staring them right in the face, carved into the wall.

"A horse's head," Grandpa said in an exuberant manner.

"We've found it. The De Gruchy Stone," William replied.

They began hugging happily and jumping round in a jubilant manner.

"Now what do we do, William?" Grandpa asked.

William fixed his glasses and took a closer look.

"All will be revealed with just one touch," he said to himself.

"Look at the eye, William." Grandpa pointed to the different coloured stone that resembled the horse's eye.

Together they pressed the eye. Then they looked on in anticipation.

The stone retracted. William and Grandpa took a step back. Loud thumps, one after the other, one, two and three could be heard. A stone staircase was revealed.

"Right. This way, then," William said as he descended the staircase. Grandpa followed.

They were inside a tunnel, a tunnel that Hector Hornsmith spoke of in his diary. They were back on the quest.

William took out his lantern from his satchel and using the matches he lit the wick and they were now able to see in front of them. Carefully and quietly, they ventured down the tunnel. This time it was just one tunnel and William saw that it headed directly towards the Abbey.

They reached a wooden door, but it was already open.

"That's strange," William said.

"What is?" Grandpa replied.

"This is the first door that has ever been open on this quest. Normally we have to do something or at least use a key." William was bemused by this.

They both stepped in, amazed by what they could see.

"There is light, William. Do you think they were expecting us?" Grandpa said.

"No, Pa, I have a feeling someone has already beaten us to the prize," he replied.

"But look at that, William! A golden cross! It's beautiful."

They both moved in for a closer look, crossed the stone pathway and admired the golden cross for all its worth.

"So this is it, then; this is Redcap's treasure. It's marvellous," Grandpa said as he walked round the object, admiring it.

William was not quite convinced.

"Surely there has to be more to it than this." He noticed one of the wooden chests was empty. But two were still left unopened. He reached down to open the first one on the left of the cross in anticipation.

"Careful, William, this could be a trap," Grandpa said.

William unhooked the latch and opened the lid.

"What is it, William? What is in there?" Grandpa asked excitedly.

William stared into the chest.

He reached down to pick something up.

"It's another riddle." He sighed.

"Another one? But look around us! We are in the temple, the gold and gems are there for all to be seen." Grandpa was sure of it.

"I guess not," William replied.

"Well, what does it say?"

William held up the stone tablet for a closer view.

To Ye Black Rock, you must depart
Back track your steps, to the start
The route you seek has been forsaken
Beneath Fort Perch Rock, you'll be taken

No knock on door that you can make
You must tunnel beneath this lake
Queen Victoria herself, she holds the key
Then Mother Redcap's treasure soon you'll
see

"Well, what are we waiting for? Let us go and find our treasure," Grandpa said in an enthusiastic manner.

"Now that sounds like a great idea," a voice shouted.

William and Grandpa turned in anguish. There stood Ellie-May, John and the Professor in the doorway.

"Not again." Grandpa sighed.

"I knew it, I just knew this was not all of the treasure," the Professor said to Ellie-May.

They walked over to the golden cross.

"I'll take that, thank you very much," Ellie-May said as she snatched the stone tablet out of William's hands.

Using her other hand, she once again produced her pistol. "Let's head upstairs, shall we," Ellie-May said as she pointed the pistol at William and Grandpa.

Once again, William and Grandpa had been defeated by Ellie-May and her crew. No matter what they did, they always seemed to be outdone by the woman who would not rest until she gained her prize.

They ascend through the cellar back towards the front door.

"Well, Professor, it seems our journey continues," Ellie-May said as she stepped through the door back into the garden of the Abbey.

"Maybe a slight miscalculation on that, Ellie-May, my dear," he replied as he placed his hands in the air.

Ellie-May turned and stood before her were several monks, but not only the monks, there were several men in blue uniforms too.

"Well, well, well. What have we got here, then?" a policeman shouted out.

"Oh darn," Ellie-May said before firing her pistol accidentally.

A loud bang was heard.

"Owwwww, my foot. You shot me! You shot me, Miss Grangeworthy. How could you?" John shouted as he leaped about on one foot holding the other, trying to stop the bleeding.

"I, I, I am sorry, John. It was an accident, I swear," she replied.

"Ellie-May Grangeworthy, I am arresting you all on the charges of trespassing, theft and now, attempted murder," the policeman said boldly. Still holding the scrolls in his hand, the Professor tried to make a run for it. He was quickly apprehended.

William thought he would intervene.

"I shall take them, thank you very much," William said as he carefully removed the scrolls from the professor's hands.

"Sergeant, send for another carriage. This one shall be heading straight to Denbigh Asylum," the Detective Chief Inspector said as he handcuffed her.

"Do you know who I am? I am not mad, I am not mad, I am not mad," she shouted as loud as possible. She was enraged. "This won't be the last you hear from me, Withens, you mark my words. I will be back and when I am back, I will collect my treasure." Ellie-May laughed as she was escorted to the carriage.

"What treasure would this be?" the Detective Chief Inspector asked William.

"I don't know, sir, she has gone mad," he replied with a smile on his face.

"Indeed she has," he replied. "She won't be troubling you for a very long time. Now, go, leave and be on your way."

William shook hands with the inspector.

"Before leaving, there is one more thing I should do," he said.

He walked over to the monk and placed the several scrolls in his hands.

"I believe these belong here."

The monk nodded gratefully, then returned to the Abbey.

William and Grandpa had one final journey. That journey was to end in New Brighton, where all was to be revealed.

Chapter Twenty-Nine

Several days had passed and William and Grandpa had returned to New Brighton. As usual the roads were busy as ever, day trippers enjoying a leisurely stroll, merchants stood outside their doors encouraging customers to come into their shops. William waved as he passed by, giving a toot on the horn of Free-Way. Still getting odd looks, thanks to the unusual vehicle, but his signals were exchanged. People knew William was always creating things of an extremely unusual nature. Heading down Victoria Road, they went to the New Brighton Hotel. No longer did they have the threat of Ellie-May and her crew, so they were to continue to the finish in a graceful manner.

Entering the New Brighton Hotel, they were greeted by an empty room with just one man stood behind the bar.

"Good day gentlemen, what can I get you?" the bartender asked.

"Two of your finest ales, please sir," William replied.

The bartender served them and they quickly sat on the nearest seats available. They were not there to drink, they were there to get into the cellar.

"Will you men be alright if I just pop across the road for one moment? I must replenish my stock," the bartender asked.

"Yes, certainly, we will be fine. You go about your business," Grandpa replied.

The bartender was thankful that his only customers seemed so trustworthy and exited via the front door.

As soon as he was out of sight, they sneaked behind the bar and opened the hatch. They went down several steps into the cellar where they had been guided by the diary. There was a hidden door behind several empty barrels.

William and Grandpa looked at each other.

"Well, here it is. The end of the beginning," William said.

"It has been an emotional journey, William," Grandpa replied.

They both hugged each other and together they moved through the doorway.

As they entered the tunnel, it began to look rather familiar to William. He felt like he had been in this tunnel before.

He had.

Another doorway was directly in front of them. But this doorway; there was a now familiar device placed on the door.

William had passed this device once before, but had never really taken much notice. This time he took a closer look.

"De Gruchy symbols. So that's the connection," William said.

He looked at the stone and it was covered in symbols. There were stone hearts facing up and others facing down in a line of four.

"I have seen this in the diary, I am sure of it. Hold the lantern one moment, Pa," William said as he retrieved the diary from his satchel. "Here, look! It's right here," he said as he pointed to the drawing of four hearts.

"But they are not the same, William, look. They are facing the wrong way," Grandpa replied.

"You know what this means, don't you?" William said

Grandpa's eyes lit up.

"Go on, I will let you do it." William pointed to the wall.

Grandpa passed William the lantern, straightened up his jacket and put out his right hand.

"Well, here goes nothing," he said.

Moving the second and fourth symbols from down-facing to up, matching the drawing in the diary, they heard a large click. The stone moved slowly and it revealed a doorway.

"It's got to be here, I know it,' William said.

They both took a step forward and walked through the doorway into another tunnel.

They travelled down this tunnel for several minutes. It sloped further and further down. They brushed aside the thickest cobwebs they had ever seen. Nobody had been down that passage in a very long time.

"We must be heading beneath the lake, William," Grandpa said.

"It must be the Fort! We are heading underneath Fort Perch Rock," William replied. He became very excited.

It was all beginning to make sense. Everything the diary had mentioned was connected to the quest. Hector Hornsmith had spent the remainder of his life constructing buildings for the people, but they were not just for the people. They were built to protect the treasure of Mother Redcap. And all along, the Fort that was never to see battle was actually the key to everything. The greatest cover story of all. The Fort guarding the fortune that was Mother Redcap's treasure. The Royal Navy themselves were guarding the very thing they had spent years in search for.

The tunnel came to an end and before them was a stone doorway.

"This is it, the final destination. What we have been through during the last few months has all been for this moment, a moment we will remember forever. I am glad that I have done it all with you, Pa," William said patting his father on the shoulder.

"Me too, William, me too," Grandpa replied. They opened the door and in they went.

The smiles were soon wiped from their faces.

The room was empty except for three large golden tombs were positioned in the centre of the room. On the first, the inscription said, *Here Lies Captain Bones*, on the second it said, *Here Lies Poll Jones* and on the third, *Here Lies Hector Hornsmith*.

"What is this? This is not how it was supposed to be," William said with pain on his face.

"My boy, nothing is ever as it is supposed to be. Maybe there was... maybe there was never any treasure. But what I do know is, we have completed the quest. We won," Grandpa said. He no longer cared about the thought of any treasure. The last few days had been the greatest time of his life. Even better than his time sailing the seven seas. Spending time with his son meant more than any treasure in the world.

"You're right, Pa. You're right." William sighed.

They had completed the quest. Before them stood the three tombs of Captain Bones, Mother Redcap herself and Hector Hornsmith.

"Maybe these are the hidden treasures of Mother Redcap," William said to himself and laughed.

"Come on, my son, let's go home," Grandpa said, putting his arm round William.

"I have one last thing to do first," William said.

He walked over to the tombs and kneeled before them.

"Thank you," was all he said.

Chapter Thirty

It was Christmas day. William and Grandpa exited the tunnel and climbed the cellar steps of Mother Redcap's Inn, somewhat disappointed, but glad to be nearly home; just one final stop remained before they could do so. One thing about Christmas Day they loved the most was the gigantic dinner that would be waiting for them when they arrived home. They were famished. But, a surprise was in store for them. As they entered the main room, they were greeted by the sound of talk and laughter.

William and Grandpa looked at each other, wondering what was going on. The inn had been closed for good, last time they were here.

"Father, Grandpa. You're back! Merry Christmas!" Mark and Michael shouted as they ran towards the startled William and Grandpa.

"Merry Christmas, my boys," William shouted as he opened his arms to greet them.

"We've missed you," Michael shouted.

"Can we have a ride on Free-Way now?" Mark asked.

"Oh, boys! Give him a minute, will you?" Melinda smiled.

William had forgotten all about the ride on Free-Way he had promised the boys. That had been a long time ago.

Melinda ran over to give her husband the biggest hug and kiss possible. She had missed him dearly.

"Merry Christmas! I have some wonderful news for you, William. Look at the front of the paper," Melinda said as she passed him today's edition of the Liverpool Daily Post.

William adjusted his glasses so he could read properly.

"Liverpool Girl Molly Maquire gives a star performance in London." William was bemused.

"What happened here, then? Good for Molly," he replied happily as he had seen the struggles that his friend had come through to succeed. He was thoroughly delighted for her.

"I met an extremely interesting gentleman you were away. He would like you to write to him about some of your inventions. I'll tell you all about it later," Melinda said.

They both hugged and kissed again.

Barney Browne appeared from out of the kitchen to greet William with a smile on his face.

"Welcome back! Merry Christmas! I trust all is well?" he asked.

"I am afraid not, Barney, afraid not."

"Oh, and why is that?" he asked.

"We completed the quest, but the treasure was gone. However, we did find the tombs of certain people. We have come to the conclusion that they represent the treasure of Mother Redcap."

"Well, that is a shame," Barney replied.

"One thing has been puzzling me though, Barney. Why would Hector go to all that trouble of creating the quest just to hide himself at the end of it? It does not make sense." William sighed.

"So you never found any treasure of value, but you have found what you have had all along. Look at you. You have your whole family around you; surely that is the greatest treasure of all. Can you not see that maybe Hector thought the same himself, being buried for eternity next to his two greatest friends?"

William agreed. He was richer than ever at this moment in time. He had really missed the family and was glad to be back.

"That's right, Barney. They are all that matter to me," William said as he hugged his family.

"So what's next then, William?" Barney asked.

"I don't know. I met a new friend who had some fantastic ideas. Maybe I can produce something similar for the manor house and fields. And now I have two new assistants to help me down in my workshop and the tunnels. Who knows? Anything is possible," William said as he patted Mark and Michael on their shoulders.

Mark and Michael were excited. They had always wanted to see what their father had hidden away in his workshed. They were going to be even more surprised when they have seen exactly what else was down there.

"And what about Miss Grangeworthy? What has become of her?" Barney asked.

"Oh, I think we have seen the last of her," Grandpa interrupted. "Let's say she is entertaining the asylum right now."

"And what about you, sir? Did you enjoy your little adventure?" Barney asked Grandpa.

"Indeed I did. There is life in the old dog yet." He smiled.

"Don't be getting too carried away now," Grandma Withens said abruptly. She came over and started fixing Grandpa's shirt collar and dusting him down.

"Remember what I said about that marvellous invention at Gerald's house,

William? May need that quite soon," Grandpa said as he winked at William.

William smiled and winked back.

"Well, I would love to stay here and chat all day, but I have to prepare for the grand reopening of Mother Redcap's," Barney said. "We have new staff starting today, preparing our Christmas dinner."

"Reopening, new staff, Christmas dinner?" William replied, looking confused.

"Ah yes. You were out on your quest. The most peculiar thing happened! I was out on my travels and my cart seemed to fall apart somehow in the village. Then I met these two delightful ladies. We had a nice little chat, introducing ourselves, and we got talking about good ole Mother Redcap's and then we got chatting about you too. They said what a delightful man you are. So I offered them a deal. Redcap's will be open once again. We will even sell food, the best ham and eggs in the land. I may have a bit of business to discuss with you about that, William. It seems the Irish ladies have decided they want to work in the kitchen. Who knows what else they might serve? But they were adamant that we must stay traditional and as the sign says 'our Ham and

Eggs, they are of the best.' They have even decided to wear the red bonnets."

Barney laughed.

"Just how it should be my friend," William said happily.

"That's what it's all about, William. The Redcap's legacy lives on," Barney said.

"Until we meet again then, my friend," William said as he shook Barney's hand.

"Indeed, Mr Withens, indeed."

Barney turned to walk away from the Withens family, heading back to the bar. The Withens family was leaving.

"Oh, William, one more thing. I nearly forgot."

William turned back to face him.

"You may want to take a look at this," Barney said as he took something out of his pocket.

William walked over to Barney, who passed a rolled up paper, tied with a red piece of ribbon.

"What's this?" William asked.

"Something you have earned. It's the last part of the quest."

"The quest? I thought it was over," William replied.

Barney grabbed hold of William and whispered in his ear. "I completed the quest several years ago. The treasure is where it should be, at Mother Redcap's. It's beneath your feet. I had to know for certain that you would be the right person to protect the Redcap's legacy, and that you are. You have shown strength, courage, kindness and loyalty on your quest. That was the true quest you have taken. Everything is yours now."

"It does exist! I knew it!" William shouted.

"It does indeed and it awaits you."

"I must ask, Barney. Just exactly how much treasure are we talking about?"

"Go and see for yourself. Complete your quest. Your answers are right there in your hand."

William looked down again at the scroll of paper. His eyes were now more enlightened than ever.

"Oh, and William, don't forget to read the rest of the diaries. There are more adventures for you yet." Barney winked as he walked away.

William stood, looking at the rolled up paper in his hand.

"What's that you got there, father?" Michael shouted.

William untied the ribbon and opened the scroll of paper. Slowly he prepared for what was about to be told. The question was finally about to be answered.

"What ever happened to Mother Redcap's treasure? I have the answer right here in my hands," he said to himself

The scroll was now open.

"It's the deeds and ownership of Mother Redcap's estate. It now belongs to the Inventor, William Withens."

William laughed to himself and turned to look at the whole family who were standing in the doorway, waiting for a reply.

William now understood the reason for the quest.

He had been given the key to Mother Redcap's fortune. It was time for him to take the final voyage and finish the quest.

"Who wants to go on an adventure—but not just any old adventure?" he shouted out loud.

The boys immediately stopped what they were doing and jumped for joy and cheered. William walked towards the huddle of the waiting family.

"This time we will all do it together," he said as they walked out of the door.

"Where are we heading, Pa? Is it far from here?" Mark asked.

"Will there be wild animals?" Michael hoped.

William smiled.

"Boys, we are about to start the greatest adventure of all."

The End

10538101R00223

Printed in Great Britain
by Amazon.co.uk, Ltd.,
Marston Gate.